GOD KILLERS

GOD KILLERS

LIAM SHARP

MACHIVARIUS POINT & OTHER TALES

GOD KILLERS: MACHIVARIUS POINT & OTHER TALES

This second edition published 2009 by Mam Tor Publishing Ltd.
PO Box 6785, Derby DE22 1XT. United Kingdom

Cover illustration by Liam Sharp
Book design by Richard Johnson
copyright © 2008

ISBN 13: 978-0-9549998-8-9

Printed by CPI Antony Rowe   www.antonyrowe.co.uk

www.mamtor.com   mamtor@mac.com

MAM
TOR
Publishing

For Christina

CONTENTS

ACKNOWLEDGEMENTS

For Christina McCormack-Sharp, my patient and gorgeous wife, who read all my stories out loud to me so I could hear my mistakes, (the most useful advice ever for new writers!) trusted me, and stuck with me – despite what all my whims and preposterous dreams have thrown her way.

For China Miéville, for proof reading *Machivarius Point: Mercenaries*, *Amongst the Trees* and *Fluxium*, and for validating, for me at least, these written words with his kind spoken ones. But mostly for his wonderful books which remain a huge inspiration.

For Kieron Day, Paul Squires and Linda Sharp who all read very early drafts, offered sage commentary and at least appeared to enjoy them. You've no idea how much I appreciated it.

For Tom Muller, for faith, design genius, and for laughing at my attempts to produce work like his. Thank you for sticking with us Tom. It means more to me than you know.

For Rich (James) Johnson for feedback, enthusiasm and formatting!

For Dean Sharp, because (though he never really read much of this) I've never given him a dedication before, and I know he loves me much better than I love myself.

Finally for the rest of my family, and everyone who has been a crutch or a shoulder, a steadying hand or soothing voice - those that have made it possible to keep going when I have occasionally lost sight of the point. This book is for you.

There was once a cold and empty place.
Lonely civilisations lived beneath blind stars.
Stranded sailors died on desolate rocks, their ships
splintered upon the hostile shores of faraway lands.

The Weeping God loved Its children, despairing
that they did not know one another, living alone
as they did in such emptiness.
So it spun for them a great web, casting it out over
the stars, so that It's children would never
again know loneliness.

And we, the children, have walked those gossamer
trails that bind the stars, and we are not afraid,
for we know we are not alone.
And we know we are loved.
The Weeping God has forged for us a way home.
A bridge across the darkness.
Sailors need never die alone on cruel shores again.

He has bound us all in the infinite web that they who
know of it have come to call:

"KIAZMUS!"

Anon. 1700BC.

MACHIVARIUS POINT

Brec, self-lashed to a half empty wine barrel, watched as ragged golden sails pitched, dipped out of view once more, and were finally gone altogether.

The sea was brutal. He hated the chill and wet of it. One long campaign had taken him across the endless peat bogs of Kos Moor and Dunn Fell, themselves rutted like earthen oceans. There perpetual rainfall had challenged the mercenary's sanity, but the sea's waters were far crueller than rain could ever be.

He felt he should be at home upon the sea - in some obscure way it reached out to him. Yet it engendered a troubling sense of loss, so he granted it only hatred.

That night was spent in churning isolated darkness. Distant calls from other survivors occasionally punctuated the monotony. In time they waned, became ghostly delusional echoes, and eventually ceased altogether.

Now the sun bobbed at the zenith of its low winter arc, suggesting warmth, but offering up none. The abrasive hemp lashing of the inadequate raft chaffed swollen white fingers. His body dangled obsolete beneath the waves, the moronic rhythm of which - peak after trough after peak - lulled Brec into a stupor.

His mind lurched, drunk on fractured memories.

A tribe of Mercenaries called the Umbriani chanced upon the Village at the foot of Wealdenhead Tor. Breeden, a chaotic huddle along the banks of the river Florth, had been a yolk to Brec, though it was all he had ever known. The Wulf-shanked mercenary Chieftain noticed Brec's stature, the steady gaze of his cool green eyes. He gruffly compelled the boy to undertake a succession of tasks - completed with a belligerent ease. An understanding was reached with his parents. Wine was consumed. Tears shed.

The following morning the Umbriani were back on the march, their numbers swollen by one. Brec watched sunlight strike the summit of Wealdenhead Tor, bathing it in flame as he left.

Clinging to his makeshift raft, he could not recall having thought about his parents a moment beyond that day.

Gingerly he opened salt-stung eyes, blinking against the light, but there remained nothing but sea and sky. No lonely jutting spur of a rock, or loom of distant islands. Not even the sharp coasting outline, the fluting caw of a Ghull.

The cold seemed to burn now, engulfing him in waves of feverish heat that suggested other memories.

Back in the Suusa Desert. Back in that breath robbing swelter.

Back in the Patthylyon campaign, fighting for his life.

Cut off from the bulk of the Umbriani, he had bulwarked himself and his men in a fissure of scorched earth. For five fraught days they kept the red-eyed Maasoom at bay, but were, themselves, trapped. A thick, craggy wall was painstakingly erected, rough steps hewn, and on the sixth day they broke free of the defile and rejoined the relieved mercenaries – finally shifting the balance to their advantage.

That evening they gorged themselves on triple rations, accompanied by the severed heads of two hundred braves mounted on an arc of wooden staves.

Brec could no longer distinguish day from night.

Vaguely he hoped a Trillon, or some other oceanic predator, might take him - honour him with one last battle. The kind of heroic ideal for death he had been raised to approve of.

It would have been an ill-made match.

The thuggish slap, the monotonous swell and retreat of waves, continued to lull and confuse his senses. The inescapable cold awoke another memory in which he shuddered, half buried under dank, snow-beaten bracken.

The Umbriani had been decimated.

Brec, a handful of others – the remnants of three hundred - had escaped into the largely uncharted gloom of the Tollos Forest. There a huge Kaddn had chanced upon his hiding place. It had reared, startled, falling on him like a landslide, its serrated tusks gouging chunks out of him, its four red eyes wide, wild.

It took him months to recover his strength - he remained terrifyingly scarred - but he had crafted a fine cloak out of that Kaddn's thick white-furred hide, and for many years it contributed greatly to his legend.

(He imagined the bedraggled thing now, spiralling down into unknowable depths - a belated resting-place. The waterlogged skin had threatened to drag him with it, but he had managed to cut it free.

No other man would claim it as a trophy at least, and he contented himself with that.)

Time had seen his reputation grow, precede him – he almost smiled at the recollection. He had become a famed mercenary, sometime bodyguard, and, if work was scarce, assassin. He balked at the thought of this last, preferring open notoriety - the fearful appraisals the Kaddn-skin mantle drew - to fugitive deeds.

It was also true that in near global travels Brec had seldom looked far for a soft bed, a willing fuck. His large cock (though not the legend it was purported to be) and surprising tenderness perpetuated an entirely different fame. Yet such trysts had been little more than sport, or relief. He felt nothing for the women who writhed in his rugged embrace, vainly hoping to add his name to their own, his legend to their meagre histories. There was a gap within him - he knew it, but not why - and though he couldn't remember it, he knew that the gap bore a name.

Darkness subsided, giving way to a throbbing golden-red beyond his eyelids.

Brec, half-open mouth invaded by swirling tumultuous brine, groped his way urgently toward wakefulness. Supporting himself upon shaky elbows, he hauled in a long, shuddering breath. Puked, violently, in the shallow seawater, numb fingers curling in sand.

And yet - land!

He cut himself free of the barrel, made his way up the beach on unsteady legs he felt did not belong to him.

The sky was cloudless. Only a faint bite in the wind suggested winter. He was, he supposed, on one of the many volcanic islands that huddled conspiratorially a days sailing west of Corthallia. The nearest dry land beyond these was in Hulffennland, where they had been bound, a month's journey northward. He would build a raft - there was plenty of vine and wood - and head back to the Isthmus of Corthallia. It should take no more than three days, he calculated.

By that evening he had located a source of fresh water and butchered a fat and fearless Plattofowl he found foraging in scrub. He built a small fire and was soon dining on the tough, rich meat of the flightless bird. The stars glittered above and upon the tranquil mirror of the sea, and the greasy carcass of the Plattofowl filled the air with a sweet oily scent.

The following morning he awoke feeling much more akin to his usual self. It was in sitting up, opening his eyes, that he discovered how wrong that initial perception had been:

Where once the sea swelled, there now stretched an ocean of ochre sand. Behind him the landscape had also inexplicably altered. The verdant undergrowth, giant Galmeetha Palms of the previous day had been transplanted with a wall - more impressive in scale than any other he had born witness to. But most troubling of all - to his mind at least – was his new nakedness. He was weapon-less.

Brec had always been decisive, capable of making the most of unusual, or unexpected situations. Unable to rationalise his disconcerting circumstances, he chose to accept them. He walked alongside the featureless construction in the cool of its ominous shadow, waiting for reason to makes itself clear. Either he had stumbled there delirious in the night, or he still dangled from a barrel, close to death in the open sea.

Day wore on. Soon a too-high and exacting sun beat unmercifully down upon his broad umber shoulders. He could take that. His skin had almost turned to leather over many years of stoic service and often self-induced hardship. Nevertheless, by midday the magnitude of his situation was unsettling him, as there had been no window, door, or opening of any kind within the inscrutable expanse of the wall. Bitterly he surmised that had he somehow walked there during the night then it must have been from the other direction – half a day's walk had not returned him to the sea after all. At best, he could hope to be back at the sea's edge by nightfall. At worst, the dawn should see him there. With this in mind, and armed with his dogged resolve, Brec turned around and retraced his route with scarcely a break in pace.

There had been cause for wonder in his life, Brec recalled, tracing the immense curve into the shimmering distance with his eyes. He had once hunted alongside the dusky-skinned Ostrider-men who had two toes on each foot and ran like the Patthylyon-wind. They had laughed as he tried to keep pace with his huge, unwieldy frame. But they had also grown to respect him when, at the end of each day, he arrived - often hours later - having tracked them through the heat and dust.

Another occasion he had discovered a fellow Umbriani warrior; an Ottwhan outcast named Farro, half dead in the Kythruu Forest having been brutalised by some unknown assailant. Brec stood vigil by Farro's side that night, waiting for his Manna to ascend into the Ottwhan After-Where. Yet in the morning he watched, awed, as Farro threw back his cloak and stood, whole again in his bloodied rags.

Two nights later he witnessed another spectacle: Awoken by howls, Brec discovered that Farro had grown a whole shin-length in height. His nails had blackened, thickened and curved into claws, and he turned his bright, sorrowful eyes on Brec, bayed like a wounded Hund, and bounded off into the pitch weave of the night forest.

But the wall was something else entirely.

All through the cool night he marched, and yet, in the broad morning shadow of the wall, he found himself still no closer to either sea or sign of life.

Then the last wonder Brec would ever witness occurred:

Fatigued, he had sought to rest himself against the wall to consider his predicament, and in doing so discovered there was nothing substantial there. He simply fell through it, landing not on sand, but on soft, deep grass peppered with a bright efflorescence of tiny meadow flora. He could not help but laugh, as for some reason he had not once thought to touch the wall in his long night's journey - a subtle etherwork, no doubt!

Reaching into the hide satchel at his hip, he found his gilt butterwine horn and removed the finely crafted gold and leather bung. He raised the vessel up to his parched lips and, grateful, took a deep slug of the smooth liquor. He closed his eyes, savouring rich tannins, berry and pepper flavours exploding across an expert palate. He felt amazing. Opening his eyes again he glanced down, smiling as he replaced the ornate lid of the drinking horn. It was with a shock that he realised his hands were not his own.

Casting the vessel aside Brec sprang quickly to his feet, gawping at the utterly alien, hauntingly familiar clothing he found himself wearing. It was not only the garments that were strange to him; it was his whole self; body and mind. He took out the small oval mirror, which he somehow knew was nestling amongst other trinkets in the hip satchel, and gazed into it. It was a relief that at least the face that looked back, though less broad, was recognizably his own. The same cold green eyes still *blazed beneath a strong, straight brow. But the wild golden mane was gone, shorn to the skin, little more than a shadow. The nose swept unbroken and equine, and he wore a short, sculpted chin-beard and fine silver loops through both ears. Most striking of all was the thin scar that crossed his forehead in a diagonal line, cutting through his left brow, reversing back on itself to slice through his lips, finally terminating right of his chin. He touched it gently, wondering how he had received such a wound. Why he could not remember it.*

He was glad to discover a long slender blade sheathed in an elegant scabbard at his left hip. The tough black leather jerkin and leggings were of exceptional quality, and his right arm was sheathed in remarkably crafted silver plate armour that appeared to mimic the working of his muscles and danced with glowing cyan slithers - alchemical flares from precious inlaid minerals.

"Shit," he whispered. "I forgot. Again."

AVATAR

I

The city of *Tantrix-Alumnae* glowed like a caged aurora. It nestled comfortably in the foothills of the Ornisbach, and myriad lights illuminated the low clouds above with a faint golden radiance.

Brec's name, he remembered, upon *this* world - this planet Arddn - was *Hergal Ban Egan*. He felt unbidden tears dampen his eyes as he gazed down upon the city. Tantrix-Alumnae was a favourite amongst those places he had thought of as home. Neither the largest nor the most ostentatious of Aetuland cities, he yet thought it the most beautiful - though from where he stood it promised little of any virtue. The city wall was rutted, inelegant, rising out of the ancient landscape like a shear crag, three hundred and fifty spans high. It curved away from him in both directions, a coarse arc to oval the city; an imposing casing for what lay within. Black smoke rose in slowly burgeoning gouts from vents and chimneys, like giant spectral fungi. It spread out across the sky, lending a purple hue to the failing twilight.

Hergal was feeling extremely fatigued after the initial exhilaration of his return. It was always the way. But he could not allow himself the luxury of sleep. The fast fading memories - gathered over half a lifetime as a man named Brec - had to be sifted through. Important elements had to be firmly secured in his mind if the experience was to have any purpose at all. And he had to be careful how he managed his emergent memories of Arddn - dancing between twin sets to create a new whole.

He felt giddy with relief and confusion.

Between Tantrix-Alumnae's great outer-wall, and the first of several lesser inner-walls, there ran Pontifrax's Parade; a wide panoply of cloistered shops, free houses and opiate spas. *The Sayer's Alms*, an old, unselfconsciously decadent haunt in the western reaches of the Parade, was one of the first places upon Arddn he could clearly recall. A good place to review his situation, he judged.

At Methen's gate he sought out a guardsman, barely noticing the desperate crush of people. They petitioned for access with official looking documents, earnest desperation, or bribery. A very few might slip unobtrusively through in the midst of the melee, but most would fail. The amassed fortunes of the Island's wealthiest citizens had been proffered for property within Tantrix-Alumnae's walls, to little avail. It was a proud city burgeoning with a host that could often recount their generational heritage back over a thousand years. They would give up their birthright only at the very last, clinging to their meagrely apportioned acreage as though it offered physical sustenance.

Hergal reached inside his hip satchel for a certain artefact: A silver ring, too large to wear, upon which was mounted a chunk of amber containing an ugly prehistoric beetle. It was priceless, and singled him out as a Lordt. There were no more than twenty of these rings in the city. Other noblemen would bear a similarly priceless broach, clasp or buckle - all decorated with a lump of amber within which some ancient creature had met a sticky end. He presented the ring to a guardsman who hastily dismounted his shaven and heavily armoured Rafasi, removed his iridescent blue crested helm and bowed.

He escorted Hergal swiftly through the mob, clearing a brief passage with his powerful mount. The desperate hoard begged Hergal to help them, grabbed at him, pleaded - but he was soon through to Pontifrax's Parade where the crowds thinned and the guardsman bid him good day.

Once inside the city Hergal could more clearly recall its geography, as old familiarities awoke his long-slumbering memories. Concentric circular terraced parades echoed the outermost ring - like ripples in a pool - Peribold Walk, with its many-coloured guesthouses and ancient elms. Ardinax Street, with its ostentatious Banker's-Guild Hall, imposing granite facades. Penn and Willow Street crowded with a cacophony of artisans. Merchants and craftsmen competing for attention with brightly coloured awnings, inventively manufactured signs. Finally, running up against the city's immense central inner-wall, there ran Duhn Ring, home to silk merchants, silver-smithies and other purveyors in the excess of success. This vast wall was supported by five hundred and ninety-two flying buttresses. It reached vertiginous heights, five hundred spans and more. Light danced off the tough ground surface in faint swirls of azure and rose pearlescence. Within it lay the Old Town, the city proper. Here dwelt the descendants of the city's forefathers in archaic marble-veneered houses perched precariously on the top of Skaff Hill. None of the confusing rat-runs between the houses were named, though collectively they were known as the Flacks. No one could remember why. A final flint-cobbled wall ringed a small fortress and the tall Ornish temple at the city's apex.

Striding along the gentle curved walkway of Pontifrax's Parade, Hergal glanced up at the snow-capped peaks of the Ornisbach, often called the "Aetuland Spine". A pale and unappreciable mass, it loomed above Skaff Hill like some colossal fallen deity. These were the mountains that cut the island of Orn into two halves, neatly dividing Sutzeria, in the north, from Aetuland, in the south.

Sutzeria, he thought to himself. *So then - What's going on up there now?*

A large, simply carved sign in stained Cherry-wood spanned Pontifrax's Parade and announced The Sayer's Alms to would-be patrons. The Inn had been built by the giant race of the Ornish many centuries earlier. It had once been a grain mill and warehouse and was massive when compared to the surrounding buildings - standing a third again as high, despite its being likewise constructed over three floors. A fresh coat of Mantis-green paint glistened on the ten-span oaken doors. The window boxes overflowed with a cascade of vermilion and peach Porthalia, filling the air with their sharp sweet scent.

Inside, to Hergal's relief, the inn appeared mostly unchanged, though the plump Landlady was - not surprisingly - unfamiliar to him. Granite juts punctured the cream walls, which in turn supported a cross of broad oaken beams. These bore the weight of a complex wheel-like wooden structure, which splayed outwards from the centre in elaborate curves, forming a platform upon which the upper floors now rested - all that remained of the original Ornish machinery.

The Sayer's Alms entertained a cosmopolitan host. A large breasted merchantess, with a sardonic bent to her forked smile, threw Hergal an inviting glance. He nodded in her direction, his clear eyes fixing on hers momentarily. A faint smile danced fleetingly across his lips, but he had other things to deal with before allowing such distractions to develop. Three local musicians pelted out a familiar shanty in the smaller adjoining bar - to hearty applause. The main bar was peopled with nobles, mercenaries, merchants and soldiers in the employ of the city. They traded banter like blades. Others, practitioners of the Old Arts - alchemists, Fakkirs, philosophers and such - huddled at tables, arguing in hushed tones. Reconstituting abstractions and theorems in new, exciting variations. A palpable divide had grown between them and the nobles, it seemed. But the city's traditions were holding. Any bar room brawls would have seen the perpetrators cast out of Tantrix-Alumnae indefinitely, and that was more than either the nobles or alchemists were prepared to risk. Disagreements could be dealt with outside in the courtyard if it came to it. There was a designated square for violent confrontations at all of Tantrix Alumnae's inns, but losers faced possible exile and the squares had become more symbolic than anything else.

A Soul-less Ornish mercenary towered gloomily in a dim corner, his tattoos charting his downfall. He appeared to be looking for someone, his tragic violet eyes briefly settling upon Hergal before restlessly flitting on.

Hergal settled himself in a hermit-stall opposite the crackling central fire, and ordered a Long Ale and a Merchant's Platter. As Brec, beer - not wine - had been his drink of choice, and that part of him still fought for dominance. He was finding it hard to come to terms with the plain reality of the situation: He did not, as Brec, truly exist anymore. For thirty-nine years he had been that other man: The powerful golden-haired mercenary in the shaggy white Kaddn skin, famed across three continents! Hergal looked at his manicured fingers with distaste. They were the hands more of a poet, not the hard-come-by hands of a warrior. He was a highly accomplished swordsman, he recalled, but he had grown accustomed to Brec's thuggish barbarism. He mourned the loss of a life more simple.

The platter and the flames warmed him. He rediscovered the carved soapstone pipe; it's ornate Mahoghanni stem inlaid with a silver thread, the pouch of aromatic Tobbach. He began to relax.

"No. It's never easy." He said to himself, like a mantra. "Try and remember that the next time."

It took monumental self-discipline for Hergal to regard the larger sweep of recent events with a dispassionate eye. What had been going on in Aetuland since he had been away? He was back again, but what - if anything - had been learnt in this protracted foray? What had he achieved in undertaking it?

He waved over to the barmaid, who's name, he had discovered, was Mola. It was early, and his taste for expensive butterwine was returning.

AVATAR

II

Tunny Mal-Tuboly swung his booted feet up onto a stool, belched, and closed his eyes, luxuriating in the warm afterglow of a faux-traditional Hero's Portion and three so-called Rafasi-bladders of Nettle 'n Grudd wine.

"Not bad," he muttered contentedly. "Not bloody bad at all."

"Mal-Tuboly? May we speak?"

Tunny stumbled, cursing, half to his feet, hand fumbling at an empty scabbard – they're being no weapons permitted in The Sayer's Alms.

The Ornish Soul-less pulled back the stool, which had moments earlier supported Tunny's feet, and carefully sat down, so that he met the now standing man eye to eye. Tunny was a stocky ball of improbable muscle beneath a sloven's fat. Black coils spilled around his shoulders and were, along with two dark, sparkling eyes rimmed with curling black lashes, his only claim to beauty. A vast beard hid the remainder of his podgy features.

"Great Orn, man! Can't a fellow drink in peace?" he spluttered, red faced.

"I did not wish to startle you, Mal-Tuboly. May we speak?" The voice, as with all the giant Ornish, had the quality of sounding like many in unison. At little more than a whisper it commanded regard. Tunny scrutinized the enormous tattooed figure, perched precariously on the seemingly diminutive stool, with wary eyes.

"You're not from Thurford are you?" he paused. "You know, what happened in "The Fine Prospect" last night, well, it wasn't really my fault old chap…"

The mercenary looked confused.

"No? Well, then. Good. Good. A sticky matter, best forgotten. No harm done."

The Soul-less giant gathered his brow, looking troubled. He stared down at his own huge hands, spreading them palms up as if he were looking for answers there, then abruptly balled them into two minutely shuddering clubbed fists. He raised his magnificent, shaven head; met Tunny's eyes again - who calmed, suddenly filled with compassion. He was, if nothing else, a man of empathy. It was in part what made him so endearing. Here sat an Ornish Soul-less - a son of that rare, ancient and most sacred race. The legendary offspring of Orn, the god who gave his name to the island within which Aetuland and Sutzeria nestled restlessly: Tunny also perceived a profound sorrow in the giant, and that reached out to him, instantly snuffing any misgivings.

"Right o." he said. "All right. Please. Go ahead."

The Soul-less looked over toward the window, beyond which - though they could not see it - lay the Ornisbach, and beyond that, Sutzeria.

He returned his gaze to Tunny.

"My name is *Iutzparthi-Llud Pellaquial*, though most know me as Pellaq. I am, as you see, an Ornish Soul-less, and a mercenary. I have been told you are well connected, Mal-Tuboly. That you might know where to find a man. I also have an offer you yourself might be interested in."

Tunny peered intently into his companion's troubled eyes.

"An offer, eh? And what might that be, old chap?"

"I do not wish to go into all the details now. It is a fragile matter. However, the man I wish to talk to is a soldier; one *Woebeg Ban Errieu*."

Tunny's eyes narrowed. "I may have heard of the fellow. Then again. It would help if I knew your particular interest. It might help me, shall we say, narrow it down a bit?"

Pellaq stroked his bald pate with a vast left hand. "Regarding Ban Errieu; his skills as a fighting man are well-known. We seek warriors. The finest. You've a certain fame yourself, Mal-Tuboly. There's hefty payment on offer. Ornish gold."

Tunny was a master of the blade, though cursed with a rogue streak of cowardice. Too wilful to be a soldier, he found himself a wandering sword-for-hire. His nature suited only the briefest of loyalties. His bold declarations of honour, love or fealty were noisome and expansive, but they were sickly, and prone to wither. He was a romantic, a dreamer, hoping to find something great in the world, something worthy of his life - his death. The heartiest of companions, however, he enjoyed a peculiar kind of fame throughout Orn. His gift was to be beloved of most who met him - and a kind of small magiq there was in that.

Tunny nodded his fat round head gently.

"Sounds interesting. I'll need to know more, of course, but give me a couple of days, all right old chap? I'll see what I can come up with."

31

AVATAR

III

I'm shaking and I can't see properly, and there's a monologue running in my head, falling through my head, that's taking my mind off the pain. I think I've lost my left arm but I can't be sure, there's no time to look, no time to stop the blood that must be pouring, gushing. I'm screaming like Thotlan, and the blade that writes the Karnaghk in the air should be a two-hander, but she sings beautifully all the same. Bloody vapour trails her passing, clotting my nose, I breath through a grin; a grim grin. And the faces are (scared/angry/mad/sad) all exactly the same, the same face, cut in two, in half, like fruit, an opening, so slowly, like a red bloom, in a cheek, an eye. Small explosions of crimson, bursts of salty metallic blood-sweat-tears. Clawing pleading hands. I'm laughing because it's the best they've got, the very best. And it's not enough because I'm nearly there and they can't stop me. They can't stop me. And the last ones run as I open their friend/brother/comrade neck to groin, shoulder to hip, wide open, like a flower, a big bright flower opening, red, facing the sun, opening up to the sun.

And I'm out, I'm out, and I'm laughing/crying blood sweat tears...

Hergal awoke to sodden sheets and an unfamiliar ceiling. A young noblewoman whom he did not immediately recognise stroked his forehead gently, mewing. He felt a knot of distaste writhe in his guts. Not physically unattractive, the girl was yet blemished by a smug, patronising air that hung about her like old sweat. She pouted in a manner that only contrived to intensify Hergal's sudden distrust, eyes too full of questions. He bemoaned his lack of better judgment the previous evening having consumed far too much alcohol.

"Leave." he whispered.

"Are you all right? You were dreaming..."

"I *was* dreaming, yes. Now I am awake. So please, do as I ask, and leave - preferably quietly."

Any pretence at liking Hergal fled in a cold instant from the girl's face. She stood, abruptly, wearing her nudity like a challenge, breasts jutting below a similarly jutting chin.

"So, what then, you're just going to kick me out? Did I do something *wrong* - or was I just a *fuck* after all?"

Hergal did nothing to hide the frost in his eyes. "Don't pretend it was ever anything more! Your being here tells the lie, so let's not fool ourselves shall we? We're not old friends. Look, please, I need to be alone. My head hurts. I don't care in the slightest who you are. It's an irrelevance. I have no idea what I

33

said to you last night either, or how we came to be here – sorry if that bothers you, but I was very drunk. Regardless, I need you to go. Right now. Or do I owe you some sort of payment?"

The furious girl scooped up clothes strewn in ribbons and bunches across the floor. "How dare you! You're definitely not the gentleman I *thought* I met last night! Fuck you!"

"*That*," said Hergal, chuckling despite himself "is certainly true enough!"

Later, emerging from a modest guesthouse on Peribold Walk, Hergal pondered his dream. It caused him to rub subconsciously at his left arm beneath the elbow. He still sweated lightly.

"So, you are back to bother me some more, eh?" He reflected gravely. "*Nuddfegh-Ho*."

Barachal Tush, the Sayer, found Tantrix-Alumnae much changed. Whilst Sayers had always induced a little fear in the human citizens of the city, and distrust in the Ornish, the outright disgust he now encountered on the streets verged on the alarming. His golden robes were spattered with globules of spit. Inn doors were noisily barred shut at his passing as word sped up the streets that a Sayer was amongst them. It grieved him enormously. He took it all as a sign that the Tells were right. That what he had gleaned in the *Echoes-To-Be* was coming to pass.

He knitted his gold and black furred brow into furrows. He was here at least. And those he sought - those whose futures would impact on that of the planet Arddn, on that of the very universe they all dwelt within - they were here also. Now. With the fate of uncountable lives resting heavily on his shoulders, such dark murderous looks as Tantrix-Alumnae's ignorant populace cast him were of little consequence. He continued his troubled search through the streets, and, to the extent he was able, paid them little heed.

*

"A word, if you please sir!" A young male voice barked suddenly, at Hergal's left. To his right another older man appeared, and Hergal was aware of at least two more people behind him.

"I'm in a hurry," growled Hergal. "Speak as we walk, if you must."

"If you are obliging, *Munger-lover*, and allow us to escort you out through the Lion Gate, you will come to no harm. There have been changes in Tantrix-Alumnae since you disappeared. Your kind, my Lordt *Warloq*, is no longer welcome here."

Hergal, frowning, turned to the younger man - a city noble by his dress and bearing, quite at odds with the accompanying thug.

"Well, then, what have we here?" he said. "You know, clearly, that I am a *Lordt* of Tantrix-Alumnae – though not by my ring I would guess. As such I would normally expect better manners from someone of your evident standing. But then you are correct - I have been away from this place for a while. Things change. So tell me, how is it you know so very much about me? And why exactly is it that you choose to address me as both a *Munger-lover* and a *Warloq*?"

The youth wrinkled his nose in distaste. "I've spent some hours this morning - shall we say - researching you, Lordt Ban Egan. And, do tell: Where have you been for so long, and yet *not aged a day*? We, here, know of your kind. But these are modern times. Our times. As I see, you still favour the fashions of the Ornish. Quaint. It was a look my father embraced in his youth. My generation chooses not to look to the *past*. Indeed we would rid the city of all the dark, dangerous ways it once embraced. Warloqery - all *Munger* associated trickery - are practices we are committed to purging from these lands. The Ornish themselves are not above our scrutiny, sacred or otherwise. Let the shit-eating Nefarean scum be ruled by the fear of magiq and it's like, we shan't be so easily cowed! You see - we are armed with a new knowledge; the surety that *the world does not barter in dreams*. This is a harsh, solid reality we live in, and we will defend the honesty of that with our lives. We say the practitioners of our enemies' dark arts are themselves our enemies. And we watch for any such people as might return here; we have eyes in many places. *In sleep you damned yourself...*"

Hergal burst open the older man's left eye with a ringed finger, then ducked as a thin blade sliced through the air above his head. He rolled lightly on the cobbled street and was up again. Spinning around, sword now free of sheath, he carved a blur of intricate patterns in the air. The young noble was shocked to find fine slits opening across his forehead and both cheeks, weeping red rivulets.

"A man's *dreams* are his *own*, and not subject to the laws of this city, let alone this world." Said Hergal, a frost in his eyes, as he peripherally noticed his carnal companion of the previous evening fearfully backing her way through the gathering crowd with a hand over her mouth. Her eyes were wide with shock, and she pointed at him but could utter nothing. He cursed her silently.

"I suggest you get your friend here some medical assistance." he hissed. "And I certainly hope you're paying him well enough, poor sod. Now then, I have been friend to Tantrix-Alumnae for longer than you can guess, and may it always be so. As for my whereabouts these last how-many years - *that* is none of your bloody business. But I tell you: It was spent in service of this realm, and this island, Orn. My age is my own concern - but as you see; I take care of myself."

"Fuck you, Warloq! We'll get rid of your kind soon enough! We'll put you all to the fucking Torch..."

Hergal's blade flashed again above the bridge of the noble's nose, pricking him. He stared along the blade's length, meeting the man eye to eye.

"I don't know you - not yet. But, if I were you, I would get out of the city. You have no idea who you're messing with. I don't forget faces, and yours has some - let's say - distinctive features now. I'll enjoy finding out who you are, what games you play here. And I'll relish hunting you down. Rest assured, your own ignorance will be your downfall. Now piss off, boy. I'm bored of this."

The man glared at Hergal, crimson blazing in his cosseted blood-streaked cheeks. A hand hovered uncertainly above his still sheathed rapier. He seemed to be deciding on what his rejoinder might be - but then he grunted abruptly, gestured that the two others attend the injured man, and shouldered his way belligerently through the gathered onlookers dabbing a handkerchief at his bleeding face.

Hergal kept his sword poised and steady until they had all departed then sheathed it in the manner of a larger, rougher man - Brec's legacy. Bile burned his throat. A slight tremor danced up his spine, bristling the hairs on the back of his neck. Blood throbbed up around his temples.

Turning brusquely, Hergal marched to the next throughfare into Ardinax Street, where he puked against a wall. A short while after that he refreshed himself with a drink from one of the many spas, cleaning his bloodied hand and splashing his face in the naturally warm mineral water. Then he walked shakily on, via Penn and Willow Street and Duhn Ring, arriving eventually at the Raven Gate - the only way into the Old Town.

AVATAR

IV

"Pellafinn, you old bastard," croaked Hergal, head swimming.

The Ornish priest raised himself up to his full seven spans - short for the Ornish - and turned, a little unsteadily, to face him, standing in the enormous study doorway. He regarded his student intently for perhaps the thousandth time, squinting myopic eyes, before customarily shaking his head. For many years - three hundred? More? - he had not much liked the man. He found Hergal's cold green eyes too full of secrets. His manner overbearing, arrogant. Above all, he had hated Hergal's vanity. However, too many decades and common causes had created a unique bond between them. Hergal, as far as Pellafinn was able to judge, was his equal in age, and time had eroded those sharper edges, as experience in many forms heightened his regard for the other man. There was so little to marvel at in their epoch, yet Hergal was a genuine quandary, a throwback to a time when magiq had been commonplace. He intrigued the old priest. Tantalized him with his metamorphic, world-striding energies.

Perhaps a little vanity was understandable in such a being after all.

"Ah! Lordt Hergal Ban Egan no less! Come in, come in." said Pellafinn eventually, with an ironic crooked smile. Hergal found himself startled and immediately drawn to Pellafinn's mellifluous voice - so at odds with his appearance, and which Hergal invariably contrived to forget about.

"You've been gone from us for seventeen of our Arddn years! Well now. Have you recovered anything of use? Uhm? Were you many years in that other place?"

Predictably Pellafinn had wasted no time on pleasantries. The infamous and ancient Ornish priest was not only frustratingly recondite, but caused Hergal to feel mildly nauseous - a sensation exacerbated by his current condition. Pellafinn was distressing in appearance, pallid and cadaverous. The fastidiously polished black leather jerkin, satin pantaloons - also black - finely decorated with symbolic patterns of golden thread. The knee-high, fur-lined and buckled boots - all contrived to create an image more of terror than splendour. No amount of finery in his dress could conceal his physical shortcomings: Sickly-yellow bones raised parchment skin - his blood, weakly coursing through broken veins, faintly palpable beneath it. What muscles there were seemed more like ligaments.

Pellafinn's eyes were ruddy and brown in the whites, and the pupils exactly matched the colour. They bulged, Kameleon-like, from hollows above sallow, sunken cheeks. Beneath an impressively long crooked nose a thin, blue-lipped under-bitten mouth chewed continuously on Tobbach - the reason for his blackened teeth. A strange double-cleft chin faintly trembled above his pronounced Ponti's Pear, which jiggled distractingly in a sinuous neck when he spoke. Completing the horror were the deeply etched tattoos that covered the lower half of his poorly shaven head in swirls, dots and zigzag lines.

Hergal could hardly believe he had grown to love this hideous old man as though he was his own father. He smiled, but when he spoke, it was with an air of loss, even of waste.

"*Seventeen years* you say? Bloody hell. I suppose I should expect things to change, but I never remember. I'm never prepared for that. Ah, Pellafinn, you remain my only constant! What little I did learn, though, may have scant use this time. I've brought nothing, nothing at all back with me - except maybe a fraction more knowledge of land warfare, and a perception of what it is like to be a rougher man of cruder intellect! I do know that the Great Powers continue to fade. On the planet I've returned from there were few ether-works, less even than here. Indeed, having forgotten completely my true self - I was born into the body of an infant - in thirty-nine or so years abroad the greatest marvel I encountered was a wall! It appears the Kiazmus is hidden in this guise, and in another layer of deception was rendered as an uninhabited island. Great energies were clearly tapped there once, but time has stolen such skills from its natives. And yet again, as always, I stumbled across it: *The Kiazmus*. Drawn to it, and so back to here, in some way I can't even begin to understand. But I never get lost!"

Turning his back on the Hergal, Pellafinn cast his filmy eyes over yet more intricate charts with the aid of a magnifying lens.

"The *paranatural energies* continue to fade, yes. I've gleaned it."

Hergal fought the rising urge to throttle the old priest for his apparent lack of empathy - *half a lifetime in another world!* But it was his way.

"So," he asked eventually, with studious calm. "What's going on in Sutzeria? Is it still - free?"

"Ah. Indeed," replied the priest, not turning around. "Of course. The memory thing. You'll have some catching up to do. Most frustrating."

"Perhaps you wouldn't mind filling in some gaps? Tantrix-Alumnae certainly has a fresh - edge to it."

Pellafinn carefully placed his precious charts in the wide shallow drawer of his plan chest and turned around to face Hergal at last. He took a deep breath.

"Since your departure, Hergal, there was - let me see - five years of peace, before the *Nefars* crossed the Sutzerean Straights again - hundreds of thousands of them. They sailed their Dragships up the river Rae, to *Duhn*. And, again, the city fell - Ornish designed siege engines, I'm sorry to say, and extremely efficient they are too. There are too many Soul-less Ornish mercenaries these days. Too many. It bruises the soul. So, the new walls succeeded only in delaying the city's agony. As we witnessed, another pointless tax raised for another pointless wall, bringing about another pointless famine in Duhn's poorer quarters, and utterly failing to bring any new element of defence to Duhn what. So. Ever. Do we learn from history, Hergal? Do we though? It's the old-mans-rant, I know, but still. The army went east after that - as usual. Through the Forest of Duhn, and on, parallel with the Ornisbach - the Aetuland spine. Within two weeks they arrived at Shea Pass, marched south to *Da Derga's Heights...*"

"I know that name, Da Derga's Heights."

The small giant's eyebrows arched, eyes bulging, incredulous, below. "As you should, even with your limited memory! You recall the Brookbane's Sutzerean fortress? Surely you must?"

Hergal looked up at Pellafinn with an empty, tired expression.

"Just indulge me, you old bastard. I'm still struggling with the reality of just being back here!"

"Hm. Well." The priest shook his large ugly head, collecting his thoughts. "Da Derga's Heights stand in the eastern-most reaches of the Ornisbach, right on the Aetuland/Sutzeria boarder. It is, as I'm sure you will soon remember, an architectural achievement that remains unrivalled upon Arddn. There is no structure more famed - and you have been there, in and out of my company, on more than one occasion..."

"I know the name, I just can't... the memory - my memory – it's all messed up. You know how it is, Pellafinn! Indulge me!"

"One would not necessarily think it wise to go out drinking having recently journeyed between worlds, Hergal. I've said this before…"

Hergal waved a hand weakly and frowned. "Now that bit I haven't forgotten! Enough bloody lectures Pellafinn! You're not my father – oh gods, I hope you're not my father! Just help me out a little here."

"Hm. Well, let's see. Let's see. You remember the *Brookbane* dynasty?"

Hergal shook his head slowly.

"Great Orn! What then, my goodly Lordt Hergal Ban Egan, do you recall of Arddn? I can hardly tell you what you don't know if I don't know what you do!"

"I take your point. Let me think. Alright, this is Tantrix-Alumnae..."

The priest looked hard at Hergal, quite still for a moment, until it became clear he was not going to say any more. "Am I to congratulate you on this remarkable feat of memory? Really now. And is there anything - else?"

"Orn's bollocks, Priest! I'm still two men! Two men! And only one sore head!" Hergal gathered his brow. "So, what I do know - what I know about where we are - is: We are in the heart of Aetuland, the southern half of the island, Orn. We're separated from the north, Sutzeria, by mountains, the Aetuland Spine - as I believe we in the south like to call, uh, that lot, out there." Hergal gestured through the window vaguely. "I was thinking about it last night. Thinking about Sutzeria. What might be going on there? As for names, history – it's all confusion. The Empire of the Nefareans lies to the... west - I remember that - and it constitutes most of the continental mainland. And Duhn - Duhn is Sutzeria's largest city, on the norwestern tip of the island..."

"Good. Then at least you should have understood what I have told you so far!" The old giant sighed and resumed his story in the manner of one naturally malcontent. "This is all of immediate relevance to you, so listen carefully! I won't be happy if I have to tell it twice. Time is of a premium right now, Hergal, especially to old men like me. So. *Lordt Thrall ban Duhn Ne Brookbane* - the rightful and last true ascendant of Da Derga's Heights - was a Sutzerean Warlordt by bloodline, but a well-known Aetulander in his heart. He married, as has been the custom of centuries, a noblewoman from Aetuland. In his case, she was the *Lady Pesheval Nar-Bo Tertrigal Ban Hapfthoven Ne Belorvelian-Alumnae...*"

"And how the fuck am I supposed to remember *that*, Pellafinn?"

"He met and, fortuitously enough, fell in love with The Lady Pesheval while studying here, at the Ornish temple in Tantrix-Alumnae. You drank in his company on a couple of occasions! I'd say you were close acquaintances for a while - so you really ought to remember it!" Hergal frowned, rubbed his eyes. "The courtship was brief, intense, and mutual I was told - by you as it happens. All concerned parties were content with the arrangement, and the union was compacted within a half year of their first encounter. They enjoyed three blissful years together before the Lady Pesheval became Munger-stricken and died over two agonizing months. Brookbane was heartbroken, and a certain wildness was noted in him thereafter. He remained, non-the-less, a fine Lordt to those that served or worked alongside him. Fair, generous to guest and friend - if a little dour when drunk. When Aetuland came under threat again it was he who organised and assembled the massive army that gathered up there - the largest this land has ever hosted. He had put forth his argument at the Lordt's Council, reasoning that the plunging walls of the fortress had never been breached. That if Aetuland could be defended, then it would be best defended there: At Da Derga's Heights. Needless to say, the Lordts did not take much persuading. History was on the side of Da Derga's after all, and for once they listened to such wisdom as the ages proffered.

"The ensuing battle, now laughably referred to as the 'Battle of Da Derga' (though Orn knows how many battles have been fought there!) lasted nearly three weeks before Lordt Brookbane splintered the Nefars with the assault that subsequently made him famous. The demoralized Nefars retreated, and Brookbane continued to harry them all the way back down the pass, until, tragically, a flaming arrow blinded him. A good man he may well have been, but Brookbane was also a vain man." Pellafinn shot a pointed look at Hergal who was massaging his temples with the tips of his fingers, eyes shut. The giant sighed. "Something I fear all you so-called Lordts have in common - and that includes even you unlanded Lordts! So, then - accustomed to power, shattered by personal tragedy - I would guess Brookbane was unable to adapt to, let alone accept, his blindness. Whatever the truth of it, he abandoned his responsibilities, leaving rivals to fight over Lordtsway of Da Derga's Heights.

"Twelve years on and there has been another uneasy peace, between Aetuland and the again Nefar-occupied Sutzeria. Da Derga's Heights remains the only unoccupied Sutzerean

44

stronghold."

"Never-the-less," Pellafinn leaned slightly forward, his voice dropping. There was a conspiratorial glint in the muddy eyes that Hergal had, he realised, greatly missed. "I have been hearing *tales*, Hergal." The clawed hands, with skin like oiled papyru stretched over waxen bone, writhed in excitable knots around each other.

"There is a legend growing up around some Nefarean Warlordt – and a *gemstone*. This man has won the favour of the Emperor, and now holds sway over the Nefars abroad in our lands. He operates from Duhn. *Machivarius Point* to be more precise. It is said that the man is a Warloq. That he can invoke the power of the Munger, the *Undead God*, through a gemstone. Moreover, it is rumoured that he plans a new campaign to conquer Aetuland. They're calling this man *The Wayfarer.*'"

Much had happened since Hergal had left. He met the giant's eyes with his own. "What can we do about – all this? Where do we stand?"

"You'd do well to ask what I am already doing about it! You may be surprised to know that plans have been put in motion to steal the gemstone from this Wayfarer, if it - and he – truly exist. Let me ask you something: As one of the Ornish I would *forfeit my soul should I perpetrate any act of violence.* Is it therefore imperilled, do you think, by the act of my *hiring* mercenaries?"

AVATAR

V

Baalor Dark-Eye, The Wayfarer, fell to his knees - fearful, expectant.

The prospect of again channelling energies long thought lost chilled him. He shuddered. This was now the nature of his life.

Sweat gathered in the livid holes that once housed eyes. He reached forward with an unsteady but strong hand. Felt the edge of the ebony shrine. His stomach lurched - but he mastered it. He unhooked the elegant gold latch, lifting open the lid. His fingers brushed against the padded silk that lined it - a deep vermilion, had he eyes to see - and fumbled around inside, until they found, and closed upon, a smooth gemstone the size of an eyeball. It was mounted within an intricate golden mesh, suspended from a thick white-gold chain. It felt warm.

Fervid, he fastened it around his neck and forced the gemstone into his right eye socket - rupturing delicate flesh and causing pain, and blood to flow.

The gem's paranatural energy surged out of it into bone and nerve - downwards, and then back, upward, coiling round and slicing through his spine. It exploded within his skull, bursting out through ruined sockets, around the edge of the stone, bilious green flame bathing the darkened room in a sickly light that imparted one of the things he most craved:

Sight.

He smiled.

MERCENARIES

I

The snug in The Sayer's Alms afforded the three mercenaries
a fine view of the landlady's generous arse jiggling beneath a
threadbare linen skirt.   Woebeg smacked his lips, nodded his
head in appreciation. Once Captain of the Brookbane Elite, he
would recount his exploits to anyone within earshot - if they sat
still long enough. He wiped his mouth on a stocky forearm,
heaved himself forward, elbows on table, chin on back of hands.
"So anyways, Brookbane is going fucking crazy, see? The flanks
are taking too long, much too long to close in on the damned
Nefarean shit-swillers, so he's loosing men quickly." He drew
a diagram in a spill of ale on the tabletop to illustrate. "So now
the bastard - I swear you've never seen anything like it - the

crazy bastard pushes his personal guard aside and runs at the Nefars, just runs at them! And he starts screaming, screaming like a fucking lunatic: "You fucking dog fuckers! You fucking shit-eating fucks!" Hah! That huge black axe of his took down a good ten of them with one fucking blow - no shitting you! - And they just, well they just started to fall apart around him. He was this black whirling death. They couldn't even get close."

Woebeg reached for his Long Ale thoughtfully, sank a throatfull of the bitter liquid.

"What got me though, what I really couldn't believe if I hadn't seen it, witnessed it with these eyes, was what Brookbane - big fuck - did next: He just stopped, didn't he? Stopped dead and stared at them! And you know what? The stupid crap-eating bastards just stopped and stared back! They didn't know what the fuck to do! Brookbane, cool as you like, reached up and pulled off his helmet. Handsome fucker he was, grin like a crescent moon. "Give you a fair chance," he shouts, "you dog-shagging Munger-fuckers!" and then he rushes at them again! This time he takes twenty, thirty of 'em, and we've - you know, after seeing that - we've all got our helmets off and are going crazy too! We've all gone fucking feral, fucking berserk, and that's when - finally! - the flanks closed in and finished the fuckers off. Shame is, you know, that if he hadn't taken off his damn helmet..."

Remorse flitted across Woebeg's wide face like a shadow.

"Well. You know the rest." He drained his glass. "I assume, Tunny Mal-Tuboly, that the next round is yours?"

"I believe, old mate, that you are correct in that assumption! Same again chaps?" Tunny, rotund face barely visible behind black locks, that vast beard, rose unsteadily and weaved a passage to the bar, leaving Woebeg and the Ornish giant alone.

Pellaq had been studying Woebeg throughout the evening, looking for signs that he was the right man. He sensed in him something not quite whole - an absence - but otherwise, nothing.

Pellaq had expected to know immediately if Woebeg was an ether-worker, a Warloq - wielder of magiqs, a power capable of turning events so that Arddn, and this whole perception of reality, might have a future. Pellaq was distraught to find Woebeg such a disappointment, but he buried his feelings deep. "It must be so," he thought, "it must be he."

The former captain was a short man. His red hair was thinning, unkempt. While not long, his broken nose took up a large portion of his face width-wise. He had a strong jaw, intelligent blue eyes. Eyes he now fixed on Pellaq, searching the giant in turn. "So, Pellaq, why are you here, eh? Clearly not to visit the old temple!"

The giant adopted the accepted role of his kind when he answered, predictably: "There are no temples for the soul-less."

For the Ornish, an act of violence, no matter the provocation or circumstance, would lose the perpetrator's soul to the Munger - the Undead God. "Soul-less" Ornish often became mercenaries, their lives rendered pointless. It had become a death cult.

But giants die hard.

"What I'm looking for," said Pellaq, "is someone to organise; put together - let's call it - a recognizance expedition. There are a lot of important people worried about what's rumoured to be brewing in Sutzeria, specifically Duhn. Tell me, have you heard of "the Wayfarer"?"

Woebeg snorted. "Baalor Dark-eye? So-called "Soul-pike" and "Munger-spawn"? Yes, I've heard of him, every soldier has. I bet every child in Arddn knows some dark fucking story about the Wayfarer just now. Good fucking propaganda that! Scare us shitless first, eh?"

"Yes. The Warlordt of the Nefareans." said Pellaq. "He's commanding the Emperor's operations from his base at Machivarius Point, we think – but there's a lot we don't know for certain. I'll tell you it as it is, Woebeg, as we have very little time

I think. No time at all, really, so it has to be so. We – those who have entrusted me with this operation - need to create a small, pretty much independent affiliation of mercenaries, fighters - the best. People we can trust, or who's trust we can buy. And we need a leader. Someone prepared to try and infiltrate the Wayfarer's inner circle. Maybe even attempt an assassination. Failing that, we require information. Captain Ban Errieu, your fame precedes you. Wherever I look, I find you. Aetuland is in danger. So I'm asking you; do this for us out of love for your country. And if not that, well then, do it because there is a great deal of money and land on offer.'

"How much up front?" asked Woebeg.

Outside, in the shadow of the Sayer's Alms, Pellaq leaned heavily against the wall. No ordinary Soul-less, for reasons even he could not as yet fully comprehend, he chose to continue his immersion into the Echoes-To-Be - ripples across the membranes of existence, agents of future possibilities. He studied under a tolerant Ornumnae Priest called Pellafinn. At first the priest had thought working with a Soul-less was distasteful, but he soon found it had many advantages. Pellaq brought with him knowledge of the politics, the hairline balance of power abroad in the continental mainland. Information Pellafinn could work with. The arrangement was clandestine, but it suited both well. Pellaq had learned of the end-of-times, the "Lynchpin". He gleaned who presented the only possibility of a future for their reality. Over time it had been revealed - in whispers and smoke, frail yet compelling - what he must do. Yet now Pellaq was disheartened. He questioned his knowledge, all he had learnt. He railed. How could it - of all the men, all the Ornish, the Sayers - how could it be this man?

Woebeg.

*

"Ah, but y' are a fine woman!" Woebeg breathed into Heron's ear from behind. "I've a proposition to make..."

"You'll remove your hands from my breasts or be barred!" She swung round and faced him, narrowing her eyes.

"But Heron, you don't understand..." He lurched - another attempted embrace - twisted awkwardly, and spiralled into an ill-kempt heap on the floorboards.

"You're drunk." There was disdain, fists balled and planted on full hips.

"I've got money now, Heron love! Lots of it! Damn it woman! Can't you see I want you? How much I - I fucking love you Heron? You, me, we could go somewhere; set - I don't know - something up together! Just you and me, love. You and me." He gazed up at her, tried to muster a little charm, but he was ill advantaged, and, less still, liked.

"Oh! I see now. You think you can buy me!" She shook her head, smoothed the sheets on the guestroom pallet - more out of irritation than necessity. "And what kind of a woman does that make me? Is that the level of respect you have for me now?"

Woebeg frowned. "Lordt, no, woman, that's not what..."

"Do you think I'm looking for wealth, Woebeg? Is that it? I have all I ever wanted right here. This was my dream, nothing more. You've nothing you can add to it. I see what you're up to - all those declarations, flowers, endless gifts - they don't impress me. People talk, Woebeg. And I've heard you drunk, bragging about being "the thumb on Lordt Brookbane's right hand" in the "grand old times". But soldiery; it don't hold a glamour for me. Never did. Conflict, killing people... You're all bleedin' fools! Like big bloody children you are, all fighting over bigger children's playthings! Tonight I heard you boasting about how, apparently, you've been "entrusted with a secret mission for the Ornish"! Secret? Secret in what way exactly? Half the patrons of the "Sayer's Alms" are waiting outside every night to relieve you of some of that gold you've been flashing around! So. What is it all for, Woebeg? Did the Ornish give it you to spend trying to impress me? Or do you really have something of value to do with it?"

Woebeg's gaze dropped.

"If you're any kind of a man at all you will do the job you were employed to do, and you'll leave me bloody well alone. I don't love you. I'm sorry. Never will. You've got to understand that. I'm not a soldier's girl, Woebeg! Go do the thing you're supposed to do. Do something right, if there is such a thing for a man like you. Do it *well*."

"But. Heron. Please."

He watched from the floor as her buttocks disappeared behind a slammed door.

Unexpectedly his eyes began to sting.

Thrashers plummet, their wings flaming. The riders strain to control the dives, but the beasts, consumed with pain and fear, spiral in chaotic panicked arcs to bloody deaths on rocks below. Nuddfegh-Ho raises a slender white arm and a boulder, ten footfalls across, shoots into the air trailing sulphurous death.

A mauve arc of light splits open a thumb-wide gap in the world, horizon to horizon, severing Nuddfegh's left arm below the elbow. He turns, quickly; as if it has not happened, runs forward, pulling his double-handed sword single-handedly from its scabbard. It parts air with preternatural grace, writing the Killing Karnaghk. The defenders go down with appalling ease, and Nuddfegh keeps charging forward, towards the "Temple in the Deep", screaming like Thotlan.

Then he's before it, his blade high, descending fast, too fast…

*

Hergal opened his eyes. Blinked. It took him a moment to remember where he was, the little guesthouse he favoured in Peribold Walk. It had been another long boozy night in Tantrix-Alumnae, and he felt old. Had it been his doing, all of this? Could he in some way be tied to whatever energy – malignancy - was rendering null the paranatural across so many worlds?

"No." he muttered. "I did not start this." But the stated conviction was not echoed in his thoughts. He sat up, rubbed his brow with the heal of a palm. "Stop fucking haunting me!"

His old memories played tricks, often undistinguishable from persistent dreams. He thought it might be his basic magiqal essentia conjuring a Djinni, a phantom abhoration. That his great age had fouled his essence, made it impure with too much accretion - too many harboured memories of other lives to remain true to himself. All those angry other-selves - lives he had lived over appropriated centuries, upon other worlds - crying out to be set free, to be manifest again, and solid. A succubus, he had worn the bodies of other men as an Avatar, annexing their life spans. But he always returned to Arddn, to this body, this mind. Lordt Hergal Ban Egan, frost-eyed, fastidious, complex. In quiet moments he longed to be them all again. He had loved them. But the disturbing recollections concerning Nuddfegh-Ho confounded him. He could not recall how long ago he had been Nuddfegh-Ho. Where he had been Nuddfegh-Ho, or if he had ever been Nuddfegh-Ho beyond the confines of a fever-dream. His cognizance was dissipated, incomplete, confused.

Hergal shook his head, rose groggily and shuffled to the window. "I am who I am. Whoever *that* is."

Peribold Walk reverberated with chatter in the mid-day balm. Hergal regarded the circles of animated discussion with awakening interest. There was something occurring nearby. Numerous mercenaries, swiftswords, curmudgeons and dicers, filed down the narrow cobbled street towards the throughfare to Pontifrax's Ring, and more specifically he guessed The Sayer's Alms. Soft-skinned nobles passed comment in hushed tones, their faces revealing distaste and envy. A hush descended as a large Sayer passed by - horned, golden robed, elegantly feline. Some nobles spat, but quickly looked away less he touch them eye-to-eye.

Hergal's mood further darkened. Such ethereal creatures withered under the crush of time, unmarked graves awaiting them.

They fear what they no longer know, he thought. *Well then. Let them fear*.

The man who sat facing *Cherry Longorn* in The Sayer's Alms did not instil her with confidence, regardless of what his reputation suggested. It was said he had neither compassion nor fear upon the battlefield. That he was murderous. A butcher. Uncanny in violence.

Cherry thinned her lips, not liking him. Woebeg might be their leader, but it was an Ornish endeavour. She would be part of it whatever. It was a matter of history. There had been promises.

Woebeg had heard many tales of Cherry Longorn. An implausible creature of profound exotic beauty, she was a mercenary's legend, an almost-myth. Though her true heritage was unknowable, it had been culled and crafted, improvised out of hearsay, a very few facts, into something credible. Over battlefield campfires, in a thousand Aetuland barracks, her story had been told and retold:

The daughter of a Soul-less mercenary and an Aetuland Noblewoman, she should have died long before birth. It was near unheard of for such unions to result in conception, and they never went full term - Idle Noblewomen were known to tussle with Soul-less mercenaries for this very reason. Cherry proved to be the rare exception. Her mother died giving birth to the enormous child after carrying her more than a year - it had been assumed that early signs of a pregnancy had been mistaken, and later that she carried twins. Cherry was bundled off to Ork on the isle of Gann, to be raised amongst the Ornish priestesses at their high temple. Of course her aristocratic family would wipe all trace of her from their histories. She would never be allowed to discover who she really was.

She would also never reach Gann.

A Nefarean Dragship, it was said, attacked the heavy-laden sea-barge, killing the sailors and looting the stores. They found the jet-black baby girl - whose eyes were as dark as a Kushnan night, even in the whites, but who's hair blazed crimson, like the setting sun - and carried her off to Nefarea, a treasure.

At twelve years old Cherry, named for the red "o" of her lips, was six spans in height. Stronger than most men. Lavished with gems and exotic garments, yet caged in a gilt chariot, she was hauled from city to city, an exhibit. Men would pay to wrestle her. Nobles to bed her. Cherry Longorn was the most outré spectacle the continent had witnessed in a thousand years. She represented a fading past, was a last flourish of ancient legerdemain. She was also a captive, a slave, of unknown parentage and dubious origin.

At fourteen, Cherry sickened. Her satin skin began to dry, breaking open in raw cankers and weeping. Her celebrated hair fell out in clumps. The tendons of her hands began to constrict, tighten, curving sinuous fingers into claws. Her Nefarean masters were quick to realize there was little profit to be made with her in such a condition. Exhaustive treatments failed to return her health, so she was abandoned by the Silk Way in Ypo-Polaria, ailing, and frozen half to death.

Two days later there had been a rescue, of sorts. Despite her distressing condition the fat merchant recognised her for who she was. Never wealthy enough to enjoy her at the time of her celebrity, he had often been amongst the spectators. He clothed her, watched her lasciviously as she picked at the dry salted meat he proffered. All the while he thought of the stories he would tell. Cherry Longorn! He could hardly believe his good fortune. She should thank him, he had thought, for his kindness. Maybe she would beg to stay with him, who knew? He smiled to think how he would say he had spurned her while she begged - begged him! - for the comfort of his arms. How he would relish the incredulous gasps of fellow merchants! But he would need some kind of proof. A lock of hair perhaps? It was no matter. He would think of something.

That night he took what he obviously felt he deserved in a singular, brief act of rape. The following morning she killed him, along with his two attendant mercenaries - her training had made her lethal. Life had not bred her for compassion, and the merchant had little deserved it anyway. She took from one of the paid armsmen a short Kushnan stabbing sword, twisting its hilt painfully into the claw of her right hand, binding it there. The scabbard she fitted pointing upwards at her left shoulder, a leather loop to keep her hand, and the sword, in place while she got on with living. She could now defend that life.

For the first time ever, she was free.

She became a thief and an outlaw. Sometimes she chose to travel with mountain bandits, way-lay men. On occasion they would overpower and rape her. It would have been better had they killed her, as they would all suffer for their betrayals with imaginative, terrifying deaths. Her reputation soon ensured it happened less and less.

But her condition remained unstable, and eventually

worsened. Once more she was dying, alone in a russet autumnal forest, somewhere east of the grand steppes of Nefarea. The rags she wore bonded with raw, seeping skin. She was unable to open her eyes for the cloying matter that caked them. Cocooned in her own discharge she shivered, cradled in the roots of a twisted Elm, awaiting the Munger's kiss.

A clutch of stocky Dolomites waited nearby, sniffing the air for death. The blind scavengers shifted their maggot-white bodies impatiently from stump to stump, but scampered away screaming as the traveller neared.

He gently lifted the wretch, cradled her in his vast arms. A day later she sipped a little rabbit broth infused with medicinal herbs from his satchel. A week beyond that she lay naked in his arms as he bathed her in the warm volcanic pools that welled in the Ypo-Polarian foothills. He was entranced, watching intently as she recovered beauty lost to her. Laying her on his roab-skin cloak he bound up the remaining lesions that marred her legs, her arms, placed a compact - root extracts, crushed barks and fungi - over her still closed eyes. Finally, painstakingly, he eased open her hands, removed the sword, and bound them too with a medicinal compress.

Later, as he cooked a Marsh Hare over a small fire, she spoke to him for the first time.

"Why? Why are you here? Why are you doing this?" she whispered.

He paused some time before answering, and when he did his voice was tremulous. "Because we are the same, you and I. Because you are young enough to learn, I think, that not all men are the same. But you can, you must try to, see the goodness that also exists in this, in all worlds. There are echoes in everything that can be read, did you know? And they told me to seek you here – but it's more complex than that. Sometimes we don't own our destiny, not really. This part of my life was not my own, it was yours. Come here, do this thing. I saw it, so I came. Because, even if you have no soul - especially if you have no soul - life is always sacred. It may be all we have after all."

"But - why wouldn't I have a soul?' she asked.

"Why?" The Ornish wanderer was aghast. "Don't you know what you *are*?"

Cherry looked momentarily scared. She had never met anyone who had any idea what she was, or where she had come from. If they had, they had not told her.

The traveller could not fill in the details of her conception, her birth - he did not know them - but there were legends of her kind amongst the Ornish - of the rare survivors of human and Ornish couplings. It was most likely, he said, that a Soul-less warrior had sired her. That therefore she would have no soul. It was a cruel tradition, but such was the Ornish desire to avoid violence it had become inviolable.

Neither one could recall how interwoven their tragic yesterdays had been, and he did not dwell on things yet to come. He could not help but see the wounded child as anything else but that which she was. She cried herself to sleep in his arms that night, and something within him broke for a second time.

When the bandages were removed from her eyes Cherry's rescuer had gone. She squinted into the dim light of the room, tried to find details in the blurred shapes moving around her, affix images to the voices and names. Whilst unsure how long she had been travelling, Cherry did know she had passed through the eastern reaches of the Nefarean Empire, crossing over the dark waters of the Sutzerean Straights into Sutzeria itself. The loss she felt when her companion left was profound, and this without ever laying eyes on him. He had been the first to show her any true kindness, but that was not all. Instinctively she knew they were bonded to each other, irrevocably.

"One day I will come back for you." he had said.

He never told her his name.

Once her eyes had recovered she was led from Nor-Thal, a small settlement in Nudd Bay, to Tantrix-Alumnae. Here an Ornish priest, Iutznefydd-Baal Pellafinn, took care of her. He provided a small apartment in the Flacks, continued her treatment. She grew strong, became quite a celebrity in the bright oval city. After years travelling the continent she was an adept with language, could stand her ground with the city wags. But Cherry had lived a harsh life. She found it hard to settle in the little city. The narrow walkways, dimmed by tall, overhanging Ornish buildings, grew oppressive. She was restless. The fight with life had been cast in her and it fuelled her. Without the need to fight she felt unsure of herself, so she took the path chosen by her father and so many other Ornish Soul-less: She had the saga of her life, as she understood it, gleaned and charted in fine red tattoos across her skin - interweaving the faint pink scars of her prolonged illness.

She became a mercenary.

One brisk winter dawn she marched out of Tantrix-Alumnae into the world. She did not return for seventy-six years.

The message Cherry received in Aetullia had seemed urgent. She was needed, it said. When she arrived back at Pellafinn's chambers asking questions the old priest had berated her for her absence, the stories of her exploits that had caused him such worry, but he had told her to go down into Tantrix-Alumnae and wait. She would be found. Cherry was about ready to move on again when the Soul-less mercenary had come for her. Giant, even by Ornish standards, his arms rippled in motion like the surface of an energetic stream. His were the wide flat shoulders of a born swimmer, and there was something of the hound in his long torso - deep chested, narrow at the waist. His expressive hands were strong and fine. They matched his face. His violet eyes were hard to look into for the torment that haunted them, but with profound clarity she realized that she loved Pellaq the moment their eyes met. She would have given him her own soul, had she one to give. She saw the sorrow he endured, an unspoken, terrible loss. (Cherry thought she knew about loss.) Though he would not say it, she also knew that it had been he who had saved her. That he had been true to his word: He had come back for her. Moreover, she knew he loved her. Had always loved her. She trembled inside, noticed how his hands shook - almost imperceptibly - whenever they spoke together. (In truth this shaking had stayed with him since he first caught sight of her, turning heads in Peribold Walk days earlier, and he was fighting a loosing battle to keep it under control.) She did not want to know why he had left her, the source of the fear that troubled his eyes. It was unimportant to her, passion made it irrelevant.

She was with him again.

In The Sayer's Alms Woebeg Ban Errieu was running through plans. Maps of the Ornisbach were laid out across a large wooden table, marked in varied colours denoting different routes. They would not be taking trade routes, or any of the more direct paths - they wished to be as inconspicuous as possible. Woebeg was committed in his manner - almost resigned Cherry thought.

"I'll say it - I'm impressed with what I've seen, Longorn." Woebeg said. "You're certainly formidable, that's clear enough!" In various corners Ornish and human alike nursed cuts and bruises inflicted by her. Woebeg had been diligent in his trials. "But you must understand, we could all die. This is not some petty campaign to put down a bunch of Ghull-Raiders in Suddfenn! If they ever suspect us, if the shit-eaters get wind, we're fucking dead. Simple as that."

"Out there, on the battlefield, I'll be yours Captain. I've

crossed the Ornisbach many times. It's not a place to hang about, but it's just a big hill after all."

""Just a big hill" eh?" Said Woebeg, looking up at her.

"Captain Ban Errieu, I'll be coming along with you whether you want me there or not. You can stop your worrying about me, and start being glad of it. I don't have to prove myself to you."

"All right then, Longorn. I won't stand in your way. Some important people, people who have concerns about Aetuland's immediate future, are privately funding this undertaking – they apparently want you along. The Council of Lordts has - bloody typically if you ask me - failed to come up with any kind of resolution. War is more than bleedin' well likely, far as I can see. Our employers seem to think so too. Now. Upfront the funds will get ten of us there and back I reckon. That'll include new gear if we need it - but nothing too flashy! We don't want any undue attention. The amount we will receive on returning - which I have already secured at the Methen Banker's Guild - is enough to keep even you long-lived Ornish content for a couple of lifetimes. Alternatively there's some substantial offers of land. I have contracts in my quarters if you want the extra security, but you do have my word on this as a former Captain of the Brookbane elite."

"When do we leave?" asked Cherry.

Woebeg bit deeply into the forefinger of his left hand, breathing heavily. He had found a storeroom adjacent to Heron's bedroom on the third floor of The Sayer's Alms and the slatted wood and plaster divide had warped enough over time for slender cracks to appear - cracks just wide enough to peer through. He had picked his moment carefully. It was early. Crew Finches warbled in the Golden-Ethné tree, which dominated the small courtyard at the back of the Inn. The clatter of market stalls setting up - shouts, laughter, and the flap of pigeon wings - danced in on the gentle breeze. Heron, woken moments earlier by the hubbub, rose naked from her pallet. Woebeg's heart lurched.

"Orn…" he whispered. "Oh, shit. Sweetheart, yes."

She swayed, groggy, stretching her arms above her head. A brief, energetic yawn gave way to a single high, pure note that faded into birdsong. Woebeg quivered at the sight of her large breasts, rising with her arms, nipples engorged in the cool air.

"Heron," he stammered quietly, urgently. "Oh you fucking beauty, you fucking fucking beauty."

With a languorous gaze he caressed the contours of her body, fixed urgent eyes upon the dark curls of her pubic mound.

It was not long before he ejaculated; semen spurting between shuddering fingers, pent up passion released with a violent scream that was barely a sigh.

He waited until she had dressed, gone below, and then let himself out of the storeroom. Crossing the hall he entered his rented quarters, coiled himself into a bundle on his pallet, wretched, wracked with guilt, the dreadful hollowness of the unrequited.

Two weeks passed. The duels and contests, organised with Heron's begrudging permission in the courtyard, had paid off. A lethal ragtag alliance emerged. When Woebeg Ban Errieu finally left Tantrix-Alumnae he marched with nine others:

Tunny Mal-Tuboly. It was his kind of venture. "And Orn! If we pull it off we'll be rich, man!"

The Ornish Soul-less; Iutzparthi-Llud Pellaq, the half-breed Cherry Longorn, travelling with him under their own mutual terms.

Two swarthy brothers from the south, Cass and Drum, lethal with numerous up-close weapons.

The pale, slender Arcassus Ban Tetrial wielded two short blades with brutal efficiency.

Balorvel Ban Kuss, a seasoned mercenary.

Marrat Ashemen-Hlot, who claimed he could track a wraith through fog.

And Nufeg Hagnodsfyorge, as fine a Bowman as any in Arddn.

Woebeg had not said goodbye to Heron. He did not think he would see her again.

Barachal Tush, the Sayer, watched from the shade of the Raven gate as they disappeared up into the foothills.

MERCENARIES

II

The band of spies and would-be thieves arrived at Dutwerth's
Leap on the afternoon of the sixth uneventful day following
their departure from Tantrix-Alumnae. Dutwerth's Leap had
once supported an impressive castle, perched like a great black
Rook on the edge of the precipitous overhang of rock. The castle
had long since been dismantled and rebuilt as the small town of
Dutwerth, clinging to craggy rocks like a child to its mother.
Access routes were steep and meandering, but not overly taxing,
and the hospitality in Dutwerth was legendary. Woebeg, Tunny
and Balorvel Ban Kuss had enjoyed many visits to the foothill
town over the years and were happy to be back. They each knew
where to go for the best food, wine or ale available. After all,

there was only one guesthouse in Dutwerth, "the Poniard of Bellthoria".

Thom Ban Nutton, the Landlord of "the Poniard", was fittingly a chiselled old rock of a man. He had served his time up at Da Derga's Heights when Pesheval Brookbane, Thrall Brookbane's father, held Lordtsway. Above the fireplace in the main bar hung an enormous seven-span sword, and he liked to tell its story.

"Iutzethra-Llal Bellthoria was the largest damned Ornish Soul-less that there ever was alive in the world. As I stand, six and one half spans, so he stood fifteen – no lie! He once carried a cart and two Oxen - an Ox under each arm. The cart, fully laden mind, on his back - across the river Wynne. He could dam up a river with one of his Dragboat feet, and I watched him vault the walls at Tantrix-Alumnae - so wide was his back he could not fit through any of the gates! I swear, he washed his face by poking his head up into the clouds, uprooting an Oak to scrub those tombstone teeth with its roots.

"When I served Pesheval Brookbane, Bellthoria was said to be at least six hundred years old, but for the cracks around his eyes and the pain in his knees you'd swear to a third of that! He was Brookbane's personal guard, his closest confidant. He went everywhere with the aging Lordt. We've all seen the statue of the pair atop Methen gate at Tantrix-Alumnae, back to back-of-thighs at the Battle of Tuffin Hill. So it was no surprise when, in answer to the crap-eating Nefars invasion of Free Nochentia, Lordt Brookbane sent old Bellthoria to attain some assurances - against any possible invasion of Sutzeria and Aetuland - as much as to convey the acute displeasure of the High Council of the Lordts at the Nefars most recent aggressions.

"Bellthoria refused to be escorted though, and chose to go to the continent by his own means. He ran - with a great rolling and grunting and grinding of the knees - traversing the Aetuland Spine in three bounds, which nearly broke the island in two! On he ran, and his running whipped up a hurricane, which sunk twenty Nefarean pirate Dragboat hiding in Nudd Bay. And still he ran, hopping over the surging wild whiteness of the river Rae, as a child would a brook. The huge mountains that used to puncture the sky at Brows Well in Gwendd were laid low in the fury of his passing - so that it is now the flattest land in all the kingdom of Orn! Still, on he ran - to the Point of Fridd, and there leapt from those great jagged cliffs out over the Sutzerean Straights. The first mighty bound brought him to the Isle de Roche - where the hole he made filled up and became a great lake. The next took him to the Isle de Florettia - which sunk and is no more. And the third bound brought him into the false dominion of the crap-eating Nefars and their Munger-loving Emperor.

"So it was that Bellthoria was taken before the Nefarean Emperor, Khatzach ai Baden Shevic - the Majestrix-Rexae himself! The two of them talked into the night, for the emperor was impressed with the great stature of Bellthoria, as well as his noble bearing. For four days and nights Bellthoria kept the Emperor amused with feats of strength, tales of times passed from the world. At last, Shevic could resist no more. He could not help but comment upon the incredible size of the sword Bellthoria kept strapped across his back. The Ornish Soul-less - having drunk twelve barrels of the Emperor's finest wine and six hogsheads of Long Ale - replied. "Sword? What sword? This is my hunting knife! Our swords we keep for battle, and those who would threaten our freedom!"

"It is said that Shevic became enraged and struck off Bellthoria's right hand while a hundred and twenty eight men restrained him. He had the hand – which killed nine men even after it had been so rudely separated from it's rightful owner - strapped to the hilt of the giant sword and sent back to Pesheval Brookbane with a note, bearing the legend:

""If you come into Nefarea you had best bring your swords, not your knives.

"Until we meet in Orn.

"Shevic, Majestrix-Rexae."

"And there it is, the poniard of Bellthoria, by fucking Orn! And though you may scoff, it truly did look much more like a dagger than a sword in those bloody monstrous hands."

Everyone knew that the sword over the fireplace was just a shabby, somewhat rusty, replica - though no one would ever say so out loud. But in the dim of the large bar it commanded some awe, if not in its craftsmanship, then in its sheer size.

Woebeg enjoyed the tale for maybe the tenth time, snoozing in a warm corner, and waiting for things to start getting lively.

"Oh fuck," said Tunny, "This looks bad, chaps."

Above them and either side of the narrow pass rogue Nefars stood, bows and blades poised, Nefarean brandings livid on serious brows.

"Quiet Tunny!" hissed Woebeg, breath spiralling in the ice-haze of low cloud. They had all left Dutwerth in high spirits, moving swiftly up into the Ornisbach via the relative shelter of Terrek's Pass. Two days into the climb they arrived at an old border hut settled on a jut of rock, which punctured the glacier abutting Mount Jenedd. Here they spent the night, and Pellaq had revealed his plan to go on ahead into Sutzeria, once he had seen them across the glacier between Mount Tunday and Mount Durgh. He would say no more, but that he would be going to Orn, the spiritual centre of the Ornish, and that he was going alone. (Cherry had gritted her teeth, confusion a scream within her. She was loosing him again. But she said nothing.)

Marrat Ashemen-Hlot was furious at himself for not spotting the signs that should have given the Nefars away. He knew instantly they were out-numbered - seven, eight to one. He began frantically searching for the best way out of their predicament.

"What are you doing up here?" asked Woebeg as coolly as though the Nefars were old friends chance met.

"I do not think" said the stocky leader in a rolling voice of round vowels and clipped punctuation "that you are in the position to ask questions here. But what's it matter, eh?" He laughed throatily. "We are, as you see, Nefars - is it "crap-eaters" or "dog-fuckers"? I cannot remember – and I suppose we don't have masters now, see? Nevertheless, it is a shame, all right? As we do not like pissy Aetulanders much, so where do we go? It's good you are here though. We are hungry, and I am sorry but we are fed up of eating our own crap. Maybe we eat some of yours, eh?"

The Nefars - those that understood - laughed darkly at the joke.

"We're going to Sutzeria," said Woebeg, scratching his head. "Aetuland is falling apart. Doesn't stand a bloody chance if this "Wayfarer" fellow really is coming. Not from what we've heard anyway. Truth is we don't really care where our allegiance lies any more. Perhaps we could join you?"

"No, I don't think so," replied the rogue Nefarean leader. "We are hungry through being too many as it is."

And upon a barked order the Nefars attacked.

The first to die was Nufeg Hagnodsfyorge. He barely had time to fire a single arrow before one of the rogues pierced him below the ribs from behind, lifting him off the ground in the thrust. He died without a sound.

The same could not be said for Drum. He killed four of the attackers in quick succession, assorted blades dicing them, laying open their stomachs, throats, eyes in a wild flurry of motion. When the tendons behind his knees were sliced he toppled backward onto an awaiting blade and screamed like a child until his throat was slit. Cass stumbled towards him, the fight forgotten. He barely noticed the relentless puncture of arrows as he held his brother in his arms, rocking him as his own life, in turn, fled.

Marrat Ashemen-Hlot secured himself in a narrow fissure. Shortly thereafter the tough veteran, Balorvel Ban Kuss, joined him. The two of them worked a deadly magiq together, killing upwards of fifteen Nefars before long pikes were brought in, gouging chunks out of them in sickeningly slow systematic thrusts. Finally, Balorvel, in an act of mercy, hacked off the appallingly wounded tracker's head before falling upon his own blade.

Tunny Mal-Tuboly danced through the Nefars in a manner that belied his bulk, but an axe blow opened his head and he went face down into the snow and lay still.

Arcassus Ban Tetrial and Woebeg had both run forward into the enemy, Woebeg screaming obscenities, Arcassus silent. The effect was the same: Both managed to break through the ranks of Nefars, killing and wounding them. They fought a fast-moving battle weaving through the mountains, the attackers in pursuit.

Woebeg felt the rise obtusely. He grinned. Shouted. He executed his strange stiff dance, killing more by far than he should have by rights. It was a gift of sorts, but he was blind to it. He's methods were as unknown to him as those that died by them. He was an automaton, industrious in his slaughter. He spat fear at his opponents in great gouts, smothered them. His killing was arcane.

Arcassus fought with fury and desperation, though his soldierly discipline was telling in the numbers he sent screaming to the Munger. Yet eventually their flight brought them to a dead halt against a featureless granite face. They turned to find themselves facing another wall of fifteen grinning Nefars.

Woebeg laughed. "Come on then, you dog-fuckers!" He yelled, "Shit-eating dog-fuckers!" He ran at them once more.

Behind him Arcassus yelped as an arrow pierced him in the hip.

Techen Phippe watched as one after another of his comrades was dispatched. He could not make sense of what he was seeing. The man jerked, twisted, laughed, and from him came fear. It was palpable, almost physical. It weakened them. Weakened him.

"Dog-fuckers! Shit-eaters!" he shouted, and Techen Phippe watched his companions die.

Fifteen were now ten. The other man was down, clutching at the arrow in his hip, trying to stop the blood. Ten men circled this crazy jigging old man, and yet, *And yet*, thought Techen, *we could loose this fight. We could fucking die here, all of us.*

Now there were nine.

Eight.

Techen had once been a student of more peaceful ways. In the mountains he had studied the mysteries; nature, ether. Time - what had he learned amongst the priests of Ypo-Polaria so many years ago, when still a boy? Before the Nefarean army had razed the temples, stolen him away, branded him, made him one of them? What was it the Priests had taught him about fear and time? That in some way they were connected. Etherworks wrought in time could change it's passing. He had been adept, skilled. He could have been Magus, should have been - but that was another life. If he could only now conquer the fear starting to infuse his bones, slow him down, then he had a chance. They all had a chance.

Seven.

Techen Phippe watched, stepped back, changed his perspective, and this time, as the warrior cut down the next man, leaving six, he saw how the blood spread like a fan. Growing and blooming. Still growing...

He saw the scene at another angle, with ancient disciplines

he'd only ever known as a means for enhancing the thought process. Etherworks, deep meditations, to better understand the world, not to destroy it. Techniques that slowed down time...

They could have saved themselves, thought Techen, *the Priests, they could have saved us from all of this.*

As the world danced slowly around him, Techen advanced upon this dealer of death and raised his own sword. He and Woebeg were in another realm, alone, just the two of them. Techen noted the looks on his companions faces as they tried to focus on him, understand how it was he also moved, how he was doing this. They looked shocked, scared.

Woebeg caught a motion, an intrusion, in his peripheral vision - something moving too fast. He turned in time to avoid the cutting edge of a sword, but it's flat connected violently with his skull. Woebeg felt his consciousness shift again, slipping away now. But still the soldier in him reflexively struck back, a brute cut of little grace, his sword thudding into Techen's side, almost halving him.

Not right. That wasn't right. There's something fucking wrong about this. thought Woebeg, senses dimming.

It was Cherry who caused most grievance to the mountain rogues, killing the leader with a thrust upward through his groin to the base of his ribcage, a wide savage smile like a gash across her face, his spurting blood saturating her. She moved with deadly purpose through a tide of tiny men, giant, ebon, an effigy of some forgotten goddess dragged screaming back to life by bloody sacrifice. Sheer numbers brought her down in the end, but they would not be killing this rare prize.

Woebeg gritted chattering teeth as yet another of the Nefarean warriors raped him, fucked him.

He was naked, spread, face down in the snow, arms and legs

lashed to stakes. Beaten, his mouth oozed bloody saliva onto the ice, body shuddering with cold and horror. He was a soldier, a veteran, but he had never been bested. Rape was an act he had not fully acknowledged in warfare. It was a denial, almost an abstraction. But he had born witness to it. ("All right lads, that's enough now. That's enough.") He was helpless. There was no way free. He could not fight his way out of this. *Bested*, he thought. *Beaten. I'm beaten.* ("That's enough now lads. Fucker's had enough.") *I'm fucking beaten.*

He turned his head to where Arcassus had been suffering a similar fate, but the swordsman's eyes had glazed over. The Nefars kicked him anyway, joking with each other.

"Maybe you like to try some of this, eh? Is good, yes?"

Woebeg looked up as best he could at the man who was speaking and noticed with rising horror the lump of shit in his hand.

"N. N. N." he stammered, but was cut short as the Nefar pulled back his head by the hair, smeared the vile matter around Woebeg's mouth, forcing it between lips and teeth with rough, filthy fingers. Woebeg instantly gagged, puked, gasped for breath, but the man carried on, retrieving lumps from amongst the contents of Woebeg's voided stomach, forcing them back in.

"Try it, please. It won't kill you. Actually it might, but it will have been worth it." He sounded almost offended in his tone. "No really, you will like it…"

Cherry turned her head away from the spectacle and took, in turn, her share of the Nefarean abuse. It was nothing new to her. She knew how to survive it.

There was cutting, pulling, and suddenly the tension was released. He felt strong arms role him over, lift him gently onto soft furs. Slowly everything was drawing closer, looming out of the night.

There was a face, looming, looming out of the darkness. Coming towards him. Out of the night.

"How are you?" Asked Tunny Mal-Tuboly.

"Oh shit, Tunny," whispered Woebeg through chattering teeth. "I've seen better days..."

And he slipped back into the darkness.

MERCENARIES

III

"The Ornish say the *Munger* was trapped," said Tunny, fingering the Mountain Marmot bone he had completely stripped of meat, eyeing it with melancholy. "In what they call *Vile-space*, and that was inverted into the *gemstone*. They trapped a *God* inside a *stone* ten thousand years ago! The only way the Munger can be freed is by uniting the gemstone with the Torc it was mounted upon. Listen, mate; there is more truth to the Ornish legends than you might like to think. You may not believe them, but I - by Orn's nads - have seen things with my own eyes that say different!"

Woebeg shook his head minutely, almost a shudder, his frown deepening. But he refrained from comment.

"The Torc is lost now, long ago. Hidden by the Ornish when they first came to Arddn from their own world. But - the gemstone never got where it was supposed to go. It was taken onto the continent, but never reached its destination. The Ornish Warloqs, to whom the gemstone had been entrusted, were attacked. The stone - lost.

"Some centuries ago, a gemstone with certain paranatural properties started appearing in Nefarean folklore. You've heard the legend of the *Dealing Stone*, right? Well it seems our Ornish benefactor believes it might actually exist, and be one and the same stone, by Orn! So, that's what this is all about. I'll tell you what though, mate; my head is fucking sore…"

Tunny Mal-Tuboly's eyes fluttered momentarily in the firelight, he gingerly touched the blood-caked bandage dressing the festering gash in his forehead.

"Why didn't fucking Pellaq tell me all this?" asked Woebeg, shivering in his furs the other side of the fire.

"Who can say?" replied Tunny, looking off towards the fading red tear of a sunset over the Ornisbach. "Maybe he witnessed me telling you in the Echoes-To-Be? Maybe he knew you wouldn't risk your life for what you'd think was a pile of Rafasi-crap…"

"Well he'd have been bloody right there!" Rumbled Woebeg through gritted teeth.

Tunny's face creased suddenly, a portrait of agony, and he hunched forward into a ball, shuddering.

"I'll be glad to be off this damned mountain and inside some nice warm tart with a belly full, I can tell you!" He said. Woebeg nodded his agreement but was too wrapped in his own misery to be overly concerned about his friend's condition.

"Woebeg." Tunny continued, the uncharacteristically serious tone returning once more. "The fate of the world, mate, is down to us. You, me, and this fucking stone. And what a right bloody mess we've made of things so far! Looks as though the bastards have got poor Cherry too - still, I know enough about that one to almost pity the crap-eating swine that's got her! Oh shit. Tactless bastard. I'm sorry Woebeg."

"What for, Tunny?" Woebeg asked, distractedly. "What the bloody hell for?"

The sun had completely sunk behind the peaks and the now familiar utter blackness of the mountain night engulfed them.

Raised a slave in the conquered lands of the Nefareans, it had not taken long for Cherry to talk her way into the hearts of the rogue Nefars in the Ornisbach. She shared their language and customs. She was beautiful, exotic. They soon forgave her the deaths she had brought about, allowing her to become one of them. They fell in love with her.

Within a week they were all dead.

Cherry came down from the Ornisbach alive, but alone. There was only one desire within her - to find Pellaq. The Nefareans heavily controlled North-Eastern Sutzeria, where the grand and ancient city of Orn sat mouldering upon a dusty plateau. Armies patrolled it systematically; much of the area had been raped. Pellaq would have had to take great care in reaching the city, and Cherry, if she was to be crossing Northern Sutzeria also, judged it best to do so in a position of employment. She went to Duhn to find a Nefarean merchant bound for Orn.

A vast, ill-treated place, Duhn sprawled by the river Rae in cosmopolitan confusion and unpredictable subjugation. Savaged and over-run more than any city in Sutzeria - or indeed on Arddn - Duhn was peopled by ragmen, gutter-wags, nomads, politicians, merchants and the soldiers of whichever nation held power there at any given time.

It was a city of towering scarred architecture, dusty grey parks, and long hedonistic nights. It existed for trade, was sick in its heart because of this. The impoverished were drawn to

Duhn, motivated by the false hope that it might deliver them into wealth; transform them into creatures of cunning, devoid of weak-minded morality. But it grazed on the poor, its streets littered with their bones.

Duhn was, however, a survivor amongst cities. It was ancient, and at its centre an Ornish temple still stood impassively. No invader would completely lay waste to it on account of its prime plot: It was the gateway into Sutzeria and Aetuland from the continent. Its trade halls were huge, generating vast revenue. It was essential to all that it be maintained – at least in the districts where fortunes were being created.

Cherry liked Duhn; she had taken on many commissions there. It was a city that thrilled her, appealed to her damaged nature. The rubble of Duhn's recently breached walls bit unevenly upward through the ground like an enormous mantrap. The poverty and death permeating the outskirts safeguarded the inner city, driving many away. Walking northward up Prospect Place, Cherry noted huge pyres of smouldering human debris, belching malignant black clouds in the shadowy twilight. Packs of master-less Dogren - feathers tattered, colourless with dust, their spherical eyes refracting morsels of light - fought for gruesome titbits to swell cadaverous shanks.

A wide avenue, Prospect Place ran alongside the Great Union Canal, upon the putrid foamy waters of which barges ferried the city's shit and debris. The grand cloistered houses, which ran along the opposite side of the rutted, sucking road, were, without exception, windowless. Small splutters of wane light hinted at pockets of life within. Above, upon the few hundred-span-high columns that still remained standing, were the lifeless mottled green husks of the *Machivaria*. Cherry recalled how once they had been the envy of Arddn. Cast in bronze, they were made in the image of a four-headed Lionid, each head facing outwards from the centre. Lazrus Machivarius had found a means by which energy could be harnessed, increased exponentially, and put to good use throughout the city. He initially discovered that lightening could be employed to generate light. By containing the power it produced within a Tantric Sphere he could light one room for up to twelve days. Eventually columns topped with Lionid-headed *Machivaria*, as they became known, were placed strategically all over Duhn, adhering to the lehlines and co-ordinated with other geographical energy fields located above and beneath the city. Lazrus Machivarius - taking the principles of the Tantric Sphere and applying them to what he named "Tantric Tubes", ether-work tunnels - linked up the Machivaria in a huge network above Duhn. The city blazed into light and for two centuries Duhn traded day and night, never sleeping, basking in the glow of the Machivaria.

It was darkly humorous to Cherry that, as it later turned out, no other city upon Arddn had energy fields of sufficient scale or complexity to maintain Machivaria in such numbers. They were unique to Duhn as, in time, other more efficient methods of creating light were devised elsewhere. It seemed fitting somehow.

Eventually persistent invasion and warfare damaged too many of the ingenious tantric-machines. The lights went out over Duhn, never to come on again.

Prospect Place ran straight up into Flackminster, where it joined Griphon Road, Torpe Street and New Haddly Street at Chittin Circus. Cherry paused to gaze at the large roundabout bearing the wreckage of a once fabulously ornate fountain. Now a mound of dead bodies adorned it, half obscured beneath a cloud of ravenous Rooks, Ravens and Wyrats.

No one had bothered to set the pestilent heap alight.

By the time she reached the inner walls it was midnight, but Duhn had still not revealed its true, ravishing, ugly face. She hid for a moment in the ruined fetid lobby of the formerly prestigious

Hotel Valdenpoliére, as a troupe of truculent Nefarean soldiers sauntered past, whooping. From there she could make out the remaining left wing of Pertinax's summer palace, looming like a hollow in the darkness, and next to that, the old courthouse in Utoxiter Road. The legacy of the ancient Ornish settlement asserted itself here, in the grand scale of the facades, high doorways and bridges. Ornish architecture had always been beloved of Duhn, though no self-respecting Ornish - but for the wayward Soul-less - would any longer step foot in the cursed city. Cherry could hear far-off sounds of revelry; smell the culinary delectations of all-night restaurants. She was nearing the river Rae, and the gaudy shops and bars that festooned her banks.

In the dusk she meandered through hearty throngs on Celebration Row, smiling at admirers, enjoying the crush. Music pounded, oozed and throbbed out of bars, cafes, or erupted from the street itself. Charming beggars tipped hats. Others, less charming, swore, or spat, or stumbled in drunken stupors into gaps people made for them. An Epicurean paradise, as far as Cherry could see people milled, drank, ate, danced, fucked, spent - and made - money. She wandered delightedly along the whole great stretch of Celebration Row, through Aetuland Square, with its million lamps, down Florrid Road, Gray's End, into Iuddydd Park. Here, a quieter crowd gathered around the enormous fire that perpetually burned, a place for lovers. Cherry skirted the blaze at a distance, not wishing to be reminded about matters of her own heart.

Finally she came to the Ornish-crafted canyon that was Iutzettra-Hai Crescent. Two titanic structures that curved, parallel to each other, in a gentle arc stretching from Iuddydd Park to Trypeston Station and the northernmost inner wall. Twin aeries in white Moniath Marble - massive slabs shipped over from Ypo-Polaria - each stood six hundred spans tall. The monolithic structures were featureless, but for the slatted windows, impressively huge doorways, and at night the candlelight. Magnified through lenses, it shone up through strategic ground-level holes ringed with railings, and danced over the buildings - creating the illusion that they were themselves made of light; gargantuan spectral structures of purest white.

By daylight their age was evident, however, for they were pockmarked with the scars of three thousand years of strife.

Cherry had long maintained rooms in Iutzettra-Hai Crescent. There was anonymity to be had there - a rare and blessed thing for her. Nowhere was safer in that ever-changing city. She found her way uneventfully to spacious penthouse chambers just as morning sunlight blazed through the slender windows, painting golden strips across her bleached white walls.

"I'm sorry Woebeg, I just…" Tunny Mal-Tuboly was leaning hard on Woebeg, breathing heavily.

"I just need to, to…"

He slumped to his knees and swayed unsteadily.

"I'm sorry old chap. Can't seem to…"

Woebeg tried to lift him, move him from the path to the shelter of a tree and the comfort of soft grass. But the big shaggy mercenary was not responding, seemed not to notice.

"Come on Tunny, fer fuck's sake…" he breathed through his teeth with the effort. "Let's get your fat arse over here…"

The bigger man just pitched forward into the mud, rolled onto his side, panting.

"Woebeg!" he shouted. "I did tell you, didn't I? About the stone?"

"Sod the fucking stone! And yes, you told me!" shouted Woebeg; frustrated and verging on what he assumed must be panic - a feeling he was unaccustomed to.

"No no no, Woebeg, listen to me. The stone. You've got to get it back to them. To the Ornish. They'll know what to do."

"Bollocks to the stone, Bollocks to the fucking Ornish, and bollocks to you!" yelled Woebeg, a crimson bloom high in his cheeks. "Get up! Get up man! Look…" he pointed down the hill towards the hazy horizon. "There. It's Duhn, fer crying out loud! No more than half a day's crawl I'll wage ya! You remember old Duhn, don't you Tunny boy? Times we had! Who was that tart you met down Celebration Row? Emmer? Edina? Ran your flabby arse right out of town in the end, didn't she? Come on Tunny," he said, as the panic turned to sorrow and found a way out in moist rivulets down his ruddy soldiers' cheeks. "I've got nothing else left but you, sunshine. Nothing. Just a little further, eh? We'll get that head of yours cleaned up. Nothing a good night and a warm bed in Duhn can't sort."

But Tunny Mal-Tuboly - the jovial, jocular barrel of a man; the infuriating unreliable sloth; the fool, coward, drunk; the gem and salt; the hearty and compassionate, beloved of men and women alike through all mighty Orn and the emerald isle of Gan - this man had died on his way to Duhn. Slumped in a rut on a filthy path and a hopeless quest.

VILE-SPACE

I

Winter draped itself over Tantrix-Alumnae like a fitted gown, softening the city's edges and making it all the more beautiful. Finely dressed nobles glided down the hard-packed snow covered streets, on skis and skates. Gas lanterns sputtered their warm light and the scent of spiced wine permeated the night air.

In "the Sayer's Alms" spirits were high, the seasonal increase in patrons lending more comradely comfort to the already inviting atmosphere.

Tersis Halvern was a middle-aged wine merchant from Aetullia, two weeks south of Tantrix-Alumnae. He had known Heron for most of her life, and had done business with her directly, ever since her father had died. She had sold the family vineyard in neighbouring Ghuppio to him then, and moved up to Tantrix-Alumnae, taking over patronage of The Sayer's Alms. He and Heron had since enjoyed an easy trading relationship, his butter wines being amongst the most popular in her cellar, and she had long been the unknowing custodian of his affection.

Heron regarded Tersis from out the corner of her eye, as he fretted about, not knowing quite where he should look. Unusually, for the soft-spoken, reserved merchant, he had remained in the Sayer's Alms for most of the afternoon, hovering around the bar area long after his business had been completed. He half turned, again, as if to leave. Hesitated, scratching his nose. He removed his floppy black velvet cap, smoothed back his thick grey hair before once more replacing the hat and turning again towards the bar. He looked flustered. She smiled, and had the feeling that he wanted to say something to her, but could not find either the words or the courage.

Her heart quickened slightly at the prospect, which surprised her a little.

He was a handsome man, she supposed, having not really considered it before. Hard working. Strong. His features were even and his eyes gentle. He was not a tall man, true, but what did that matter? She was a little under five spans herself! Not one inclined to indulge in idle chatter - indeed he spoke only when he had to - his lined face none-the-less betrayed his good humour. She thought him as fine a man as any she was likely to meet, and after all, she knew him well. Trusted him.

As she turned back towards him Tersis once again removed his hat and sought out her eye.

"Ah, Heron?" he said, "Could I - a word perhaps? If you, if you're too busy I could always -"

"Of course, Tersis," she replied. "What's up, dear?"

"Hm." He looked down at the hat, as if he could not think why he was holding it. He looked up. "Oh. Ah. About tonight

- You haven't any rooms left by chance have you? Only it's late, and usually I -"

"I haven't, Tersis love. Time of the year." said Heron.

"Ah," he said. "All right. Never mind. I will be getting off then. Lovely to, ah - I mean, It has been, as ever, a pleasure seeing you again, Heron."

"Patience Tersis!" she scolded, warmly. "Did I say you couldn't stay? There's always a corner for you here. My house is your house; you should know that. We're practically family after all!"

"I wouldn't want to, ah, to put you to any, ah…"

"I'll have Mola lock up tonight. Let's eat upstairs; maybe spoil ourselves with a bottle or two. What do you think?" The look she threw him was not subtle.

II

Woebeg Ban Errieu shut out everything. He chose not to dwell on the last half-year. He would not be broken so easily. He had a warrior's asinine pride.

The quest he had embarked upon had been more for profit than anything else. He had led eight doomed warriors into the mountains of the Ornisbach and, to his knowledge, had been the only one to come down the other side alive. But it had been more a fool's crusade than even he had imagined. The whole truth - that his Ornish financier had required him to seek out some mythic gemstone - had not been revealed to him at the outset. The entire endeavour had ended with his dreams of glory dead in the snow, buried in a shallow grave alongside his closest friend. He would not be returning to Tantrix-Alumnae in fine silks and velvets. He would not be entering "the Sayer's Alms", proclaiming himself a hero and stealing the heart of its landlady after all. He would not be returning to claim the land and wealth promised him either. How could he? Woebeg was a modern man and a sceptic. He'd seen no great wonders in his lifetime. No small inexplicable occurrence had dented his perception of a stony, rational reality. He believed, as many others believed, that the great paranatural occurrences of former times were bloated truths, made grander to perpetuate the majesty and heroics of dead Lordts and fallen nations. They were legends to inspire armies, and bogies to scare children. He did not believe in any of it. He did not believe his skills were anything other than martial. He did not believe in Orn, or the Munger. The revelation, that the true nature of his quest was to steal an enchanted stone, had turned his stomach. A great cost for a hoaxer's trinket; a Fakir's trick.

And anyway, he had failed.

The Wayfarer's men had found Woebeg as he rolled Tunny Mal-Tuboly, his oldest friend, into a shallow grave dug out with his own bloody fingers. He put up quite a fight before they overwhelmed him. Starved and ill-treated, the swarthy Aetulander had perplexed the Nefarean soldiers with staggering martial prowess belying his condition and accompanied by a torrent of expletives. Time had seemed to warp around the man; he would in one instant be facing forward, and the next, back, another crumpled body bleeding at his feet. But eventually their numbers wore him down. Soon they were dragging him to Duhn in chains, scratching their heads and nursing their wounds.

And yet Woebeg was in some ways a lucky man. The Warlordt, *Baalor Dark-Eye*, this 'Wayfarer' who had taken control of the vast city, insisted on giving captured warriors a chance to join him. The Nefarean soldiers who had captured Woebeg were obliged to present Woebeg to him, rather than summarily killing the man. And clearly, Woebeg had proven himself no ordinary soldier. It was a sound policy, for the majority of the warriors taken before the Warlordt chose life, and swelled the ranks of his army - such was the man's charisma.

VILE-SPACE

III

Machivarius Point loomed above the city of Duhn, a phallic monstrosity in bronze. Its domed over-hanging head was pitted with two hundred circular portals framed in the mouths of roaring Lionid effigies. It was the Central Machivaria, from which numinous energies once spluttered, bringing light to the city. The structure was an oxide green, mottled with the black, white and purple of Wyrat and pigeon shit. From here Baalor Dark-Eye - so often called Wayfarer - gazed out over the city with contempt, as though it were some repugnant saprophytic organism, consuming Sutzeria, relentlessly eating away the country's beauty, field by field. Duhn was an affront to him; a product primarily of currency, and all he considered wrong in the world. Even as a young man he had not liked the city - though he could trace his lineage to near it's founding. Raised in rugged splendour amongst the mountains, the complex fortifications of Da Derga's Heights. Educated in gentile Tantrix-Alumnae's oval embrace, Baalor Dark-Eye had a dual love of natural open space and high culture. Duhn, in his consideration, offered little of either.

The Wayfarer's thoughts drifted, as he recalled Da Derga's Heights. Looking southeast, in the direction of Shea Pass, the looming mountains of the Ornisbach, he considered the fate of the blinded – now legendary - Lordt, Thrall Brookbane.

In agony, Brookbane had fled his home, his responsibilities, and his people. What kind of Lordt, or General; what kind of soldier could any blind man be? With this wretched knot of candour in his heart he was taken in secrecy to Duhn, shamefully disguised as a wounded Nefarean officer. At least he could not see the foul place any longer, he thought. But in his sickened mind it quickly assumed an even more frightful aspect.

Doctors were sought out, brought blindfolded to the hidden place. They eased the pain with deft ether works, filled in his livid eye-sockets with an assortment of pungent poultices. But the damage ran deeper than any physical lesion; it gnawed at his vitality, his fortitude; soured such nobility as was carefully nurtured over a lifetime of courtly machinations.

Vanity, his worst feature, emerged to dominate him. He became a fearful inversion of his former self, embarked upon a fanatical enterprise to seek out a particular miracle cure-all with all the passionate cruelty of a zealot. If a thing could be bought, it could be bought in Duhn. And so a large portion of his immense wealth was adroitly attained and smuggled into the over-grown, still partially glass-enclosed Arboretum - his discretely acquired home of late. With this he purchased certain specialised information, which in turn led his agents to the *Dealing Stone*. Purportedly anything was possible, however unlikely it may seem, if one could strike a deal with the entity imprisoned within the gemstone. Many people died attesting this. Thrall Brookbane, therefore, decided that the stone – and its improbable wish-granting entity - would be his at any cost. He would know he had tried everything, no matter how seemingly demeaning, to achieve his end. No matter that his retainers, his agents, all those in his employ, thought him a fool. He would see again. He would be Lordt again, the returning hero of the Battle of Da Derga's Heights. He began to search for the "Dealing Stone" in earnest, staking all he owned on this lunatic gamble; this most unlikely and futile dream.

A year, then two more, passed, turning up gemstone after gemstone. Some crackled or hissed, full of illusive paranatural potency, aflame with wispy black swirls or cyan shimmers of ether. Others bayed like Dogren or screamed like children at certain hours of the night. One large ugly stone bled copiously, shuddering like a slaughtered hog, its form turned flesh-like at full moon. All miraculous gems indeed, but none curative.

Yet, eventually he did find it. Reputedly stolen from a Chio-Wei temple in Ypo-Polaria, it arrived clad in an ornate black box, like a shrine, *Ornish in design*.

Thrall Brookbane would never forget the night.

The finders had been blindfolded, hastily paid, gruffly dismissed amongst a cloud of disinformation. What matter the perils of their search? Most likely it would yield him up nothing, as all the rest. He had groped inside the box, not believing. But the stone within it was remarkable. It was more, much more than it seemed, and not really a gemstone of any kind at all. It was an inverted space, infinite in size - and terrible.

Intuitively he plunged the mounted sphere into an eye socket – as though it had been crafted to fit such - heedless of the scraping and tearing of his barely-healed flesh.

It was an act of self-hatred, cavalier hubris: A challenge.

He could not have suspected the outcome.

In darkness he sweated, kneeling before the black box, gripping either side of it, the attached chain trailing, dripping freshly drawn blood into it.

"All right, you fucker. Piece of fucking shit fake. Fuck you!" he growled.

The sensation was little more than a tingle at first, as though his circulation was impaired by tension. It emanated from his fingertips, his toes, spreading in increments up through his arms and legs, his spine. Then Thrall Brookbane experienced shock. He lashed out, yelped, as he felt the thumb of his right hand being apparently severed below the knuckle. Standing up, swaying, cursing his blindness and his supposed unknown assailant, he floundered about, sweeping the air with his other arm.

"Where are you?" he shouted. "Where the fuck are you, you fucking cowardly bastard! Attack a blind man would you? Well come on then!"

But the thumb had not been severed, not in any physical way, though the hand gripped under his left armpit continued to experience the terrifying sensation of being mutilated, finger by finger, joint by joint. To Brookbane it was as if the flesh was somehow slowly being burned, flayed; the bones broken and digits removed - and he could not stop it. There was nobody for him to fight.

Soon it was happening to both hands, to his feet, the length of his arms, his legs. He fell to the earth, gasping, pain curling him. He writhed snake-like on hot coals. He gagged, expelled hissing arcane acids that ate away his lips; dissolved his innards, turning them to slop; emerged in steaming black rivulets through his flesh.

At a point when all he regarded as self, psyche, ego, was almost lost, and barely a glimmer of his rational mind remained

- it got worse. And yet within that final moment of being he discovered calm. A part of him was able to secure itself there, and rest. Re-grow. Inside out. The agonies that had battered him started to cling, and leave layers. He began to take on a semblance of form. The pain became rapturous, and he regained a whole new kind of awareness.

Within the inverted reality of the "Dealing Stone" Thrall Brookbane opened new glutinous eyes to chaos:

Thrall Brookbane witnessed networks of churning tunnels, constantly shifting and confounding.

Everything alive! Warm. Wet.

It brushed up against him, smeared itself upon him.

It cut him, left long mucous trails and deep jagged wounds in the flesh of his skinless new self.

Jag-toothed screams formed a physical wind that tore everything apart, but it rebuilt itself constantly into new and ghastly assemblages, grim arrangements of bone and blood.

Thrall Brookbane gave himself up to it.

He dived into it, swam within it, breathed it.

He dressed himself in it and made himself a God of it.

He punished it.

He fucked it.

In time he became it.

He had endured ruin.

He allowed himself to become enslaved, and yet he had triumphed.

Cloaked in a billion aspects he tore through uncountable hells in search of the Munger.

Thrall Brookbane awoke.

He was curled up, shivering upon the cold floor of the Arboretum beside the Ornish box.

But he could see.

He stood, shakily, looked around at all that was left to him.

"All right then. What is the price?" he muttered darkly.

Almost in answer the ground trembled. The huge expanses of glass and once ornately decorated walls shuddered, shifting apart stone by stone, pane by pane, falling away from him, shattering, exploding - upwards. He found himself upon a column of earth, rising, gaining speed, bursting through floor after floor of the near derelict structure.

Pinned to the column's pinnacle he shot up into the night sky.

Lordt Thrall Brookbane stared at the plate before him. The venison was just as he liked it, tender and rare. It steamed in the cool air of his favourite hall, the Armourium at Da Derga's Heights. The table was laden with meat and vegetables. Bread - spiced and un-spiced, laced with onion, black Olives, garlic - begged to be dipped into the warmed Peelo oil, or the steaming salty broths that lay scattered about.

At the far end of the table an empty chair awaited its sitter.

She strode into the hall with all the regal majesty and sublime beauty his memories afforded her:

The Lady Pesheval Nar-Bo Tertrigal Ban Hapfthoven Ne Belorvelian-Alumnae – his beloved wife, Munger-stricken and dead for over a decade - sat down opposite her husband, looked deep into his adoring eyes, and smiled.

He fucked her as if he would never make love to her again. She wrapped her legs behind his back, pressing her heels into the small of it. He held her at the waist, looked down at her, as she enjoyed the sight of her own hands fondling firm breasts. She gasped, laughed, came for a second time, as he plunged himself into her again and again.

*

"I love you, Pesheval." Lordt Brookbane said, rolling over and gazing unbelievingly into her dark brown fawn's eyes. "More than my life. More than even I knew."

"Oh, oh dear," said the Munger, it's voice a blast of madness, rot and shit from Pesheval's suddenly malevolent curled lips. "And I we I was/am having such fine. Fine so. Gone fleeting such distances drift anew/anew and now old sickness I prevail no/am more so, not more than before. Making sadness now you pay for it, indeed so."

He was broken, whimpering before the Munger, scrabbling at its feet. His new eyes burst, an explosion of dark unfurling flesh threads; unravelling gore. And yet his sight somehow remained to torment him. The former Lordt – the would-be god of an inverted chaos - cried and begged at the feet of something far more dreadful than he had ever anticipated.

"Back, I want it back. I want it I want it…" he murmured almost incoherently, over and over.

The Munger continued to taunt him with the guise of his beloved, fondling itself, caressing itself, before growing bored and ripping the skin from its beautiful face.

It pulled Brookbane to his feet and kissed him, a black tongue entering his mouth from between bloody lip-less teeth, extending to writhe in his guts. Fishing.

Bored again, the Munger cast the Lordt aside. He almost burst on the stone wall at the far end of the chamber.

"Out-out-out!" The Munger hissed, insanely.

Then it calmed somewhat and regarded him with a more curious eye.

"To die/to live. Touch fallow dark faces glean yellow. Yellow and dark, in place always, but hollow like spiders. Hollow like

95

the wind. So seeming, so empty, so touched so. Yes. That's right, that's right. Tell me my infant flown sundered metal wings and iron – what ails/calls/drives this? What wrong/right inflicts you upon mine/mine/me? You want it back, so?" It asked.

"Yes. Yes. I want it. I want it all. I want it back," he muttered, broken on the flagstone floor. "I want my fucking sight back. I want my land, my fortress. I want to be restored, to, to, to what you have shown me - I was. You can give me these things."

The Munger turned the skinless face away from the ruined Lordt.

"Fleet. Fleet the wind-footed. Partial and full, there - but not so." It said. "I'll eat you for it, and then... We'll see."

Baalor Dark-Eye, formerly *Lordt Thrall Brookbane of Da Derga's Heights*, fingered the faintly glowing green stone hanging from a chain around his neck.

"Just Sutzeria. Orn. Then that's it. That's it. I'm free..." he whispered to himself.

A knock on the Machivarius' gallery door stirred him from his reverie.

Emporate Hylat Costerman - Baalor's adviser and the eyes of Nefarea - led in the surly Sutzerean captain of a small division of surveillance troops, and with him, (Baalor realized with a jolt,) was a man whom he recognized.

The captain detailed Woebeg's capture.

"Leave him with me," said Baalor, and he found himself alone with the former Captain of what had been his own, Brookbane Elite: Woebeg Ban Errieu.

Woebeg did not recognize his erstwhile Lordt, Thrall Brookbane, behind the mask of Baalor Dark-Eye. Chittinous, like a beetle's carapace, ribs of thin black steel traversed a narrow section horizontally from above his eye level to below the nose. Almost a cowl, it swept backwards into two short, curled horns decorated with fine, faintly glowing cobalt symbols. It appeared grafted upon his head - sewn there, or grown. The back of the helmet was hung about in knots, braids and thongs, which draped over his shoulders and down his back, a bestial mane. The bottom half of the front was open, providing evidence - had Woebeg been looking for it - as to the wearer's identity. The heavy jaw, outfitted in a refined black beard, was graced with the same seductive mouth he had known years earlier. Starlight-white teeth, straight and unbroken. He dressed in a variation on the current Ornish vogue: A tight-fitting and heavily stitched black and brown jerkin, fur-lined and secured down one side with flamboyant gold clasps. His sinuous, impressively muscular arms were adorned with Ornish tattoos in the style of the soul-less. (Indeed he believed himself to be soul-less, though he claimed no kinship with the giant race.) Steel bands armoured heavy forearms, and a high, bulkily elaborate Tetradon-hide belt bore effigies of mythical beasts. Tough leather breeches, banded with more steel, terminated in highly decorative fur-topped boots which appeared riveted to his legs - and lent an extra three thumb-widths to his already impressive height. Though he would not show it, Woebeg was instantly awed by the shear presence of the man.

Baalor turned, walked over to one of the gallery windows, unafraid to present his back. He resumed his brooding contemplation of the ever-changing parasitic city.

"This is an evil fucking place," he said, finally. "A dreadful, bitter fucking place. Orn, how I hate it."

He turned again, framed by rays of swirling mote-filled light that streamed in through Machivarius Point's small circular portals.

"Such places, I believe, reflect our darker, truer selves. I knew a man, many years ago – a man who perhaps might have

97

been thought good, in better days – and he resembled this city, resembled it more closely in his soul than the entire world would have guessed! I knew him well you see. It resembled him more than he himself ever knew, or could know, at that time. Over the years he became, I'm sad to tell, a dreadful, bitter man. This city held up a mirror to his face and reflected his soul. And he saw it. He was able to see that - everything he truly was. A terrible thing, that. To see such truth. Where, you might wonder, lies the reflection of your own soul, soldier? Perhaps you are a creature of the wilderness? Are you a mountain man, soldier? Or rather man of the city? And if it is a city, is it Tantrix-Alumnae that reflects that inner truth? All those – layers, like an onion. Wall after wall, you see? Closer, closer to the core, the truth. A temple at its heart! Ha! Oh, I suspect not! That's no soldier's soul! Leave that place for the artists – or politicians! So maybe it's the city of Orn? Neat blocks. Tidy. Pure - in a way. Old. Full of treasure. Knowledge. Does that sound like you? No. No. I think not. Aetullia then? Ancient Ork? No?"

The Warlordt strode back to tower over the chained Woebeg. He stood silent a moment, studying him, looking for something in his eyes. Eventually he chuckled breezily.

"I suspect, if you think about it, you will find you bear the same soldier's soul as the man I was referring to. I suspect that this fucking ugly city we stand in is the ungodly reflection of every soldier's soul! It consumes, you see? It does not question. It lives; it dies. It is eternally replaced with more and more of the same shit that it sprung up out of. It is ugly; it is ignorant. It is a mindless beast dining perpetually upon itself. There are no true masters here - you see that? Not really. The great politicians, emperors, Lordts, builders, traders, all those that think they understand it, think they actually run it - They are blind, fucking dumb, fucking bloated, arrogant fools! Do you not think so, soldier?"

Woebeg's mind spun. The man was reaching him, somehow; winning him over, despite himself. It was true, he could see it: His soul, as a wretched gnashing thing, gnawing away at its own marrow. Yes, it - he - resembled Duhn all right! And he loved and loathed *himself* as he loved and loathed *it*.

Baalor Dark-Eye turned away from Woebeg once more, walking over to another portal on the other side of the gallery, gazing out over another aspect of the sprawl below. Misting up the glass with breath.

"There can be no prayers for the soldier," he said. "As soon as a man decides he can – that he has the right to - take another man's life, for any cause, that man is damned. Forever. As long as armies are created, so wars will be fought. As long as wars are fought, so souls will be lost. Duhn is your soul, soldier. Tell me - what great power bent your already lost soul to its noble, I'm sure so very meritorious plight, eh? Which Lordt earned your respect, your loyalty? You're not a young man. Why not retire? What country, which city is so fine and so grand a place you would give up your own life to serve and protect it? Is money the beast that holds you in its fist? That bends and tempers you? That drives you to kill for it? Perhaps it is love, eh?"

And here, again, questions Woebeg had never considered.

"Let me tell you, there is a way to end all this - though not for you. You're lost forever, as am I. You know that don't you? I can see it in your eyes. But you and I can still change things. Change the very nature of the world we walk upon. We can choose to die for the only cause that really matters: We can die to bring peace. Lasting peace. I will show you that there is a way. Roses grow in shit, soldier. Forests grow over battlefields. The earth claims it's dead. You can join me, if you chose. Or you can die. All is not as it seems, old friend. Nothing ever is."

Woebeg lay in a cell for a week contemplating his position.

Contrary to expectations, he had been well fed. Unleavened bread and thin, but flavoursome soup arrived twice a day. His piss-pot had actually been emptied, three times. His pallet was not only reasonably dry and relatively free of infestation, but warm. He had suffered no beatings or abuse, and his guards had even passed him a little butter wine in a gilded horn.

He did not, in that time, forget the reference to his being an 'old friend'. This consumed a good portion of his thoughts. There was something in the way it was said that haunted him, something horribly familiar.

"So, 'all is not as it seems' eh?" He muttered to himself. "What the bloody hell is *that* all about?"

Woebeg put his past behind him. It was of no significance any longer. He had rediscovered his calling. He was his master's hound once more. He was doing what he excelled at. He was killing people.

"Well then, Captain Ban Errieu." Baalor Dark-Eye said to the fighting man. "Tomorrow we March."

"'Bout bloody time, sir." Said the soldier.

VILE-SPACE

IV

Shivering in her furs, Cherry Longorn was once more cradled in the embrace of a gnarled Elm's roots, wanting for the Munger to steal her away to what ever hells the Soul-less were condemned to. Barely visible beneath twists of wood, a thin blanket of snow, she pulled her Roab-skin cloak tighter. For two days she had stumbled, directionless, through Duhn Forest, and nothing had desecrated her misery. Only the long whoop of the wind in the trees, the rustle of stirred frozen leaves, the dull footfall of an Elk in the snow nearby.

Her reason for living - a reason she had searched long to find - was gone.

She closed her eyes in the failing light, wishing for the longest of sleeps. But a feral moan weaved a ghostly path through the trees to her ears, plaintive and somehow desperately beautiful. Soon snatches of words became clear, until at last Cherry was no more able to stop listening than halt the flow of tears that warmed her cheeks.

"How like the wind:

A free captive of ancient rules,
Moved by memory, stilled by walls.

How like the sea:

The Mother - and Death.
Dancing out of the waves,
Though far we travel,
It is she who will embrace us
At the End.

How like the Sun:

But it is cold,
Where the wind only can touch me.
Stand, you, thresher, harvester and thief, and spill your blood gladly.
Eat, that hearts be weaker.
Darken the doors of sanctuary.
They fear you, still, they that shiver within.
But fear you the bright soul that burns
And sings
And warms us.

How like ourselves your reflection."

The guttural song stopped abruptly. There was a sense of hesitancy, and then the footfalls grew nearer, until Cherry found herself staring, like a child, at the beautiful orange and black striped face of a Sayer. His horns swept straight downward to his strong, white-tufted jaw-line and they shone with beeswax and resin. From within the deep set of his amber eyes there spilt light and wisdom.

"Out of the gleaning, we are well met at last!" he said. "My name is Barachal Tush. I have come for you, Cherry Longorn."

The Sayer gently wrapped the giantess in his yellow robe, his warmth passing into her. He stroked her head as she wept; mewling and rumbling softly like a great cat.

"You cannot die now, child. It is not yet your time. This much I have seen. Will you trust me?" He whispered, and as she nodded a gossamer trail, a ghostly projection of ether, spread forth from the stump of his severed right arm, swirling like the smoke of a dying fire about them and gently probing the lonely confines of her mind.

Images surged into him, teasing free deep and forgotten memories. The phantom arm of Barachal Tush drew from her such exquisitely painful jewels of experience that he moaned a low lament, as he endured Cherry Longorn's suffering:

In a loveless life, love became her obsession. She had never known it until her kinsman, Pellaq, had found her near death, nursed her back to health, and for the first time she felt it. In Tantrix-Alumnae she discovered, in the tragic violet of Pellaq's eyes, herself reflected. She saw his love in the trembling of his hands, the tension in his shoulders. And yet the consolidation of their feelings remained elusive. He would turn from her always, seeking ways to be apart.

At Dutwerth's Leap, away from the bustle of the city, she

had contrived to confront him with her feelings. But Pellaq had made some mumbled excuse to absent himself. Cherry had followed him. Called his name a few times, tapping gently on the door to his room.

How could he refuse her? Whatever blight marred him, burned where once hung a soul, he could not keep himself from her forever. He opened the door, turned away; moving round-shouldered to the window, and there sagged. And Cherry kissed away tears that night. She held him as he shuddered, and the little strokes of comfort turned inextricably to broader gestures of passion. They cried and laughed and cried some more. They fucked, as though in fucking they could redeem their souls. It was their time, a stolen moment.

It was their right.

Soon after that fearful circumstances parted them once more. Cherry underwent ritual - and perversely familiar - humiliation in the mountains. Pellaq had found rough passage to Orn. When later she warmed herself by the great fire at her apartment in Duhn she did not dwell on the abusers she had eventually slaughtered in the Ornisbach. Instead she thought about Pellaq, and how she might find a way to be with him again, in Orn.

She spent the next months trawling Celebration Row for a merchant bound for city, and in the ostentatious surroundings of the "Moneyed Fist" she found such a man. Well-read and widely travelled, Calcox Mal-Vitch was none-the-less a dull and narrow-minded fool. But he was suitably impressed by Cherry's feral, exotic elegance, and he was going to Orn. As a hired guard she would be less likely questioned by any Nefarean soldiers along the way, indeed it was more likely they would question Mal-Vitch.

"I mostly trade in salt and rare spices," the shapeless merchant drawled. "But I must confess to a passion for books.

My dearest, Ms. Longorn, let me tell you that I have sought out the finest literary treasures from all over Aetuland, Sutzeria and the continental mainland! It's a great sadness to me that I have never been able to grasp the finer points of Ornish literature. Frankly I find their phraseology, the staccato and rhythms of the prose, somewhat mannered and elusive - No offence intended, of course my dear! However, such Ornish classics as I do stumble across I usually take to Orn, to further complicate the impenetrable collection within the Sed Library. I'll say one thing about the Ornish however: They certainly pay well my dear! Oh yes!"

As if to demonstrate his wealth and good fortune he slapped the table and called for more butter wine. He was trying to get Cherry drunk. His leering stare was brim-full with salacious intent. He wanted her.

Let him try, she thought.

The journey to Orn took a month. Mal-Vitch was not one to hurry and the ravages Cherry witnessed in rural Sutzeria did not appear to overly bother him, despite his being Sutzerean. He sauntered through deserted and often still smouldering villages with the air of a man who had seen it all coming. He made proclamations along the lines of; "I told them, but would they listen? Poor bloody fools." Or "That was my uncle's forge. I wonder if they saved the mare?"

It was a blessed relief to Cherry when they finally arrived at the Ornish capitol. At last Cherry was able to take her pay and leave of the insufferable merchant. They parted at the city gates and did not see each other again.

Orn was a small city comprising of monumental architecture. Whilst it was known to be ancient, it was built with such care and elegance, such simplicity of form, that in many ways it appeared the most modern of Sutzerean cities. It was built on a grid system and defended by a high bleached wall, now crawling with vines and honeysuckle - dark veins dusted with frost. The walkways were wide and smoothly paved below the compacted snow, making them perilous to walk on.

A white city, full of space and light, it yet yielded surprises. Once in a while the clean lines of the ageless etiolated walls would be broken by an eruption of colour, creativity and splendour. The Sed Library was such a building. Nauseatingly high, and cylindrical, it was ringed with a great staircase. At its apex was the beautiful stained glass roof, depicting a burning planet below the outstretched arms of the Weeping God. This was the 'Roof of Orn', and from it you could see most of the city. On a good day you could, it was said, see Duhn, wrapped in its shroud of smog.

Relieved she might well be, but Cherry hated the place.

As always, her appearance in the city, any city, caused a stir. The priests, noting first her dark skin, then the weave of her mercenary tattoos, remained aloof for the most part. But her jet skin and charisma soon loosened tongues.

Eventually she learned Pellaq's whereabouts. He was not a man who could go unnoticed, even amongst his own race. Pellaq was at the Balcephellos Temple, deep in the heart of the city, causing serious consternation, it was said, to the Ornumnae priesthood.

Days later, she managed to get word to him, and some days after that a wrathful, almost frenzied Pellaq met her on the 'Roof of Orn'.

"You should not be here!" he shouted, shaking with barely contained fury. "You have no comprehension of what is happening! Do you have any idea what you are doing to me? I left you safely out of this! You should be at Da Derga's Heights! I saw you at Da Derga's!"

Cherry recoiled in horror, backing down a few steps into the shadow of the massive walls.

"Why? Pellaq? Why? What do you mean? You never mentioned Da Derga's!"

Pellaq bore down upon her.

"You cannot repair what has been done! Orn's shit, woman! You haunt me! Will you never leave me alone? You torment me with your fucking existence!"

"I don't understand, Pellaq, what have I done? What did I do? I love you, that's all I…"

"LOVE ME? Damn love! Damn fucking love! What do you know of it? You poor wretched fucking creature, you don't even know - you can't even know what it really is! Believe me, Cherry, you do not. You will never and can never love me. I know this. I've seen it…"

Pellaq was changed. He seemed older, and the broken part of him had erupted outwards, so that he had become it. In the face of her declarations he threw scorn and bitterness. He spat after her, as she fled in confusion and pain; wailing and cursing her; tearing phantom memories out of the air with clawed fingers.

Now - below it all, behind everything - Barachal Tush glimpsed other things, ancient and devastating, deep within the brutalized souls of these two damaged giants.

But they fled his attempts to grasp and understand them, like black wings against a night sky, leaving only a fleeting memory of despair.

He comforted Cherry as much as he was able, then he sent her on to Da Derga's Heights.

Her destiny, he knew, lay there. Pellaq had been right in that.

A few weeks later and Barachal Tush, the Sayer, rubbed gingerly at the aching stump of his right arm within the sumptuous surroundings of the great Sed Library in Orn. He had been working long and exhaustive days to find something that might help him understand the greater sweep of the currently unfolding events. Here ancient texts of the Ornish - relics from Althlathu, the world Sayers and Ornish both had long ago left behind - consumed him. He searched for possible answers in "the Book of the First Cycle of Relevance through Rational Remembrance and Reason", committing whole chapters to his near indelible memory. Yet, ultimately, he found little of use. He closed that book.

Looking at the vast oval central library, spiralling elegantly upwards to where it terminated in a dazzling stained glass dome two hundred and eighty spans above his head. The familiar musty scent of aged paper infused his nostrils and brought a momentary comfort.

Until he remembered: The Nefareans were coming, bringing with them fire and death. The city of Orn would not be spared this time. He trembled, as sudden anxiety caused his twin hearts to momentarily fall out of their steady alternating rhythm, the subsequent rush of adrenaline heating his gold and black furred body. He panted, to cool himself, his moisture-rich breath swirling in the chill chamber. Soon this wonderful archive would be destroyed along with the city. And after that, what?

He rose from the reading pallet and stretched his single great shaggy arm. It was time for him to glean again.

V

Pellaq strolled wearily through the Iutghe-Ja Contemplation Gardens that filled the courtyard of the Balcephellos Temple in the city of Orn. Snow clung to the branches of twisted bare willows and upright Silver Birches. It lay fist-thick over the neat hedges and curvaceous walls. Icicles dangled with perilous beauty and a fine mist of snowflakes danced, bright golden motes in the twilight.

He was tired and his heart ached.

Ahead, in the high arched gateway, stood Barachal Tush, his yellow-gold robes glorious in that last light of day. He fairly shimmered, as it glanced off his deep orange and black striped fur. Only slightly shorter than the Ornish Soul-less, what he lost in height he made up for in bulk. He held in the claw of his mighty left arm a Staff of Becoming; the levels to which he had gleaned existence lay notched in crude striations along the dark wooden shaft. His right arm - as with all the Sayers gifted with the art of gleaning - had been struck off above the elbow at puberty.

Barachal Tush spoke, his savage voice echoing about the frost-dusted gardens:

"Pellaq. Well gleaned be this moment. With honour I come."

"May the Manifold be open, friend, and the Speaking be true," replied the Ornish Soul-less in the time-honoured formal patter of his forefathers. "Come now. Time is getting short."

"So it would seem! The Alms grow flighty and noisome. The Manifold is darkening. It is good and right that we meet now."

The Sayer and the Soul-less embraced. They were both alien races to the world they now lived upon, their true home Althlathu almost faded to legend. There had long been an unlikely kinship between these two giants. Their races shared a parallel belief system born of their joint heritage, and it would be fair to say both, in their way, understood a great truth about the complexities of the universe. They knew of the Kiazmus; The Pathway Home, that linked all worlds. They worshipped the same god of this ephemeral network; the archaic force named "Orn". But here their belief systems split and grew radically different, so that it was rare for such bonds to grow. The two giants retired to a small (by their standards) temple grotto, where they built a fire and shared a horn of butter-wine before getting down to the matters that had brought them together.

"The Echoes-To-Be have shown much, though I fear not enough," said Pellaq, the familiar tortured expression taking a hold of his features. "My teacher, Iutznefydd-Baal Pellafinn,

110

saw, as is the way, different shards. Different splinters of things to come. But the sum is the same.

"We have learnt, over millennium, that a tiny part of a future truth is often no better than a lie. What I know of my self bears this out.

"It is hard on Pellafinn that only he and I, of the Ornish diviners, have seen echoes concerning the Munger and the gemstone Torc that bound him. Within the Temple at Tantrix-Alumnae he is almost ridiculed. They tolerate his views, I fear, out of respect for his great age and the skills of former times. I believe they anticipate his death soon and so humour him.

"They are fools, many of them. They look too far, to the stars. They seek a reunion with Orn, the blessed Father, as if that was all that mattered!

"Ah, but it is hard for a Soul-less to make his voice heard here. Even harder considering what it is I have had to say! Despite half a year arguing my case I fear that sadly precious few, if any, of the Ornumnae Priesthood shall stand beside us when the darker days ahead are come. The Ornumnae Patria himself, after all, has not divined this! It is no surprise then that he finds it hard to accept a Soul-less mercenary might have!

"So, old friend, I turn to you. The Munger comes, of that I have no doubt. Old powers awaken. New powers are born. Pellafinn and I have brought together those we understand must be united. It is not clear why - and I have little faith in Woebeg, the cornerstone of our small and disparate fellowship - but we have done what we saw was necessary. This has not been without cost.

"I have – learned something of myself also. Something of the past that has always been my enemy. Barachal, a terrible deed was done. Terrible. An etherwork, a – binding up of souls. An entrapment. Something was done to me, and so all of this, everything that's happening, it's interconnected. And Cherry."

Pellaq wiped an eye, fought himself. "It's not her fault, I know that. I'm sorry, it's just not very clear, I'm not making it clear, and I don't know how it fits - how it all fits together. But I'm responsible for it somehow; and for what may come to pass. That's why I have to succeed, you see? I have to stop it, to fight it. If the Munger is allowed to manifest again, in this reality, well, we've lost too much craft. We have not the power any longer."

The Sayer slowly blinked his liquid amber eyes. His horns did not detract from the distinct look of a Tiygre. He studied the clearly tortured features of his friend, thought about Cherry, whose love for Pellaq had broken her. He gazed into the eyes of the Soul-less and saw there a mirror image of Cherry's own anguish, but also a reflection of her love. Silently he wrought a prayer for them, and his double hearts ached in the knowledge that it was only circumstance that denied them both the love that should, in fairness, be theirs.

And he prayed that he had gleaned correctly, that Cherry would find her purpose at Da Derga's Heights. Would do there what must be done.

"It is true. I have gleaned the Munger's return," he finally growled, canines flashing in the firelight. "A new Warloq is also abroad - though he does not know he is one. He works against our needs; I know this, yet it is by his actions alone that the conflict can be ended. I have gleaned fully, I think, for what it's worth. For what very little it's worth."

Pellaq nodded. "We saw as much, Pellafinn and I. It was this supposed Warloq - Woebeg Ban Errieu; a soldier - that we put at the heart of our plan. I've received intelligence that suggests he has joined the 'Wayfarer'. I'll tell you though Barachal; I knew Woebeg, and could trace no etherwork in the man. I looked hard, used all the knowledge I have, and yet it was almost as though he did not fully exist. There were no signs at all that would have marked him a Warloq, not such as I recognize them. He is himself a non-believer and disdains the paranatural. His skill as a fighting man is certainly formidable, though I believe it has something to do with perception – much like the Ypo-Polarian Magi who effect the slowing of time with mental discipline."

Barachal Tush gazed into the flames. Nodded.

"Sayers are few these days - we falter. This planet doesn't suit us. All things must end. Of those I have gleaned with - only three these last nine years - most choose to wait for whatever comes. They see this as the inevitable reopening of the Kiazmus, and they dream of their past amongst the stars. Kilchal Shem will come. She has known me a long time and trusts me - my readings of Sed. She will fight with us."

A wind laced with ice crystals sent the flames spiralling in a hot red roar. It had grown dark, but the light of a thousand fires cast a faint orange haze through the atmosphere above the white city. Tomorrow the Nefareans would be back, and Pellaq did not think they would spare the city this time. The Ornish no longer commanded the awe they had once enjoyed.

The giants were targets now. It would be an outrage - the sacking of Orn - it would rock the world and deliver great power into the hands of the Nefareans and their Emperor. Aetuland would follow. But worse, should the Wayfarer turn towards Da Derga's Heights, then all the signs foretold of the Munger's return to their existential plain. Without such etherworks as the Ornish once wrought on Althlathu, without the aid of the age's supreme Warloq – a man who was ignorant of his inherent energies, and who now served the Undead God as it's champion - The Munger could swallow up the world in moments; turn it inside out, twisting it into Vilespace. The most cankerous slums of Duhn had not horrors enough to recommend them to the hells the Munger could engender within their reality.

And when the fabric of the membrane that bound their reality

was ripped, what then of all other realities?
It was time for the two giants to leave.

VILE-SPACE

VI

Lordt Hergal ban Egan was shuddering. He was burning, sweating and shivering. His face was bloodless.

"What...What...What..." he stammered. "F. F. What..."

"Calm yourself, Hergal." Pellafinn crooned. "It has passed."

"F. F.F. F..." Hergal struggled with his senses. He was trying to speak through his eyes. He perceived Pellafinn as a spherical brownness through ears never meant for sight.

Someone far off was asking the same question, over and over, and he asked, in turn, a question of it. "What? What what? F. ff. F. f. What what? What?"

Pellafinn shook his large, ugly head. He felt responsible.

He had put Hergal into the trance in order to investigate the anomalous visions the man had been experiencing with regard to one 'Nuddfegh-Ho'. This had evidently opened him up to something Paranatural and prescient. Pellafinn suspected that Hergal had just come face to face with a part of the Munger, or something of that nature. This was worrying. He surmised that the gap they perceived in the Echoes-To-Be was widening. There was a leak in the vile-space, created to entrap the Munger ten thousand years earlier. And whatever was causing this breakdown between realities must be close – here, upon this world: Arddn. It seemed increasingly likely that the presumed mythic "Dealing Stone" was the lost Ornish gemstone that imprisoned the un-dead God.

He turned from his rapt friend for a moment to gaze out his study window at the Aetuland Spine.

"Mutton," he muttered. "We're all just fattening mutton."

He tried to picture his small army – nine of the best, a motley fellowship, but experienced – who must by now have crossed over the mountains into Sutzeria. It was the best and only thing he could have done, being no soldier or general himself. How could he be? He wondered if he had damned his own soul by financing the raiders. If violence had been done then he would certainly have played a major role in its cause. He tried not to think about this though, consoling himself with the bigger truth; if they did manage to bring back the gemstone, half the key to the Munger's prison, then it could be put beyond reach in this - or any other - world, finally and for good.

"Wind at your back, Pellaq," he whispered to himself. "Walk far with Orn - and secure me that damned stone!

"And you!" he said, looking over at Hergal. "Wake up, damn you! We need you here - I need you here. Things are going to get bad now, there's no doubt about it. There are too many bad moments; stacked, ready to topple. Wake up man!"

*

The slender Ornish Warloq, Nuddfegh-Ho, swam in the beloved element of his divine ancestor, Orn. He leapt fifteen spans out of the water, like a Great Crested Porpoise, his white-gold hair trailing dazzling spectral foam in the sunlight.

Pit black and flame haired, Iuttse Lai laughed her bright joyous laugh and dived beneath the waves into the awaiting arms of her lover. Nuddfegh marvelled, as he always did, at the sight of the ebony goddess who had wrapped herself around him. Her teeth flashed from behind those ripe red lips. The black marbles of her eyes gleamed, awash with starlight...

Pellafinn hobbled on stiff, aged legs, as quickly as he was able to, along the tall and narrow cherry wood panelled corridor, connecting his chambers with the study and guestroom. The screaming that issued from within the room had awoken him, casting him in a sweat.

The noise stopped as he reached the door. He hissed a frantic prayer for Hergal, as he fumbled with the lock. Entering the study Pellafinn railed with the shock of what had transpired within. Risen from the pallet and standing, naked, his back to the door, was Lordt Hergal Ban Egan, transfigured. He was gazing out through wide-open windows at the Ornisbach looming over Tantrix-Alumnae, and as he turned, Pellafinn dropped painfully to his knees, shaking uncontrollably, his strength deserting him.

Newly born, Hergal stood nearly ten spans in height - almost twice what he had been - tall, even for the Ornish. His icy green eyes gleamed. Cool. Ancient. Lithe, slender, he yet rippled with barely constrained power. White-gold hair framed his face and stirred round his shoulders. His elegant beauty was overwhelming to Pellafinn, who found himself weeping. Hergal had awoken from the induced trance as one of the ancient Ornish. Not the modern Ornish of Aetuland, or even this world he now stood upon, but - Pellafinn knew unequivocally - one of the "Founding Race", as near to actually being a son of Orn as it was possible to be.

His was the race that had discovered Arddn and settled here; naming the island they alighted upon for themselves, and their God, long before men had come into their precious realm.

Orn.

His was the race that had unwritten the killing Karnaghk and become champions of peace.

His was the race that had entrapped the Munger in Vilespace.

"I am *Nuddfegh-Ho*." He said, and opened wide his great span of arms as warm tears began to melt the ice in his frosty gaze. He went over to where the Ornish priest sobbed on old knees, lifting him to his feet with a fierce tenderness.

"Pellafinn, we are party to great events." He whispered. "I see this. You have been my guardian, my friend, and for that you have my love – and my gratitude."

Nuddfegh-Ho embraced Pellafinn and the old diviner shuddered. He struggled with his rational mind, hardly able to comprehend the significance of what had occurred. He felt like a child: ignorant, young. What could he know of anything compared to the man who embraced him, a man whose years of life must number at least ten thousand?

"We must prepare. The Munger will soon know I am restored. I could not remain hidden forever." Not even from myself, thought Nuddfegh-Ho. "We'll travel north-eastwards, to Da Derga's Heights. It is time for a reckoning of sorts, I think. There's much to do."

VILE-SPACE

VII

Tersis released a spasmodic explosion of pent up desire - nurtured over some ten years - within Heron. He shivered, gasping at the intensity of it, the sheer pleasure of it. He laughed like a king and wobbled like a baby. Heron - no stranger to passion – found herself similarly consumed.

"Sweet fucking Orn…" he panted, grinning. "How long? How long I've wanted to do that! I want you Heron. I want to be with you. I know it's too soon, much too soon to say, but I love you. For so long. So - just think about it, will you? Just consider it. Don't say no out of hand. Consider me."

"Oh Tersis," she whispered. "I don't want to be alone any more - "

"Then will you - " he ventured, stroking the hair away from her flushed, sweat-beaded face. "Would you ever consider... being"

"Oh yes," she replied happily, pulling him to her. "Why ever not?"

ALTHLATHU

I

Nuddfegh had argued against any attempt to convince the Ornish priests at Tantrix-Alumnae that Pellafinn's gleaned concerns were authentic. Pellafinn did not fight him. He had few friends at the temple, and was enjoying this, the greatest of his many secrets. He felt caught up in something illustrious. Nuddfegh also wanted - for reasons best known to himself - to keep his identity secret for a time. He shaved his head in the manner of modern Ornish and conjured tattoos to further enhance the deception - the resemblance to Pellaq, Pellafinn noted, was marked.

It had been a tough journey for Pellafinn. Inhospitable valleys and perilous glaciers were aspects of nature the experience of which he had long thought behind him. Bitter frost bit deep and the Great Sloth fur cloak had not stopped the wind from penetrating his thin skin, lacing his marrow with ice crystals, but finally they arrived at Da Derga's Heights more or less intact.

The legendary fortifications were a man-made mountain. They tore jaggedly into the sky, the architectural styles of three thousand years battling for dominance over the outer aspect. Within it became apparent that its true origin lay much further back in time, and historians had estimated that some parts of the structure were built a possible nine thousand years earlier.

Where the walls straddled Shea Pass, in a huge dam-like curve connecting the mountain's interlocking granite spurs, there stood a sheer dark face of Ornish-carved stone slabs placed layer upon layer, two thousand spans in height. The concourse that crested it was as wide as a hundred spans at strategic points, as narrow as two at others.

In the shadow of this great wall a small town had emerged since Brookbane's departure. Golderga, as it became known, nibbled at Da Derga's toes, stole from its table. It was the new place to be (outside of Duhn) for any merchant who counted himself a contender.

Lordt Tarq Bellafest Crookshaft, the most recent master of Da Derga's heights since Brookbane's flight, was a fat, oily, yet puissant figure. Pellafinn and Nuddfegh had gradually convinced the new Lordt that they were not Nefarean spies, and persuaded him to let them attempt to uncover some lost sections of the fortress. Little liked, seldom crossed, Crookshaft did not much enjoy the idea that it was two Ornish giants and not his own men searching for long hidden labyrinths below Da Derga's walls. He saw enemies everywhere. But Nuddfegh-Ho was a master of many subtle arts and, imperceptibly, Crookshaft's stance became altered. In time he became utterly convinced it was at his personal whim that the Ornish diviner and his enigmatic soul-less assistant worked deep in the vaults of the fortification.

The apparent rock face rudely terminating a gently sloping carved corridor deep in the foundations of Da Derga's Heights was Nuddfegh's first obstacle. It had also proven the toughest, as all the subsequent obstacles had systems based on that first. Pellafinn marvelled at the flickering ethereal webs that Nuddfegh wrought - gently probing, suddenly stabbing, writhing and dancing their way through unseen, ancient locks. They had been there for almost ninety days before the breakthrough came, fiercely defending their intentions to Crookshaft as they laboured in the gloom, apparently achieving little of any worth. Pellafinn himself might have lost heart were it not for the constant patience of Nuddfegh. Outside the walls spring had arrived, and tiny cerulean and yellow mountain flowers dappled the purple rock. However, below the ground the temperature remained constantly near freezing, and Pellafinn blew into the cup of his gnarled hands and chewed on his Tobbach for comfort. He almost fell over when Nuddfegh, with a shock of motion, struck the limestone rock-face that bared their way with both fists, hissing the strange language of their forebears, long forgotten by even the Ornish Ornumnae priesthood. He watched that seemingly impregnable mass fold silently inwards as spluttering light - from what looked like a variation on Lazrus Machivarius' tantric spheres - revealed yet another corridor in the gloom.

"And now the next!" Exclaimed Nuddfegh, stepping through the gap and setting a brisk pace down the long and unremembered passage leaving Pellafinn to hobble breathless and excited in his wake.

"Well then, Pellafinn. Should I trust you with all Da Derga's secrets?"

"Lordt Crookshaft," said Pellafinn, irritated by the swarthy-faced pretender-to-Lordtsway, "These are historic days. Your name, not ours, will be that noted in Da Derga's annals for sanctioning this work, making this unprecedented discovery."

"Indeed." Muttered Crookshaft. He didn't like Ornish Priest - he believed himself a modern man, free of religious superstition - but in truth he was utterly delighted by the finds. "I've heard it all before Pellafinn. Spare me. So, you've uncovered another three chambers you say?"

"We have, my Lordt." Said Pellafinn, his crooked and unbidden smile flashing those black stained teeth. "And it is by far the largest yet found, and the last I believe. And there's something else - something quite remarkable. You should see it alone I think, so you can best decide how to proceed. May I escort you there, my Lordt?"

Crookshaft gasped. It had taken he and Pellafinn half the day to descend into this most recently discovered, and massive, chamber. It rose eight hundred, to a thousand spans upward of where they stood. At it's centre was a black basalt cube, the size of an Ornish temple, upon which glowed writhing violet symbols. There did not appear to be a way into it. Nuddfegh-Ho remained rooted before it, arms crossed – as though he had not moved since Pellafinn left him a day earlier to relay the news.

Crookshaft's eyes were alight with wonder. "This whole place puts my beliefs into doubt! How could we have not known about this? Why have we not found this sooner?"

It was Nuddfegh-Ho, not Pellafinn, who spoke this time. "Lordt Crookshaft, this is not in any sense a part of your world. It was created outside of such concepts as "place" and "time". Ornish Warloqs, newly self-exiled from old Althlathu ten thousand years ago, built this hall. They created an inverted space - an area outside of physical reality. And they unfolded that space here. It can, however, only be reached as we have reached it: Upon this world, within this domain. This is the seventh and final chamber, which houses the "Bright One", the dread gift from Terrax, the "Temple in the Deeps". This cube. Within this lie energies that can ravage a world. The Torc, sometimes called the "Wayfarer", one half of the key to the prison of the Munger. We stand at the gates of Vile-Space."

Crookshaft strode around the black cube slowly, attempting to comprehend the meaning of what was being revealed to him, but mostly revelling in the palpable power of the enigmatic construction. He could tell it was dangerous, his hair bristled in static waves as he walked, and the air around it smelt faintly of sulphur and burning. If he could master this, then what did his future hold? He could, he felt certain, end the war with such a device. He could be the man who did that! And what then? His imagination leapt, and he found himself giddy at the thought of the Emperor Shevic prostrate at his feet, and the entire continental mainland his to control. It was with a shock that he found himself face to face once more with Pellafinn, and behind Pellafinn an image of himself. There was no time to exclaim before his head exploded in a mist of fine dark crystals, which dissipated in the dank, still air.

Pellafinn was startled, and clasped a shaking hand to his mouth, bile burning his throat. Nuddfegh was now cloaked in the aspect of Crookshaft, a counterfeit of a counterfeit.

"You would have tried to stop me." He said.

"Orn, why?" asked the shaken Pellafinn.

"Could you swear to know an agent of the Munger if you saw one? I'm sure I could not! This way we alone know the truth of what we have here. Now it is we who hold the power at Da Derga's heights. It is the only way we can be sure."

Pellafinn stammered, reaching for answers. "But... But, it is not the way of the Ornish to... to..."

"*What?*" retorted the changeling. "To *kill*? And what do you know of my ways, the old, *true* ways of our race? You weren't there! You Ornish of today are like echoes of what we were. I would rather we had become extinct that suffer the ignominy of the weak, superstitious and pathetic race we have become! I'm sickened by it. Such a thing as the *Captive Soul* - the very notion is abhorrent, Pellafinn! You have no right to tell me what I am or how I should act, what is legend to you is memory to me! I love you, Pellafinn, but do not go up against me. I would kill you as soon as kiss you. Be strong, old man. Your soul is safe. Trust me.

"Come now." He said, in the voice of the dead man. "We have found The Temple in the Deeps. There are things to be done."

Pellafinn gazed in stunned silence at where Crookshaft's body had fallen, but all that remained was a stirring of motes - less even than a shadow to his old, suddenly weary, dark eyes.

ALTHLATHU

II

The Hound tore through the city of Orn like a fury. Wholly berserk, cruelly calculating, partly insane. Swords, knives, lances, they all avoided him, shied away from him. They hissed past, spat at and cursed him, but could not touch him. When faced down even seasoned warriors knew fear of a kind they had not imagined they could ever feel again. They fell to the cold earth, begging. Pissed themselves, blubbering. He heralded the coming of the Wayfarer and there was no mercy in the man for he did not see living people. He did not think of the sobbing mothers waiting for their butchered sons to come home. He was blind to the terrible beauty of the twelve-year-old girl he decapitated, booting her head into a bloody snowdrift by the side of the road.

The piles of stripped and mutilated bodies - human and Ornish - did not resemble people to him at all. They were meat temples; red-black carcass towers erected in honour of almighty 'Time', the Liar, herself. The thunderous pulse in his head beat a tattoo for him to which he paced his swings, his blows, his thrusts. He barely had to parry as all fell before him. It was palpable, his mark on that city, it could be felt streets away; such was the fear he instilled. A dreadful ripple - it consumed the fortitude of even the bravest, the most courageous. Time, in a slow dance, kissed his cheeks and blew softly upon his neck, courting him, for he and Time were lovers. He gifted her with bright scarlet blossoms of infinite variety that swelled amongst the bitter white snowflakes, and she in turn slowed herself for him. There was no escape. Through his eyes his victims appeared to be floundering helplessly in murky waters while he danced through the pale air. To those who saw it was hard to comprehend exactly how he plied his dark trade, how he moved. There did not appear to be the balletic quality to his killing one might expect from martial genius. He progressed in a jerky, upright gait. His arms spasmed and thrust in a manner that seemed uncontrolled, as though he suffered a malady of motion. An almost comedic dance, he wobbled and twisted and looked as though he might topple over, but instead he brought death and fear and agony.

Nobody laughed as they died.

His men had grown fiercely loyal to him. They saw his unflinching bravery, astonishing ability to kill. They respected his unconditional faith in their Warlordt, Baalor Dark-Eye; the Wayfarer, who had delivered him back to his former greatness. They picked off the stragglers, fanned out to entrap those who sought to flee.

It was a massacre.

Orn, the most ancient of Sutzeria cities, fell in less than two days.

ALTHLATHU

III

For the urgent and immediate attention of Master Iullafei-Baal Porddaddynn, Ornumnae Patria, and my divine brethren the Ornumnae Priesthood at Orn.

Such things as have happened to me these last months I find hard to transcribe into the written word. None amongst the Ornish, myself included, could have foreseen the wonders that have been revealed to me in the fullness of their detail and the richness of their manifestations.

There are those of you who have thought me a fool - I feel it is only fair to say that I afforded you a similar sentiment - and this, to my shame, led me to conceal (or at least, fail to volunteer) the thrust of my findings. In this matter I have been most roundly foolhardy and onerously culpable, for I earnestly believe this to be a time of genuine and immeasurable danger to all that dwell upon this world, and others.

In the company of a certain Nuddfegh-Ho, an Ornish Warloq - one who had concealed himself within the guise of the Lordt Hergal Ban Egan and who has come amongst us from the very time and lands of our forefathers. Althlathu herself! - I have gained access to catacombs deep in the belly of the Aetuland Spine. I break his trust in telling you this:

Below the vaulted walls at Da Derga's Heights there lies a city as grand as Tantrix-Alumnae and well nigh as capacious as Duhn! Cut within the heart of the Ornisbach are chambers vast enough to house the Flacks! These are dressed with palisades, columns and great sweeping balconies. Level upon level, they conspire to addle the senses and befog the mind. Passages that appear to slope downwards break out again into higher chambers! Boundless spiralling stairwells plunge down through the surface of sunken lakes, and on, into murky depths.

It is Nuddfegh-Ho that has opened up these forgotten spaces. With incantations and wrought-ether works - the likes of which were lost to us, eons ago, when first the Munger was ensnared and we made our pacts - he has once more revealed great and former glories.

I write this down so that I know I did what little I could to convince you to come to us when the call goes out. Nuddfegh-Ho believes that it is here, in these hallowed halls, that the Munger's Torc lies hidden. That the Wayfarer - bearer of the Gemstone - will come for it.

I do not have to spell out what this would mean should it prove true.

I have been a seer of the Echoes-To-Be for as long as you have known me, most of you. It may be true that my path, and those I have chosen to ally myself with, might not have met with your approval. That, in my pride, I did not work hard enough to explain my actions and to fully disclose my discoveries. Never the less, I have been diligent. I have left nothing to chance - in as far as it is possible not to with regard to divination. I have ever worked for the greater good, as I perceived it to be, and it is for this reason that I was long ago made a High Priest of the Ornumnae at our nameless temple in Tantrix-Alumnae. And therefore it is in my capacity as such that I ask you to give serious thought and consideration to the terrible and imminent possibilities implicit within this letter.

It should also be noted that a much-changed Cherry Longorn, who enjoyed our hospitality in Tantrix-Alumnae some years ago, has also joined us here. It would appear my plans to secure the gemstone, which I believe to be half of the key to the Munger's prison, have failed. Most of the company I commissioned to undertake the task perished at the hands of rogue Nefars. The Soul-less Pellaq, whom I confess has worked along side me now for many years, resides in Orn where he seeks to sway more of our noble brethren to this cause. No mean task for a Soul-less. As far as I know he alone amongst the Ornish has seen what I have seen in the Echoes-To-Be, and I, as I know you must, have found such a notion uncomfortable. Yet, too, I trust him with all I am and have.

As should you.

I also trust good sense will prevail and that you are able to put aside your doubts and prejudice in order to ascertain for yourself, with the eyes that have justified your meritocracy, the ramifications of these great and fearful events.

In hope and humble service,
Iutznefydd-Baal Pellafinn.

ALTHLATHU

IV

Woebeg waved the scroll under the wrecked nose of the High Ornish Priest.

"So, Master Iullafei-Baal Porddaddynn, what does this mean, do you think? You can't believe what is written here, can you?" It had been a shock to Woebeg, discovering the message from his former employer, smuggled out of Da Derga's Heights in the hands of yet another trusted agent – *the old giant Pellafinn must have them scattered across the length of the world,* he mused. But Woebeg was committed to his fate, his part. The performance he called a life. Everything of subtlety escaped the man, leaving him capable only of following orders - for now. This his did with brutal efficiency.

"You are right. We did not. Did not believe." Blinded, Porddaddynn could still see the fervent Pellaq in his minds eye; urging, begging the High Ornish Priesthood at Orn to at least attempt to substantiate his claims, to try a deep communal reading of the Echoes-To-Be lent store by the guidance of a notion, no matter how seemingly unlikely. But he was a damn Soul-less! How could the lost children of Orn know of, or even comprehend such matters? Pellaq was unwelcome and unwanted, and the appearance of the unnatural Orn-spawn throwback, Longorn, had not helped his cause. The two were a corruption, a blemish within the city. But perhaps the Priests should have listened after all.

Porddaddynn heard the old saying in his head: *How often we Ornish damn ourselves.*

"Damn. Ourselves – we. Damn..." he whispered. And died.

Woebeg considered the words contained in the message, and sneered with distaste. *To think*, he thought, *that such deeds as I have done should be in the name of mythology, delusion and all that I do not believe in. The bloody irony of it!*

The soldier took the unheeded, redundant scroll and held it above a guttering torch, watching the paper blacken and break into near-weightless grey fragments that broke again into shadows and nothingness.

Baalor Dark-Eye raged through the Balcephellos Temple, up-turning the tables, burning the ancient tapestries, the wooden effigies of Orn.

"Where are you!" he screamed in his fury.

Baalor slowed and stopped, shaking as his fury waned. His shoulders sagged.

"I had hoped to resolve this, *here*," he said quietly.

The Wayfarer turned at last, the blood of dead giants

glistening on his dark armour.

"Da Derga's then," he muttered. "So be it."

ALTHLATHU

V

Cherry arrived at Da Derga's heights a vapid shadow of herself. She had gone there at the bidding of Barachal Tush - whose gentle ways had persuaded her at least to make the journey, if not to embrace a new life - and was received at the vast fortress by the current Lordt, Tarq Bellafest Crookshaft. The man had barely been able to keep his eyes from her. An elaborate feast was hastily arranged for herself and the pretender Lordt, all of which she barely registered, and yet in the immense Bullcavarach Hall something extraordinary happened; Crookshaft unexpectedly threw wide his arms and wrought out of the ether a shimmering display; places and times Cherry had somehow dreamt of, knew and had loved. She gasped as she saw herself surging amongst

Great Crested Porpoises in bright tumultuous waters. Making love to a man, a beautiful, slender, powerful man of the Ornish, the true Ornish of Althlathu. And as her eyes fell upon Crookshaft in unabashed wonder and excitement, the man transformed. He became Nuddfegh-Ho, more ancient than the nations of Nefarea, Sutzeria or Aetuland. He became the lover of these visions. Her lover. And Cherry could not resist him. Would not deny him what had so long been denied her.

"How can this be?" Breathed Nuddfegh into the velvet hollow of her ear as they writhed, ecstatic, in the false Lordts bedchambers. "I have found my beloved Iuttse Lai."

Nuddfegh awoke shouting, drenched. He rose quickly, moving to the narrow windows that revealed an impressive aspect of Shea Pass.

"What is it, my love?" asked Cherry. "Are you alright?"

"A dream, Iuttse," he said. "That's all. Go back to sleep. Everything is fine."

As he looked back at Cherry, curled up on the bed, he though himself a loving man. But he had, over thousands of years, been *all* men. And yet still Nuddfegh-Ho. He had not known - before now – exactly why he had lived so very long. His memories of Althlathu had been incomplete, faded or blocked out. His recent metamorphosis at Pellafinn's lodgings in Tantrix-Alumnae had furnished him with some of that knowledge - the nature of the Torc's hiding place, of Althlathu, his homeworld - but none of it was true memory, it was more an education. He was sparing himself the true depths of his personal living experience until the right time, and it would seem that time was now. The appearance of Cherry had changed everything.

As Lordt Hergal Ban Egan he had cared deeply for this land he called home. For so long he had worked with Pellafinn to safeguard Aetuland from dark things the priest had read in the Echoes-To-Be. He had utilised his strange ability to move between worlds and live as other people to study the patterns and flows of paranatural energies, and to learn more about the nature of them. In his last incarnation as the warrior Brec he had walked on a world whose Munger-given energies had faded much like they had once upon Arddn. Before that he had lived as a Courtier to Quene Liddya of Spaynne upon a world called Uorth, a world that treasured it's fading magiq, trading its last relics as though they were of priceless physical value. Here they could not accept the demise of the paranatural and remained in a magnificently delusional state regarding the meagre energies their etherworks actually possessed. And yet before that Nuddfegh had walked as the woodsmith Yahmus Gris on the arboreal planet Tallamuuth, where etherworks once plunged great galleons through the skies. As Yahmus he had constructed the last flying vessel of that world, a skiv large enough for one man. He had risen above the city of Gadansé full of false prophecy and misdirected belief, only to be shot down in flames, his agonising plummet and frantic etherworks returning him once more to the Kiazmus, and ultimately back to the form of Hergal Ban Egan on Arddn.

As Hergal his memory stretched back over four hundred years. It was this that revealed the difference: Here, almost imperceptibly, magiq was returning. Its strength was growing. The "Dealing Stone" had nearly vanished from folklore in the early years of his memories, and yet it had re-emerged as important. Anecdotes of its dreadful wish-giving powers could be found in variations all over the continent, from Ypo-Polaria to the deserts in western Umarica. There was the living evidence proffered by the Giantess Cherry Longhorn, whose like had long been though myth. There had even been reports of the great Machivaria spluttering briefly back to life above Duhn, bathing the city in their paranatural radiance for a ghostly handful of seconds. The dead heroes of Tuffin Hill had paraded through Tantrix-Alumnae one long winter night, witnessed by more than three hundred of the city's denizens of all race and class. The evidence was clear:

Magiq was fading, dying out on other worlds - but here on Arddn it was returning.

Pellafinn knew that without Hergal, and his remarkable ability to walk in the skins of others – itself a sign that the paranatural flourished - they could have never discovered this fact. It was knowledge they guarded fiercely.

And yet Nuddfegh-Ho's memories as Hergal receded into a thick fog of recollections glimpses only rarely in dreams. As such the greater sweep of his personal understanding of things was ultimately partial. He had wanted, as Hergal, to understand the threat of the Munger fully. The returning of paranatural energies on Arddn revealed to him that the Munger was gaining strength, as all things paranatural emanated from the Munger, and that his prison must be, as legends suggested, here upon Arddn in some form or other. He and Pellafinn knew that there must be seepage, they had identified as much. And they therefore knew that the Munger remained a real threat across worlds. He could return. It had become his wish, as Hergal, to stop it - kill it if he could. Hergal had rightly begun to suspect that it might be the "Dealing Stone" that contained the Munger. The myth appeared consistent with the theory. In ways more elaborate that even Pellafinn could have ever know, Hergal set about retrieving that stone. He identified those people who might have the means and would wish to seek it the most. In Tantrix-Alumnae he saw a hunger for power in the Lordt-Justice, Taal Brookpass, and had gifted the man with numerous small power-granting charms in the hope that he would eventually actively seek the "dealing Stone" for himself. But time and comfort had dimmed the man's ambition.

Hergal had met another ambitious man called Crookshaft in Aetullia, who had set his sights on the acquisition of a high post at Da Derga's, but Crookshaft had no belief in the paranatural at all and so proved an impossible proposition.

Then there had been Lordt Thrall Brookbane. Brookbane and he had become great drinking partners in the various haunts of Tantrix-Alumnae, and Lordt Hergal Ban Egan would fill the young man's head with tall tales from the continent. In Brookbane he found a captive audience, a great imagination, ego, and all the power and fortune his inheritance of Da Derga's Heights would afford him. Hergal's darkest and hardest deed to perpetrate was the installation at Da Derga's of a rival – a bowman, and a former suitor of the Lady Pesheval, Brookbane's ill-fated wife. Lady Pesheval, who Hergal had himself introduced to Brookbane. If anybody would have the powers and resources enough to track down and bring the gemstone to Aetuland it would be Brookbane – if he wanted it enough.

The plan had almost worked perfectly.

But was all this what *Nuddfegh-Ho* wanted?

Cherry had brought Nuddfegh fully into the world at last, and everything had again changed for him. His memory was finally, and fully, restored.

He rested his head gently upon the firm expanse of Cherry's belly.

"It was a harsh age for lovers, *Iuttse*." He said to the sleeping giantess. "Ours was a beautiful world back then, when we first met, ten thousand years ago…"

The slender Ornish Warloq, Nuddfegh-Ho, swam in the beloved element of his divine ancestor, Orn. He leapt fifteen spans out of the water, like a Great Crested Porpoise, his white-

gold hair trailing dazzling spectral foam in the sunlight.

Pit black and flame haired, Iuttse Lai laughed her bright joyous laugh and dived beneath the waves into the awaiting arms of her lover. Nuddfegh marvelled, as he always did, at the sight of the ebony goddess who had wrapped herself around him. Her teeth flashed from behind those ripe red lips. The black marbles of her eyes gleamed, awash with starlight. He entered her, as they spiralled down through the forest of flitting light, and she arched her long sleek body, matching him thrust for thrust. Taking all of him. Consuming him. Trying to become him, become one. It was a union, as were all their couplings, of unfettered passion. Once in every hundred or so Althlathun years Orn would grace Althlathu with one such as she, and a black child would be born and treasured. Iuttse-Lai was such, and she was Nuddfegh-Ho's - his light in the darkness.

Later, as they lay on the powdered coral beach beneath the fronds of a vast Borachial Fern, Nuddfegh became more pensive.

"Will you go back to him? Will you tell him?" he asked.

"Hush, love," she whispered. "Soon. Maybe. Maybe soon enough. I don't know."

"He knows about us." Nuddfegh rolled onto his side, leaning up on his elbow and stroking Iuttse's muscular belly with his other hand, admiring her exotic beauty. He went on. "I'm sure he knows, Iuttse. And we owe him the truth. These matters, they must not distract us from the far greater events that threaten Althlathu. There must be harmony amongst the factions. It is all the hope we have." He stared into her bright eyes, feeling again that flutter within, that rise and longing. But he put such ideas aside. "You have to leave him."

"How can I do that? I love you both! I don't know what to do! This is so wrong, we both know that Nuddfegh. I can't bear the thought of hurting him."

"He's already hurting, Iuttse. It's tearing him apart – as much as this war is tearing us apart." Nuddfegh rolled onto his back and sighed, heavily. "Do you think I feel any different? I'm afraid of what he might try to do."

"So am I," she said, quietly. "Of both of you."

Standing naked on the ornate balcony of his expansive apartments at Neptek, Nuddfegh-Ho breathed in the salt-rich air through gritted teeth. Below, docked in the harbour, were two enormous vessels. Palace-Ships of the Ornish Sea-Kings, they were the largest craft ever to sail upon the oceans of Althlathu. Double hulled, literally floating cities, they could sustain life without ever coming to shore. Upon their terraced decks grew many and varied crops. Fat Bor-bors and shaggy Yagshays grazed in wide enclosures of Sproose-Grass and Ypopolype Thorn. Extravagantly plumed Kirkums sucked up the worms that writhed away their dim existence in layered earth high above the waves.

Attendant to the Palace-Ships he could see a host of lesser vessels, all fulfilling different roles. At least two hundred deadly Biremes, their lower deck housing rowers. Upper, soldiers. A square sail enabled the attacking speed required for deployment of a ship-sinking ram. There were maybe a hundred Triremes, and thirty bulky Quadremes - enormous crossbows or catapults ranked along their hulls in deadly array.

The other distinctive ships in the port contained fishermen or Porthaar hunters. Diminutive cousins of the monstrous Levithians, Porthaars were a dangerous catch. Their hunters were held in high esteem and grew extremely wealthy over their generally short lifetimes.

There were Carpenter's Guild ships, whose fearless crew plundered the wood-stores of the Ypopolypi.

The strange square vessels were home to the Guild of Smithies, which gathered molten ore as it bled through fissures *in the ocean-bed. Within the dark fiery chambers of these ingenious craft proud, surly men crafted deadly curved blades and light, double-skinned armour filled with air pockets for sea-faring warriors.*

Nuddfegh shifted his gaze, across the squat flat roofs of the dockside warehouses, then on to Neptek's bustling market square from which the bustle of vigorous trade ebbed and swelled on the wind. Casting his eyes along the wide avenue that dissected the square, Nuddfegh traced its path to the foot of the gargantuan statue of Orn overlooking the city. Even from the height of his balcony Nuddfegh had to crane his neck slightly to see the statue's shadowy head, the face hidden beneath a stone cowl in a shimmering haze of heat and distance.

A slender hand slid sinuously around his waist and downward.

"Troubled?" asked Iuttse Lai, resting her ebony head against his naked back.

"No. Everything is fine," he replied. "But I think it would be for the best if you left Neptek. At least for a while. Until we've sorted things out. It can't go on like this forever."

From beneath the cowl of the statue of Orn – which housed both a small temple and a gateway into the Kiazmus, the sacred path amongst the stars – there burst a cloud of Thrashers from Terrax that surged into the sky above Neptek, their naked blue-skinned and red-eyed riders whooping and chanting battle mantras. They circled above the island like monstrous carrion Roarches before landing on the purple lawns outside the great Council House, a terrifying black squall.

Nuddfegh-Ho marched across the finely cropped grass towards them. He wore the burnished gold armour and white cloak edged with emerald symbols that revealed his status as a Neptek Warloq. Bright hair danced wildly about the fine features of his face in the churning winds generated by the Thrasher's dark and immense wings. He halted at the periphery of this alien landing party, seeking out a particular face amongst the chaos.

"Beltan!" he shouted. "Where are you? Beltan!"

There was a stirring amongst the brute animals as they hobbled awkwardly on short legs, eyes bulging, wide and fearful. They were cliff dwellers and level ground unnerved them.

A gap opened up in the ranks and there was Beltan, as plunged in darkness as Nuddfegh was in light. Beltan Fel matched Nuddfegh's height and was half again his mass. A giant amongst the Ornish, his enormous Red-back Thrasher was of a breed usually reserved for transporting masonry up and down the palatial eyries of Terrax. He sported a black beard in the fashion of his adopted peoples, though he retained his Ornish clothing. Tattooed serpents snaked their way up muscular arms and the shaggy Yagshay cloak - held in place by two hefty chains - made the man appear even bigger. His hair grew long and wild beneath a ragged Roarche-winged helm.

Beltan strode towards Nuddfegh at speed and before the Warloq could speak struck him with a balled fist, lifting him off the ground and sending him sprawling.

Nuddfegh rolled onto his back coughing a little. He reached inside his pulped mouth and tugged at a loose tooth until it came free. He spat blood then slowly raised himself unsteadily to his feet.

"I deserved that. What now?" he said, staring Beltan in the eye.

Beltan stood over Nuddfegh shaking with fury. He screwed up violet eyes and bellowed his pain and frustration. Several of the Thrashers shied, attempting to escape back to the safety of the sky. The riders steadied them, barely, with thick leather reins.

"Yes." he said, his deep, soft voice wavering with emotion.

"Yes you did. Yes you bloody well did." He looked around for a moment, searching for words, taking in his former home. "Well. Well then. Here we are. Nuddfegh. Here we are. You break my heart. So. Are we to be civil then?"

"That would depend," said Nuddfegh. "There's much I need to say."

"What might that be, Nuddfegh? Will you yield; renounce all that you are? Have you – and it would change everything, believe me, for us all - have you finally seen that there is only one real way to finish this, only one way to truly end the threat of the Munger? And will you admit that you were wrong - that you made a terrible mistake - the day you seduced Iuttse Lai, my wife?"

Nuddfegh looked into the eyes of his brother. He saw how he suffered, how he continued to hope things might change. He saw, almost dispassionately, how those gentle eyes filled up and overflowed as Beltan recognised with desperate alacrity the impossibility of such hopes, the staunch paucity of will for such change. He sighed, shook his head. "No, Beltan. I won't, I can't. I'm sorry."

The planet Terrax resembled Althlathu only in that it was a world defined by the ocean that engulfed it. A tumultuous world of violent storms and long nights, its great Eyries - within which blue-skinned natives dwelt - took the form of enormous pillars, like the ruins of ancient temples thrusting from beneath dark waters.

Beltan, and a few hundred other Ornish, had joined the Terraxian people as their beliefs dictated they should. Beltan had not been born gifted, as was his younger brother Nuddfegh-Ho, with the energies that would have made him a Warloq. A practical man, the dogma of the Eschatarchy made clear sense to him: To end the blight that threatened all existence sacrifices should be made, and whilst the inherent powers of the Warloqs could be beneficial, he knew well that life without them was not so bleak as to be unbearable. It was not hard for him to understand that giving up such power might seem unconscionable, but he had hoped that Nuddfegh would see sense. There had, after all, been a great bond and love between the two. Beltan had taught Nuddfegh everything of seafaring, hunting and fighting that there was to know, and while many Warloqs grew sickly in their studies Nuddfegh had grown strong through his older brother's attentions.

And yet the Eschatarchic churches on Althlathu had eventually been destroyed. The last great Palace-Ship of the Eschatarchy had been burned and sunk. With a heavy heart Beltan had escaped into the Kiazmus – fled across other worlds - until, in time, he had found Terrax, a wholly Eschatarchic nation.

Beltan bowed his head to the Eyrie Queen. Above, beyond the great convex lens that spanned the opening at the top of the hollowed out spire, the Gods lit up the heavens with a dazzling electrical display. Shadows danced around the circular hall. Thrasher-fat candles spluttered and spat.

"You were right. It was pointless, my Queen," he said. "But I had to try. And I have lost her, Xtina. I've lost my Iuttse-Lai, my wife. She was... she... my life hasn't as much value now as she gave it. And I don't, I don't understand. It was real, our love. She...

"I've lost my brother, Nuddfegh, also - my people..." Beltan fell to his knees, sobbing, strength fled.

The Eyrie Queen Xtina stood, descended the steps to her throne quickly, coming to a halt just one from the bottom and taking Beltan's head in her hands, kissing his forehead compassionately. She was a strong woman of thirty-eight cycles, though she would have easily passed for less. Black hair shimmered in a cascade down her curved spine, across wide shoulders. Beneath short, blunt horns and a ridged brow there glittered two intelligent deep red eyes. As the Queen she adorned her native nudity with golden bands at her wrists and ankles, black varnish on her nails and lips. In this way she exploited her own exceptional beauty. She was vain, took many lovers - her appetites exhaustive. Adoring courtiers and foreign suitors flocked around her, but she cared nothing for them, discarding them as easily as she seduced them. Fickle in her sexuality she may have been, she was, never the less, a great leader of her nation and her people. Courageous, dangerous, political and ruthless, she was loyal to those she befriended and she never spurned a fight.

Beltan's love for his wife, Iuttse Lai, had made him invulnerable to the Queen's charms and advances, yet far from angering her it only served to increase her affection for him, and a deep friendship flourished. Though the Queen had never experienced the emotions Beltan displayed she craved them, even envied them. She suffered vicariously through Beltan, for all that he had had, all that he had lost.

"Beltan," she said quietly. "I'm so sorry. You know I did not share your hope, but still - I'm sorry. The Eschatarchists were destroyed on Althlathu, Beltan, but we can put that right. We can change it, as we planned. You know what this means. What we have to do? The Munger has to be destroyed. We have a duty to do it."

"Yes," he whispered. "Orn, forgive me. I can... I can see no other way."

"Beltan..."

"I must tell you all I know, though. Things I have not said before, that I hoped not to. Forgive me that. Althlathu. It's where it all began, Xtina. In Neptek, beneath the great effigy of Orn - that's where we started this."

"You did not create the Munger, Beltan."

146

"*Maybe not, but we trapped it. And in doing that, in doing that... Who knows, Xtina? Who knows what would have happened had we not?*"

Ancient beyond memory, the Munger had survived the death of it's native universe and had had evolved to exist upon multiple membranes, within myriad dimensions. It was not constrained by the specialised physics of the individual macrocosm. From what questing source it came none of they that discovered it were old enough to know, but bitter memories clung to and tormented it. It had suffered in out-growing Its own time.

"*When we discovered the Munger we elected to fear it - and so kill it. Our grand alliance - the "Eschatarchy" – was established to implement the Munger's destruction, and soon how different was our ostensibly "scientific" movement to a fanatical cult? I do not mean to offend, Xtina, but it was the discovery of the Munger that led to our belief system, when you trace it back. When you look at the origins. We created a new religion! Eschatarchic churches grew profligate and influential upon every powerful world because of our actions!*"

The Queen's brow furrowed deeper. "*What's your point here Beltan? Are you losing your resolve, your faith?*"

"*No, my Queen. We've gone too far now. Too far. All of this, it's almost irrelevant. What we did cannot be undone. The Munger is what we have made It – too dangerous to be cast free. Our ancestors did not grasp then that the Munger was inextricably linked to the parallel energies – the paranatural; arkane; magiqal. That it's alien nature made such things possible.*"

"*You walk upon a fine line - one that many would call heretical, Beltan. Tread carefully now.*"

"*I'm telling you only what I know, Xtina. These are histories, not myths. I try only to understand, and to trust in what I must do. With immense ether-works, magiq wrought on a planetary* scale, the Eschatarchy of my world, the Ornish Eschatarchists, created a vessel to contain the Munger. We cultivated a physical body - robust enough to contain the entity, but not so powerful that we could not in turn contain that body. And we summoned the Munger, conjured It into being within that body. We made It a god manifest!

"They said it was beautiful, Xtina. That to gaze upon it was to weep, for all the wrong it contained.

"My brother, Nuddfegh-Ho found writings, old writings, detailing much that isn't known to most who follow Eschatarchic dogma. I saw them with my own eyes, sealed in casks deep below the statue of Orn. The war on Althlathu cast open vaults containing many such secrets. I suspect he was trying to change me, make me question my beliefs, my actions. Maybe... maybe he succeeded, a little. But not enough. It's still too late you understand.

"And so. Well, we asked It questions, but It would not answer. We hurt It. And It turned Its beautiful baleful eyes upon we Ornish Eschatarchists and It wept, and still we would not relent."

The Queen looked visibly shocked, and briefly her hands tightened around Beltan's face as she searched his eyes. But Beltan was immersed in misery, unaware of much else but his thoughts.

"And then, we tortured It in earnest.

"The writings say It spoke only once – and It must have known what Its fate might be. It said, "I am only that which you are not. I am other."

"The high Priests of the Ornish Eschatarchy on Althlathu became enraged that It would offer them no more than that, and having created a body for It they proceeded to rip that body apart and recreate it anew. They, we, did terrible things, Xtina. Such things as we imagined the Munger would do to us – if it was allowed. We stretched aspects of It's substance to such length and thinness that It no longer truly existed as matter. We cloistered chunks of It in elaborate dark causeways between realities. Its blood was drawn into lead caskets and mixed with mercury and incantations. Its flesh was frozen in delicately sewn symbols upon fabrics spun out of one or other fascia of reality. We had that kind of power then. And we detailed our efforts exhaustively, Xtina. It's the cruellest of Althlathu's secrets. The Munger's soul - if indeed soul you could call it - was ensnared in a diaphanous filigree carked from the echo of it's prior existence.

"Then we summoned the ancient powers of a thousand worlds that had come together as the Eschatarchy - to end the perceived threat of the Munger in as profound and utter a manner as we could collectively conceive. We trapped It in a way that mirrored Its nature, Its mode of existence. We imprisoned It in a new realm. Somewhere "other".

"Vile-Space.

"And yet we knew that in giving It form and then destroying It, we had also given It will. And we were fearful. We proudly revealed to the Eschatarchic races of the universe that we had successfully trapped the Munger, but we did not say that in the act we had driven It to desiring an end to Its suffering - to all suffering - and thus an end to all things. We did not say that the Ornish Eschatarchists were able to perceive that within the Vile-Space the Munger began to find new form and new purpose. And the portals to that place, which still lay suckingly open, beckoned and called to all the darkness's and slithers and worms of Itself that had been spread over reality, dragging them irrevocably back. We did not say that we could not stop it alone, Xtina. That the Munger grew once more. We deceived the Eschatarchy."

"It was this that led to the second Eschatarchist dogma: The horrified elders and Priests of the Ornish Eschatarchy, in their abundant wisdom, decided that all magiq should be driven away

- outlawed and caged like the Munger Itself. The new dogma was simple enough: The Munger must die; therefore all that is magiqal must die. There would be an end to Etherworks, and they that wrought them. And so the church doomed its own Warloqs - having created Vile-Space by magiqal means the Warloqs were bound by the new philosophy to cast themselves into it!

"The Vile-Space was recreated as a Torc bearing a gemstone, a piece of jewellery more precious and deadly than a black hole; an event horizon given the form of a trinket, in the hope that – should it ever be lost – it would be perceived as priceless; and guarded. Such folly. Better it had been tossed into the heart of a star while we still had the means!

"The so-called Vile-Space was then divided - a gem and a Torc; one space in two places. The Eschatarchist Leaders of many planets took these from us, communed, and made their choice of destination. It was left to the Ornish to bury the gem aspect - to find a new world, and to lose it there forever.

"Then the Eschatarchists set about their intentions to destroy all things magiq in earnest. Our times, Xtina. Our days.

"And you know, of course, that there were many who didn't like that, not at all. Althlathu became polarised - as happened on many worlds. Those gifted with the ability to channel the ether, to carve it into new shapes – those like my brother - the Warloqs, they didn't wish to give up their skills to such a dogma. They don't wish it, and they don't want it. The belief systems that had for so long existed side by side became a barrier. Opposition grew, and the children of Orn and the Kiazmus were split into factions, family against family, friend against friend.

"Orn, to think of it, Xtina! The lives and races lost! In just our brief lifetime - The Knapthagarat, the first race to discover the taint of the Munger in all things magiqal. Gone. The Seraphallus, who could build planets from stardust and founded the Eschatarchy. These people too – extinguished, unable to

resolve the matter. Gone. The Meliora and Serenae, dedicated to maintaining magiq and accepting the Munger as part of the natural order of all things - and as such the mortal enemies of the Eschatarchy. Our enemies. We killed them ourselves, Xtina. Genocide - whatever our justification. Still: Genocide. We killed them, all of them, because we feared their beliefs, and because they would not yield – not even at the end. And so - gone. All these races obliterated along with their home worlds in a war over power, and magiq, and what should be done with the Munger.

"And so you see, it was the Ornish who did this. It's why I couldn't hate my brother for loving his arts. And my love for Iuttse gave me hope for my race, and kept me from hating them for what they did. But you see also, Xtina, my Queen, you see also why I am resolved? Without these two to give me that hope there's nothing left, but the knowledge of what we did, and what must be done. This has to be ended. And it has to end where it began."

Xtina gazed long and hard at Beltan.

"There's something you should know." She said at last. "The Torc – it came to us at Terrax. Perhaps, after what you have told me, we should send it back to Althlathu for good."

"Oh Orn, I'm afraid, Xtina. So many lives."

"As you said, Beltan. Where it began. Let's take this home."

The strange Temple sat, a cleverly devised cube, a fearsome trap, upon the beach at Neptek. It had appeared within the cowl of Orn, spat from the Kiazmus, and etherworks had lowered it, crackling, to the ground. The violent violet inscriptions had hinted at what it contained. The so-called "Bright One", a cleansing fire. It declared itself the "Temple in the Deep" in symbols denoting prophecy. It was a paradox, created using the very energies the Eschatarchists reviled, and it's creators had given their lives in it's making.

The Ornish Warloqs had been intrigued by the palpable power that emanated from it, tantalizing them. They saw it as a fearful puzzle, knowing that clearly it was incredibly dangerous. But what confused and terrified them the most were the symbolic denotations that suggested that within the cube there lay the Torc, a piece of the Vile-Space. Why would the Eschatarchists gift them with such a thing? To the Warloqs whose wish was to maintain magiq the gift was in direct opposition to what the Eschatarchists would desire.

After three days the Warloqs, Nuddfegh-Ho amongst them, had still not devised a way to open it.

On the morning of the forth day there came to Althlathu, through the Kiazmus, a vast swarm of Thrashers and their riders from Terrax, and with them a host of air-borne warriors from many other Eschatarchist worlds. For half the day they poured through, darkening the sky with flying beasts and machines, and no matter the energies wrought by the Warloqs, or the flights of arrows let loose to stem the influx, many more survived than died. They spread about above the ocean of Althlathu and brought terror and death to her people. They dropped burning pitch upon the Palace-ships and Ypopolypi. They did the same to the island cities and the great floating forests.

In turn the Thrashers and riders and other alien races assaulting the nations of Althlathu were killed in sickening numbers by crossbow bolts, flaming arrows, or energies summoned by the anti-Eschatarchist Warloqs.

Nuddfegh-Ho ran towards the beach, barking orders. Cursing his brother. The strange cube glowed in the distance, etherwork spitting and swirling over its surface.

"What?" he hissed, angry and frustrated. "How the fuck do

I open it? I don't understand!"

On the sand surrounding it were a host of Terraxian and other Eschatarchist defenders, seven Ornish Warloqs and thirty assorted warriors. They had landed a short while ago and taken possession of it. At their feet lay the slain Althlathun Warloqs that had probed the cube for its secrets. The Eschatarchist defenders now wove heretical etherworks in the air, some concentrating on the glowing cube within which lay the Torc, while others directed their powers outwards at the attacking Althlathuns. Nuddfegh jabbed a fist in their direction causing chunks of the masonry from nearby buildings to tear loose and fly at them. Some of the defenders burst open. Others crumpled, pulped and bloody.

"Nuddfegh!" shouted Iuttse Lai. "I understand it now. It's a trap!"

He turned, slowly; horrified that she had followed him.

"Iuttse," he yelled, " I told you not to…"

"This is more important than us, Nuddfegh! More important than you. You can't protect me! No one can. Not me, or any one else. Don't you see? You have to get that thing back into the Kiazmus somehow – but you MUST PROTECT IT. Do you understand? Don't let anybody open that thing…"

"But… why not?"

"It's not what's inside that's dangerous!" Iuttse was scrambling over some nearby masonry, desperate to make herself understood. "It's the cube itself, Nuddfegh! They WANT it open."

"But if I can open it we'll have the Torc – it's in there, I've gleaned it! - and then…"

His words faltered as a Thrasher crashed into her from behind, it's massive rider pulling her roughly into the saddle before sweeping the beast round and back upwards in a sharp curve.

"She's my wife, Nuddfegh! Mine!" bellowed Beltan astride

the hovering Red-back. "You cannot have her. Not in this life! Not ever!"

"Iuttse!" cried Nuddfegh. "No!"

The Warloq swung his arms forward, half-mad with rage/ love/despair, and blasted the skies with ethereal fires that engulfed both brother and lover completely. Their dying screams rang in his ears, called to him, loving/hating him. He screamed - then, desperately, and mechanically, found himself creating a new etherwork: It was beautiful he realized, vaguely - genius. Tragedy/anger/violence/love conspired to build a tantric cage - a trap, an elegant vessel. The gossamer tendrils - that connected it to his aura - flung that wondrous creation out/in/after Iuttse Lai where it ensnared her soul, tore it from the ravaged, smouldering husk of her body and bound it to his; eternally.

He did not notice that in his wild effort to somehow secure a part of his lover for himself, to save what he could of her from his rash act of violence, he secured not one but two souls.

Nuddfegh-Ho gazed skyward as tears burned his cheeks.

"Orn, why? Why this?" he whispered. "Take it back. I don't want this. I cannot live with this..."

All about him Thrashers plummeted, their wings aflame. The riders straining to control the dives, but the beasts, consumed with pain and fear, spiralled in chaotic panicked arcs to their deaths on the rocks below. Nuddfegh-Ho raised a slender white arm and a boulder, ten footfalls across, shot into the air trailing blazing sulphurous death.

A mauve arc of light split open a thumb-wide gap in the world, horizon to horizon, severing Nuddfegh's left arm below the elbow. He spun, quickly, as if it had not happened, and ran forward, pulling his double-handed sword single-handedly from its scabbard. It sang through the air with mystical grace, writing the killing Karnaghk. The defenders went down with appalling *ease, and Nuddfegh kept charging forward, towards the "Temple in the Deep", screaming like Thotlan.*

Then he was before it, his blade high, descending fast, too fast...

Too fast to stop. Too fast to change history. Too fast to avoid what had become inevitable. Too fast to look back. To think. To understand.

The "Temple in the Deep" split open at the blow, blasting off Nuddfegh's right arm and leg, and with another mauve arc of light Althlathu split wide-open this time. Violent stormy energies combined with lava, surged up through the rent, the white-hot soft innards of the planet, gases, and water: The ocean boiled.

"The cube. They wanted it open..." he whispered, watching the waves of his world turn to a sulphurous, broiling beast. A fire upon the deeps, consuming everything and igniting the fine, mighty palace-Ships like tinder, as though they were of no consequence.

He saw the symmetry in it. His world, the world that trapped the Munger, would be the resting place for that god. The Eschatarchists had contrived to destroy Althlathu leaving one half of the Vile-Space secure there. Forgotten upon a dying planet.

The swarms that still circled in the sky plunged back into the escape proffered by the Kiazmus within the cowl of Orn, returning to their own worlds. It was over.

Nuddfegh saw what he must do.

"Here!" he cried, using his paranatural energies to sustain his broken body a short while longer. "I'm hurt! Quickly! Somebody!"

"It's what they wanted, the Eschatarchists. We played into their hands. Iuttse-Lai tried to tell me." Nuddfegh-Ho whispered barely audibly the small number of Ornish Warloqs that gathered

around him in a broken shambles.   "They want to leave it, and the Torc, here. We can't let them... do that."

Within the cowl of Orn a desperate few hundred surviving Ornish - and yet fewer Sayers - gazed down at their savaged world with broken hearts. Nuddfegh, bound in lint and Yagshay fur, was secured upon a litter near the temple, and the opening of the Kiazmus. Together, he and the surviving Warloqs that were with him gleaned the depths of their God, Orn, the personification of that network. They searched urgently for somewhere safe, somewhere new.

They found Arddn, and upon it an unpopulated island far east of the sparsely peopled continent. By the time its natives had covered such distances the Ornish would be long established. They would be accepted.

Another inverted space was wrought, and the exodus began in earnest.

Nuddfegh asked that he be left in the Cowl to breathe his last gazing down upon Althlathu. The others did not question this. It was clear he had little life left in him. And as they departed - with the same desperate genius with which he had bound Iuttse Lai's soul to his own, eternally - he wrought another etherwork, this time upon himself. He galvanised his hate/love/anger, his dreadful need for revenge, into a work of unrivalled originality, unprecedented skill. He bound up his soul, as he yet lived, into another ethereal vessel and cast it into the Kiazmus after them. He would find himself a new body, and he would forget. He would walk in somebody else's footprints, see through their eyes, and one day, he was certain, he would find his Iuttse-Lai again.

And so he had.

Nuddfegh lay awake, picking at his past. Many things troubled him, but strangely not so much. Cherry - Iuttse – his eternal love, slumbered beside him. He thought it best that she did not know everything he had remembered.

And so he did not talk of the Munger, of how the Ornish had trapped It in a Torc and a gemstone, and how the Eschatarchy had secreted half of that in an etherwork temple from Terrax; of how they had tormented it, and driven it mad. How it was they that had started a war that destroyed countless worlds. He had not mentioned that.

He had not mentioned his brother, Beltan.

And he had not told her that he had not listened to her all those thousands of years ago. That he could have prevented the death of their homeworld had he done so. That it was his sword that sliced open the temple and ended the golden age of his race with one blow.

Perhaps it had been the terrible guilt at these acts that had caused him to want, so badly, the Munger destroyed - to atone somehow. It was what Beltan would have wanted of him. Yet within himself he knew that he truly loved his power, what the Munger gifted him. For this reason he stood against, fought and killed his own brother - more than that, it had caused him to covet what should never have been his: Iuttse Lai.

And he had made her love him, he now recalled, with cunning and outlawed etherworks, beautiful and subtle. She had not loved him of her own volition, yet he saw to it that she would love him for all eternity. She was his, and that was enough. Why he had not similarly put an end to Beltan's love for her, he was unsure. He had never thought to do so, though it was probably the rivalry, the relish to be had in risking such an illicit affair that made it seem real. He had wanted to better his big brother, but to be punished by him also. Perhaps he didn't want to forget that what he had done was wrong.

Nuddfegh-Ho arose and went over to the window that looked

out over the vast and wild rut of Shea Pass. He understood, finally, that he was a creature of naked contradiction, cruelty, deception and ambition.

And what was more, he realised, he did not overly care.

GOLDERGA

I

A week north of Shea pass Baalor Dark-Eye called for his hound.

"I want you to go south ahead of me and start the construction of siege towers," he said. "Flatten that abomination, Golderga, Captain. Then we take back Da Derga's."

Woebeg Ban Errieu nodded grimly. He had been working with Ornish Soul-less engineers on plans for towers that could mount Da Derga's walls. The former Lordt of that place knew better than any its weaknesses. That nobody, save his trusty hound, knew his real identity led Brookbane to bear these treacheries with brooding resolve. He planned to avoid destroying his home at all cost, yet he had to appear to be intent on it.

"Woebeg. I could never destroy this place. You know that."

"My Lordt, you return to unite us. What better cause could there be?"

"Remember it." said Baalor Dark-Eye, the Wayfarer, formerly Lordt Thrall Brookbane.

Golderga crumpled. Woebeg carved new shapes out of it. He piled high it's shattered carcasses. He garrotted it, squeezing with the fist of his men.

He did not notice the man who shuddered and gasped on the point of his sword until he heard a scream at his rear that stopped his world utterly. Woebeg, the jigging hound of Baalor, went rigid and looked at the man, whose life he had surely ended, for the first time properly. At his back the scream grew in volume, the footfalls growing closer. He knew the sound, the voice, but he could not think clearly, maybe did not wish to. The man was almost dead now. It wouldn't be long. Not long at all. He looked like a good man, as far as Woebeg judged such things – and that was rare. He had a friendly face, Woebeg thought impassively, for the merchant that his garments revealed him to be. The man slid off the end of the blade and slumped to the ground. The scream behind him became a sob.

"Oh no," she choked. "Oh Orn, no no."

But then she too was cut short.

Not here, he thought, turning. *No. No. Not here*.

But there she was, swaying unsteadily no more than ten spans in front of him, a kitchen knife limply raised to strike him, blood gushing from her half-open mouth.

"Orn, no," she whispered. "Not you! *Not you!*"

Woebeg dropped his sword, shaking, moving towards her, hands outstretched, imploring.

"What are you doing here?" he stammered. "*Heron*? Why

are you *here*?"

She toppled forward under the weight of the thrown axe embedded deep in her back.

Woebeg knelt beside her, cradled her, begged for her life. He wept.

"Tersis…" she whispered. "My love."

"No, Heron." Woebeg answered, barely able to talk through his grief. "It's me. It's me. I'll help. Get you help. It's me. It's Woebeg. You remember?"

She fixed her eyes on his face finally, and they were cold. She spat blood into it and rasped at him through gritted, gleaming teeth. "I know who you are, you fucking murderer. You fucking murderer!"

"No. Don't." begged Woebeg. "Please."

"That man. The man you just killed…" Heron looked away from Woebeg as her eyes flooded in suffering and sorrow. "That was Tersis. *That* was my *husband*."

Woebeg watched as the short, makeshift inn burned. The over-size painted sign proclaimed it The Sayer's Alms, and though it was incomparable in every way to it's namesake in Tantrix-Alumnae it would have been, he realised, Heron's own place. Not rented off city nobles. He cast a blurry eye over the trampled peach Porthalia. She had always adorned her inn with the hardy cascading flowers. He wiped his eyes again with the back of a grisly hand and shook his head. It was as fine a resting-place as he could give her, burned along side her beloved, high in the Ornisbach at the foot of Da Derga's Heights.

GOLDERGA

II

"Where is Pellaq?" shouted the aged Ornish priest Pellafinn as he stormed into the Tulsun Reception Hall to confront the Sayer, Barachal Tush.

"Ah, Master Pellafinn," the elegant beast in golden robes growled lowly, "May your gleanings be true…"

"Yes yes," said the belligerent priest. "No time for that. Where is Pellaquial, Tush? Is he alive? What's happening? I hear Orn has fallen. Bloody fools. Is he coming? Where is he?"

"Becalm yourself old man." Said Barachal, a purr-like rumble swelling soothingly in his chest and throat. "All the tells show he still lives, though where I cannot say. We had an arrangement, he and I. I am come to lend what help I may."

"What? A Sayer? Help us?" snorted the old giant. "Well then." Pellafinn breathed in slowly and deeply, and then he filled his hollow cheeks with air and huffed through the black circle of his lips, brows arched. "Well then." He repeated. "Tush, perhaps it is time we got to know each other a little better, don't you think?"

GOLDERGA

III

"What troubles you?" Baalor Dark-Eye asked Woebeg Ban Errieu.

The ageing warrior frowned. "Nothing. A moment's weakness, that's all."

"Never forget, captain, that it is often the most profound weakness that lends a man his greatest strength."

Woebeg nodded blankly. As Thrall Brookbane he had once filled this soldier's head with such platitudes, and yet now the truth of them - if truth there ever was - somehow seemed obscure. This was not the same man who had won his heart and loyalty all those many years ago. This was a charade. There was none of that deeper wit and wisdom that once resonated *truth* and

164

honesty. These were just words.

Brookbane turned his ever-masked head in the direction of his most trusted soldier.

"Care to talk about it?" he asked, the gentleness in the voice at odds with the theatrically fearsome visage.

"I watched a woman I once... *loved*... die at Golderga - after I had killed her husband *right in front of her*. I had not expected... to see her again. And it bothers me how close we are getting to Aetuland. It bothers me that I am seeing no end to this fucking war, nor any sign that we grow closer to bringing your great peace..."

The Warlordt turned again to look up at his former home and fortress, carved out of the shear rock of the Ornisbach above Shea Pass, Da Derga's heights.

"I'm sorry for your loss. You know I respect you, Woebeg," he said. "I remember well enough how you fought alongside me at the Battle of Da Derga. How well you served my father before me. I know you are a practical man also. A modern man, with no time for wonders, magiq, whatever you want to call such - stuff. I understand this, but it poses a problem for me, as I cannot explain my actions without a degree of faith from you. Trust. I fear, Woebeg, that your loyalty would be lost to me if I were to reveal my plans, as they are rooted in what you might think of as false or deceptive - they are not. And so I must show you real wonder, Woebeg. I will demand your trust, for you cannot deny this: At Da Derga I was *blinded*."

Woebeg frowned once more. "So it is said. I saw you take the arrow. They were... terrible burns, my Lordt. You must have suffered. I thought you would never see again."

"What you thought is *true*."

Brookbane loosened clasps at the side of his helm, raised it free of his head.

"This mask was never meant as a disguise."

Woebeg took a step back, stunned. A shattered face stared blindly back at him. Muscles without purpose writhed worm-like in their hollows, raw sockets that had once housed eyes. Fleshy rents, never properly healed, wept viscous bloody matter. The whole head, above the cheeks, was a mess of scar tissue. The once thick black hair now sprouted in patchy clumps, elsewhere shiny and livid skin was stretched like thin papyru over the skull.

Brookbane lifted the gem, dangling from its chain behind the Warlord's doublet, and held it up for Woebeg to see.

"This." He said. "It is sometimes called the *Dealing Stone*. Others have named it *Pathfinder*, or *The Wayfarer's Gem*. Whatever - it gives me sight."

Woebeg's hand involuntarily came up to his mouth, shaking. *What is this?* he thought. *What am I seeing?* He felt bile sting his throat, covered a gag. This was wrong. He was betrayed.

All his life Woebeg had been blind to magiq. He had never believed in it and could not begin to now. He was sick to his heart, for there, before him, was the gemstone he had been sent to steal. The stone that had cost him his dearest friend, Tunny Mal-Tuboly. The mythic trinket of preposterous powers whose existence Woebeg had very much doubted.

And what should he do now? The quest for the Gemstone had seen him raped and left for dead in the Ornisbach, his men killed or scattered. His dreams of wealth, glory and love denied him. And now he served his old master on the side of his ancient enemies, the Nefareans. A man who clearly believed a great delusion - that a Gemstone allowed him to see. A man who now attacked his old homeland. His home! Who had destroyed the city of Orn and burned the great Sed library. A man who had caused him to inadvertently butcher Heron and her husband.

And there was the matter of the letter from Pellafinn to the Ornumnae priesthood – that spoke more of miracles and the impossible. A baffling scroll detailing transformations and vast underground realms, ancient races.

Woebeg crumpled inside. Everything he had done brought only death and pain. Both sides searched for things that could not exist, attempted deeds no man could ever achieve. Pellafinn and a handful of people from Aetuland could not seriously hope to save a world with the *acquisition of a gemstone?* Likewise, it appeared, now, that his new and former Lordt was engaged on a personal quest that, he believed with a controlled yet lunatic zeal, would ultimately bring *eternal peace to the world!*

Woebeg could no longer see which side was the less insane.

"Do you *understand* this, Woebeg?" Brookbane asked, insistently. "Can you see that this is a *genuine* power? I couldn't fake this, Woebeg. No man could. *I cannot see.* I have no eyes. But I have this stone, I found it. I traced it across the continent, and secured it for myself – and it worked! You are the only living man I have entrusted with this knowledge, shown this miracle to. There's so much to know! The Gods, the Weeping God. Orn. The Munger – they're *real!* They *exist!* I have met the Munger, Woebeg! It lives, if life you can call it, within *this* stone. It is the *Munger* that gifts me sight."

"I have to…I have to think, my Lordt." Said the shaken captain. "It's not that easy."

"Do you *doubt* me Woebeg? You think I *lie?* What can't you believe, Woebeg? Do you wish to poke your fingers inside these sockets? Would that help? Look at me man! *I have no eyes!*"

"Still…" Woebeg barely controlled his horror. "Still…"

"You have tonight, captain." Said Brookbane, a metal in his voice now as he replaced the chittinous helm. "I'll see you at sunrise. Please. Decide."

GOLDERGA

IV

Life knows little of itself while it yet lives, and some would say nothing at all in death. For all that it strives to understand both purpose and nature - the chemical workings and encoded genetics that make it all that it is. On the small world upon which the Ornish chose to hide the Torc and gemstone that imprisoned the Munger, a tiny war had started, the ramifications of which had a certain importance to all of the sentient beings that shared that level of existence: Depending on how this apparently insignificant skirmish turned out, reality either existed or it didn't. Like the Dogren in Lazrus Machivarius' tantric box, it both blossomed in an infinite dance of chaotic creativity and was also a yawning nothingness - a singularity without awareness of itself. This reality faced, prematurely, the inevitable: It would have never been. Would never be. It was the paradox of existence to those that saw the balance of all things at that moment, and as such was an enduring symbol of stark terror to the very few that understood such matters.

On the small, isolated planet called Arddn an emerald isle bloomed between the Ganyelse Ocean and the Sutzerean Straights. It was not a large island - its length could be walked in two months - yet it's greatest city had become the trading centre of the world. Its Lordts were respected, it's armies feared, it's wise men sought out. The great fortress of Da Derga's Heights remained the largest construction on the planet. Within the island's embrace the most ancient monuments and cities nestled.

This was Orn.

In Shea Pass, at the foot of Da Derga's Heights, an army had gathered. Compared to the armies that had fought across the stars this was of little significance numerically. The armies that now faced each other had done so before over generations - old enemies fighting the same old war, they believed. The Nefareans, who had swept across the continental mainland and created a new empire, sought again to subjugate Sutzeria and Aetuland. The besieged Sutzereans, fractured by a cycle of rebellion and captivity under the Nefareans, an uneasy alliance with Aetuland. And the Aetulanders, in this last unconquered stronghold, expectant and fearful behind the vast natural fortification of the Ornisbach. Ancient foes. But amongst them greater powers stirred, fuelled by greater ambition, fearful urgency. Amongst them, ancient beings whose people had tried to kill a god now walked. And growing dangerously close were two miraculous and terrible jewels, the coming together of which would open a gateway and free a mad alien god known across worlds as the Munger. A gemstone and a Torc. Crafted by the most powerful

Ornish Warloqs in an era become less than legend, upon a planet whose golden age had abruptly been ended ten thousand years earlier. This tiny conflict, this pointless war, carried within it the potential to free a being who's only remaining purpose was to destroy all existence, and in doing so bring an end to its own suffering.

GOLDERGA

V

As always the soldier (Merchant? Farmer? Craftsman?) moved as though through syrup. The short sword raised to attack was hanging in the air, desperately trying to find a pathway downward, and to survival. The man's face showed all the same simultaneous signs of stunned terror, regret, desperate urgency and fatal resignation that Woebeg had come to expect. He had time to whisper a silent apology before his own blade ended that misery in yet another crimson arc, leaving the man in two pieces.

It was growing late in the day. The battle was a lumpen, tired black thing. The air was filled with more grunts now than screams. Da Derga's Heights loomed dim and ominous in the cloud blanketing the combat. In places rooks and ravens already fed on the soft tissues of fell carnage.

A thin rope of blood looping through the air splattered Woebeg's face with a brief slick warmth as a severed head spun leisurely past him.

Apanatu Spenk had been raised in Thal, an isolated settlement on the southernmost tip of Aetuland, but his dark skin, and his family name, revealed his ancestry to be of far western continental origins. Non the less, Apanatu loved Aetuland and called it his own.

At seven Apanatu witnessed his first killing. A Nefarean Dragship had landed and attacked neighbouring Tuls, but word had reached Thal soon enough for the Nefareans to be routed by the combined might of the two settlements. Apanatu had watched awestruck as the war party returned with a Nefarean warrior captive. The brutish bearded man had turned his pale eyes towards little Apanatu and smiled. With chill realisation the boy cast his eyes over the returned warriors. Soon he was running, urgently searching. Hoping he was wrong.

As they broke the warriors legs, snapping them forward on the rack, below the knees, so that he could see the terrible things they wrought upon his body, Apanatu did not look away. As they twisted off the warrior's arms, first the right, then the left, Apanatu did not avert his gaze. When finally they ended the warrior's screams by stuffing his genitalia into his smashed mouth and throttling him with his own innards, Apanatu smiled.

Apanatu's father had died well, they said. He had been the first to reach the battle with the raiders, killing upwards of seven men before he had himself been chopped down. As they burned the fallen of Tuls and Thal on a great pyre upon the beach, Apanatu shuddered with grief as great tears rolled down his dark cheeks. Yet still he uttered not a sound.

By the time he was thirteen Apanatu was one of the strongest men in Thal. Alone, now that his sister and mother had been Munger stricken, Apanatu spent all his time dreaming of fighting the Nefareans. He carried the greatest burdens he could manage. He chopped wood, hunted, tracked, ran, wrestled as if his life counted on it. He made himself stronger, more resilient with every task he undertook, every moment that he lived.

At fifteen he said his farewells to the people of Thal and set out for Da Derga's fabled Heights to fight Nefareans.

Now Captain Apanatu Spenk of the Brookbane Elite rubbed his cold, aging knees. From his vantage point - squatting, partially shielded behind a spit of rock and a knot of Hatchet Scrub - he surveyed the scene below bitterly. The day was not going well.

How long ago did the siege start? A week? Two? Slowly, devastatingly, the attackers were prevailing. Spenk had concluded early on that this army must have information regarding tactics employed by the host of Da Derga's Heights, as all the hidden passages were covered or blocked. All the places where burning pitch might be poured were studiously avoided. And then there were the damn siege engines, built by Ornish Soul-less engineers - massive constructions that rumbled along on enormous tracks and unfolded, with uncanny speed, to great heights at the foot of the fortress walls. It was not lost on Spenk that they always attacked where the walls were at their thinnest and least protected. The dampened Great Sloth hides draping the tough Chumpattu wood frames proved to be impervious to the flaming arrows showering down upon them. Da Derga's Heights would fall, he realised. There was nothing he could do about it.

With a grunt, Spenk raised himself up, gestured that the eight of his men who yet lived and had not been scattered - and who lay hidden about behind boulders and scrub nearby - should join him once more on the battlefield. They howled, rushing forward with murderous intent. He knew they would not survive, but what then was there to fear? The shit-eating Nefareans would suffer before he died though. He would make sure of that. It was his purpose. They would pay, for the death of his father, the fall of Da Derga's Heights. They would remember the dark skinned Captain. Maybe they would sing of him. Arrows hissed by his head, grazed his cheek, but he paid them no heed.

Woebeg Ban Errieu, former Captain of the Brookbane Elite, hound of Baalor Dark-Eye, was not a happy man. With each new blow he delivered upon the ancient fortress he had once called home he cut himself deeply. He was winning a battle he longed only to loose. He had agreed, in the end, to remain with his new master, and to capture Da Derga's for him. Thrall Brookbane insisted that this would be the end of it. That this would be the act that finally ended the centuries old conflict and would inevitably bring peace to all Arddn. Woebeg doubted it. But he now, for the first time ever, doubted his own sanity also. He recalled seeing his master's blind and disfigured face clearly enough, but had it been real? Had it happened, or had he dreamt it? The memory tortured and taunted him. He who had scoffed at so-called magiq. He who had prided himself on being a realist and seeing the truth of things. And he wondered what kind of trickery could make a blind man appear to see? Or was it a clever mask? A cunning deception? Was it a means by which he confused his most trusted? Created awe at the horror of his visage and the wonder of his sight? Was this how Thrall Brookbane won loyalty now? With tricks and mind games?

Woebeg struggled under the burden of what he knew, and yet he knew nothing. He had caved in, it was a great shame for him to know, through fear and fear alone. He had not thought he feared death before now, and in reality he did not. But he feared death were it to come from his master, whom he had so adored and loved, and whom he had lost and found again. He feared the death a madman who suspected betrayal might bring upon him.

And, too, did the captain toil under the knowledge that he had with his own hands killed the husband of his beloved Heron, only to then watch helpless as she died hating him. The memory stung his eyes afresh. He had been little more than a walking dead-man since that day.

And so ten more good men died by his hands as he cut a swathe through tired, desperate throngs. Another five, six - now seven died as he jigged his charnel dance. And yet more and more and so on and so on, whilst neither blade nor arrow did more than nick or scratch him.

"You bastard!" Captain Spenk screamed. "Traitor!"

He had seen the man in the distance and noted the strange yet familiar gait of the killer. As he cut his own way forward the familiarity was compounded when the man swung in his direction. It was his old Captain, Woebeg Ban Errieu, fighting on the side of the Nefareans. Apanatu's stomach writhed in shock, anger and deep sadness. How could this have happened?

"Bastard!" He yelled again, surging towards the war dog.

Woebeg squinted through the sweat and blood in his eyes, seeking out the abuser. His gaze fell upon Apanatu, and Woebeg saw then what he was looking for. His way out. Here was a man worthy of his blood! It would be easy, now, to let himself be defeated. To die beneath the blade of one of his own men, and there to sink into oblivion. No recriminations, nor any guilt, could reach him in the grave, cold and mindless and dead. His treachery would be justly paid for. Yes, Apanatu would be the fitting butcher of Baalor Dark-Eye's hound.

"Apanatu..." Woebeg whispered, saluting the soldier with his blade, and then bringing it slowly down. Leaving himself wide open. Waiting for a killing blow.

Captain Spenk, delirious with confusion and tired to his marrow, raised his own double handed blade and screamed as he rushed toward his old Captain. But the blow never landed. A wrist thick bolt from a Balistra thudded into Apanatu's side, lifting him off the ground, spinning, and casting him at Woebeg's feet.

"Whu...Why?" the dark skinned warrior hissed through a cascade of blood that surged between his teeth.

"Oh no." Woebeg muttered, stunned at this betrayal of fate. "It should have been me, Apanatu. It should have been me."

GOLDERGA

VI

"When will you *do something*?" Pellafinn thundered. "They're slaughtering us out there!"

"What the priest says is true," rumbled Barachal Tush. "I doubt we have more than a week before Da Derga's Heights are overrun. If we are to protect Aetuland..."

"It doesn't matter." Lordt Crookshaft muttered. "I'm close, very close to making the discovery that will end this war for good. Let me be."

"Very well, my Lordt." the Sayer growled. "It is not my place to question your authority. I must trust you know what you are doing. I shall take my leave."

As the great figure of the golden furred giant left the Hall of Arms, Lordt Crookshaft gestured that his retainers leave him alone with the old Ornish priest, Pellafinn. The sturdy Oak doors inlaid with rosewood and gold wire swung shut, and bolts were shot into place.

Rising from the great seat of his preposterous office the Lordt Crookshaft changed. He grew several spans, his clothing shifting in ways hard to comprehend, until he stood, radiant in his true form. That of Nuddfegh-Ho. He turned at last away from the closed doors and looked absently at Pellafinn. "Thank Orn, I thought I would have to kill him myself!"

"Nuddfegh." Pellafinn pleaded, "Nuddfegh, please. The Sayer is right, and well you know it! We - you - have to do something. With your power..."

"Oh, indeed!" the Ornish Warloq spat contemptuously. "Do you *doubt* me, Pellafinn? Is that it?"

The madness that had momentarily lit up his eyes faded again. The ice melted, and Pellafinn was left questioning what he had seen there.

"There is only one thing we have to do. We have to open up the Bright One - the Temple in the deeps."

Cherry stirred in the luxurious bedchamber. She was not quite in the real world any more. Not fully upon Arddn. There were times she thought she heard battle. Screams echoing up from Shea pass, so very far below. Sometimes she fancied she remembered how the heft of a blade felt in her hands. But mostly she waited alone and knew nothing much of anything. Nothing, that is, but a desperate carnal longing.

It was always when that longing was at its most acute and bittersweet that he would finally come to her, raising her from her stupor. They would fall into each other's arms and make love again, as they had for all time. They were gods of passion now, these ancient souls. He would whisper unbearably gentle incantations, perfume the air with rare exotic scents. He would feed her grapes and olives, sliced sweet Trellin. Tender blue Chiltern meat, cooked in wine infused with garlic and coloured with blue-black Indika. Hers had become a life of softness and sensuality.

She was his, now.

GOLDERGA

VII

Pellaq's fingers tensed into claws at his sides, their shaking quite evident of late. He glared with ill-concealed hatred at the aging veteran.

"You come to me, after all I have heard, all that I know, you come to me! We put our faith in you. You are the *corner*, the *moment*, the one man that can end this, and you betray us all! I should kill you now!"

"I wish you would, Pellaq." Woebeg's posture revealed neither fear nor any sign that he would rouse himself to fend off such an attack.

"I don't even know who the fuck I am any more..."

"And you think I might care?"

The hands bunched into balls and he took a step forward, uncertain, at that moment, quite what he should do. Woebeg finally raised his head, meeting the giant's eyes.

"I'm so tired, Pellaq. You want to kill me? I won't stop you..."

Pellaq reached for his axe, sturdy fingers clenching around the shaft.

"That would be easy wouldn't it? A swift death? Is that what you're looking for? Well I won't give you that option, you Orn-damned Munger-loving bastard! You don't deserve it! I suspect that if I even tried I would be stopped somehow. There would be a stray arrow, I might trip, hit my head on a rock, twist my neck badly - *something*. I see it now. What you are. How this all works. You're immune to magiq, Woebeg, as surely as you don't believe in it! Can you see the irony in that! You can't be *killed*, that's your power - not by anything magiqal at least, and not until you have fulfilled your purpose. Orn has damned you with a place in time, and you'll play out your role. You'll do what you have to. I doubt even the fucking *Munger* Itself could touch you!"

"I don't understand what you're saying, Pellaq. Why would you think that? But you're right, I don't – I can't – believe in all that crap, the stuff that starts wars, divides people, and gives them false hope. What's in it all? It's just another end to eventual death. And so, what's left for me, giant? This bloody shit-hole of a world escapes me in every way. I only know how to *kill*. Every person I have ever loved... or hoped might love me... has either died, or they've been betrayed... or killed, by me. I don't even know how to begin to atone for everything, for the grief my simply living has brought about. If you won't kill me, Pellaq, then put me to work. Help me to do something... help me do something to make it... *right*. I am just someone else's fucking dog. I know... I have never truly had a... a will of my own..."

"No. NO! I won't give you that. Without will there's no responsibility." Pellaq shook his big handsome head. "No. I do not accept that. You're responsible. Greater powers – far greater than you could ever understand - have conspired to keep you alive, and there's purpose in that. There is a will at work here. I don't have to like it, but there it is. I've seen it, and I know. But the deaths you brought about, they're yours. You chose to be a soldier, and that's your trade. That, at least, is something we share - but I have accepted that I'm soul-less, and that's also as it should be. I expect no peace. Oh, you're fucking responsible for your actions, your treachery, and the people you've personally killed all right - don't ever suggest to me otherwise…"

Woebeg looked away, rooting with his eyes in the middle distance. Exasperated now. "I never said… never meant…" He looked back to the giant, and Pellaq saw the murderous innocent he was. "Tell me. Show me what I must do…"

"Do?" Thundered the giant. "How would I know? The Munger comes - and you, you'll never see him, never believe. How can I *make* you see that? We fight, that's what we do. We try to stop this *end of things*, this end of ourselves. We try to live, and to carry on. We try to find a point in everything that has real reason, knowing that it will all be forgotten. That's what we do. We *exist* - or we *don't*. This is where it goes on, or it all comes tumbling down. Everything is in place. All the clues have been given. There's nothing left to add. It's up to us to read them, to understand them, and to make an end for this moment."

"Whatever it takes." said Woebeg, "I'll do it. You have my word on that…"

Pellaq's huge fist thudded mercilessly into the side of Woebeg's head, and the former captain of the Brookbane elite slumped unconscious into a dishevelled heap at the giant's feet.

"Your word! Oh this is rich! So - this, then, is the great Warloq who will save us all? Orn! Forgive me, father, but I do not understand! How can what I have seen be right? How can this traitor - this fucking Munger-serving butcher - how can *he* be the only power capable of saving us all from oblivion? Can this really be the *Munger-Bane*?"

Pellaq swung a massive booted foot into the stomach of the supine warrior.

It is how it is, thought the giant. *An age too long unfinished. A god too long undead. Whatever Orn brings to bear, then let that be.* Perhaps this flawed and foolish man was the answer. Perhaps his *immunity* to the *paranatural* was what it would take to end the threat. Where others saw wonder, what would *his* eyes see? And if the Munger became manifest upon their world, their Arddn, how would his eyes perceive it? As a *man*, or a *God?* As an unstoppable force, or an ancient mad entity too long alive, weak and begging for an end?

And could such a man as this be there to deliver that end with *a single physical blow* perhaps? Or, being human, would he falter at the last, and let the Munger achieve its longed-for end of all things? Would *Orn* be there, wondered the giant? Would *his* God, silent and distant, save them?

"*Atonement* is it, Woebeg?" He sighed at last. "No doubt you'll pay. And if I survive, if this world - and all things - is granted a continuation, and if Orn in his wisdom chooses to see it so, then I'll make sure you get your atonement personally. And yes, you'll help me end this somehow, and after that I'll make sure you suffer for what you have done, for every beat your wretched heart has left to it. I promise you this Woebeg; you'll get what you wish for - *but not before my brother dies*."

Pellaq gazed into the hazy distance, out over the Ornisbach, toward the fortress of Da Derga's. A clarity had formed in him over the last few sluggish, brutal days – like a wakeful-gleaning. As though he had never truly been awake before. The gentle Sayer, Barachal Tush, had tentatively shared what he knew about

Crookshaft - whose true aspect had never been hidden from him - and they had both wept. Tush saw Nuddfegh-Ho for what and who he was, had gleaned all he could of the man in his time at Da Derga's. With the Sayer's help Pellaq had learned of his own great and ancient heritage. And he knew at last the root of all his pain. Of Cherry's - Iuttse-Lai's - pain. The great wrong that had been done to him, and to them both. He finally understood that once, in another age, he had gone by another name, an old Althlathun name:

Beltan.

GODS AND FIGHTING MEN

The Soul-Pike, Baalor Dark-Eye, Wayfarer, blind and barely human, emerged from the smog of mist and fire-smoke. His head, a slick and oily configuration of merged mask and man, angled itself on obscenely muscular shoulders in a manner that suggested contemplation. He faced Da Derga's, a walking demigod, the energies of the newly manifesting Munger barely dammed up in his ravaged body.

So close to it's twin, the powers that bound the gemstone to the torc were finding ways out of Vile-Space, into the universe. It crackled alchemically, flaring and sending out bursts like green-hued lightning strikes that crumpled groups of defenders or levelled trees and set fires. Larger than any Ornish giant, the creature that had once been Thrall Brookbane flexed the Munger's arms that had broken out through his own, integrating them in a shifting coil of black and red musculature and confounding anatomical detail. Part Manatis claw, part Levithian tentacle, they were disproportionately large and horrifically powerful. He operated on a slew of planes, existing partially in Vile-Space, and would seem to flicker like an after-image of flames in the eyes of his automaton army - themselves transformed by his presence into hollow fighting things bereft of soul or conscience. The defenders sometimes perceived him as semi-wraithlike – transparent in parts, solid in others, an aspect of the pervading smog. He prowled below the last great line of Da Derga's defence at Shea Pass, an incarnate storm waiting to break.

The excuses for war had long ceased to have meaning. Old enmities seemed false, pointless. Nuddfegh-Ho had finally abandoned his guise as Crookshaft, and his men had either been cowed, fled or resigned themselves the new situation – what else could they do? The world was no longer that which they had been born into. These were different rules played out by entities that existed in far greater realms, whose perception was not nearly as limited as those afforded the meagre minds of men. There was no hurry in this dance, no urgency. Nuddfegh-Ho revelled in the ancient arts of his heritage, carving out new spaces, chambers of ether and true blind alleys in the façade of reality around Da Derga's, and into which his enemies fell or were trapped. Yet always Baalor Dark-Eye would perceive them, tear them apart with his own magiqal essentia. The men that grappled in the shade of these beings barely mattered any longer. Both sought the same thing, the union of Gem and Torc, the inherent power implicit in that. Power to destroy or to dominate.

But Nuddfegh-Ho knew the Munger must quickly be destroyed if he, and reality, were to survive. He had to kill the man and trap the God, and until he figured out how such could be achieved the stalemate must be maintained. It was a risk he was prepared to take. His long life had stripped away any fear of death, and his self-wrought ether-work had made him question his own nature – he wondered if his universe were snuffed out whether his own soul would emerge - as had the Munger's before him - into a new universe? If he would be perceived there also, and dragged into existence as his own race had done to the Munger?

Wildly he even considered the notion of a circular creation, the implication that he was *himself* the Munger, trapped in a paradoxical circuit of damnation and creation, the end and beginning of all things.

Deep in Da Derga's Ornish-crafted heart, in the chamber that housed the Temple in the Deeps, he laboured to break open the ominous device and take up the torc. He knew that to open it could destroy Arddn as surely as it had Althlathu, but he would not be as bold as before. He would not strike it this time. He would heed Iutse-Lai's warning of so terribly long ago. He could do it with cunning and craft.

The lock gave way with a clunk that echoed down the stone hallway and set adrenal shockwaves racing through the man who had freed it. Pellafinn stood motionless, breathing hard, shivering with barely controlled terror. But all was still. After a few moments he gently pushed on the heavy wooden door, stepped over the felled guard into the room, and quietly made his way to the bed. As Nuddfegh-Ho's trusted companion, Pellafinn had found it easier than he expected to strike the guard – a singular act of violence in a long life, and an act, he realised, that only a short while ago would have filled him with horror, sent, he had believed, his soul screaming to the Munger. He chose not to dwell on it.

Upon the bed Cherry stirred, murmuring softly, consumed

with induced pathogenic ether-dreams. Pellafinn sat lightly beside her, opening a small pouch and pulling out a glass vial of yellowish liquid. Uncorking the top he held it under her nose. Black star-lit eyes sprang open and her body began to convulse.

"Wh…?" she whispered through chattering teeth, an 'o' of red lips. "Wh…?"

"My child," whispered Pellafinn. "You are sick. I have to take you away, but I need you to try to help me. I need you to walk. You must be strong, and you must trust me. Will you come with me now? You're not safe here. Will you *trust* me child?"

Cherry Longorn looked into the eyes of that familiar, loving old face. Her head swam with strange dreams of distant places, and she ached with an unaccountable sense of loss mixed with fulfilment, longing mixed with betrayal.

"Will you trust me Cherry?" he asked again, his eyes now awash with fear and tears.

"Of… of course," she replied at last. "Of course I will trust you Pellafinn."

The old giant sighed with relief, wiped his eyes.

"We have a chance, still. I've seen it. I have to believe it," he said. "Get dressed, quickly, and let's go. You'll feel a little more yourself soon, and I shall explain everything. There may yet be the end we had hoped for."

Pellafinn's thoughts turned fleetingly to the few that gathered to this end, hiding in the disorienting tunnels beneath Da Derga's. The two Sayers, the Giant soul-less Pellaq, a company of soldiers that had formerly served Brookbane, and after that, Crookshaft. And Woebeg Ban Errieu – their sole hope - flawed, and ignorant, dangerous and child-like, lost and alone, the orchestrator of all his own woes.

No worse and no different, then, than any other man, Pellafinn thought.

Soon they were moving - recess to recess, shadow to shadow - but near empty passages offered little if any threat.

Nuddfegh-Ho's ambition transcended even his lust and love, the proximity to such astonishing power proving the catalyst for such shored up insanity as always lingered in him. He had visited Iutse-Lai less, found her exotic beauty, the thrill of that illicit and wrong pairing, less profound than once he did; less consuming than the madness. He was giving himself over at last, and fully, truly finding out what Nuddfegh-Ho had become – a destroyer of worlds. The love that saved the souls of all three of them - himself, Beltan and Iutse-Lai - was no more in him, vanished over 10,000 years living the lives of other man. Such matters as blood, loyalty and love were abstractions, the lesser behaviours of lesser beings. Even his miraculous reunion with Iutse-Lai had, ultimately, stirred him more with its majesty and concept than touched his emotion. After such crimes he could not love again.

How real had that stolen love ever been anyway?

Cherry, on shaky, under-used legs - and sick from Nuddfegh's binding ether-works slowly forgotten, coupled with Pellafinn's medicinal remedy – soon found herself deep below Da Derga's with the old priest, listening to stories of her life that she barely grasped, of events she was both wholly a part of and at present entirely removed from.

"And so, Cherry," Pellafinn told her quietly, "these are the ways you were beguiled. And I also. I loved Nuddfegh-Ho, loved Hergal – whom he had once been. His life has been one of crime and regret, of terrible deeds for which he sought recompense. But Cherry, my child, he must be stopped. A madness has consumed him. Do you understand what this means?"

"Pellafinn…" Cherry croaked. "It's too much. I feel so weak." She leaned up again the harsh cold stone of yet another descending tunnel, sloping away into a blackness of hard to define space. "Can't you leave me somewhere? Leave me out of this? I'm afraid, Pellafinn. I'm afraid to see Pellaq again…"

With a rumble that caused the Ornisbach mountains to shudder, the great wall of Da Derga's Heights that spanned Shea Pass gave up its many thousand year stand against the north, and crumbled like a landslide, crushing defender and enemy alike. The fall of it took an age as rock clashed with rock and forged a path of rolling debris down the pass, obliterating the burnt husk of Golderga and the remaining siege-towers of the Ornish Soulless. And rising up out of the chaos of that, absorbing the energy from it, Baalor Dark-Eye emerged like an elemental. Da Derga's lay exposed. Gathering the smog about him like a cloak, still dancing with a swirl of dust and rock, wood and bloody debris, he fell upon his former home in triumph.

"Iutse…" said Pellaq, torment twisting his features. "I did not think…"

"Please, Pellaq. My name is Cherry. Whatever was in the past, whoever that person was, should remain there. I am who I have always been in *this* life. And that is Cherry Longorn."

"Cherry," he whispered, grabbing her with a passionate cruelty that quickly transformed itself into a sobbing embrace. "I'm so sorry for what I said, what I did…"

"Shhh, Pellaquial. I understand," she sighed into the red warmth of his ear.

Pellafinn cleared his throat then spoke into the gloomy chamber that had once been a dormitory for the giants that carved and wrought the labyrinthine passages. "The wall is breached, I'm sure of it. What else could have rocked Da Derga's like that? The Wayfarer comes, bearing the gemstone. Brookbane is possessed by the Munger. Nuddfegh-Ho, meanwhile, labours to open the Temple below us and free the torc – but his madness may drive him to break it open, in which case, as I have learned, our whole planet faces destruction."

Barachal Tush spoke up, his rumbling voice gifting the words with fearful and appropriate gravitas. "An end to all things shall surely come this day if we fail. More than just Arddn is at stake if the Munger escapes. There is no time left."

"All we know, Cherry, is that both the Wayfarer and Nuddfegh-Ho must be stopped. And that this man," Pellaq pointed an accusatory finger at Woebeg, alone with his misery in a corner, his face burning with frustration, anger and regret. "*He* is, it seems, somehow the lynch-pin. All we have to count on."

"Pellaquial," said Barachal Tush in a low growl. "Let it be. You know the Tells. We must respect them, and because of that – *him*. Don't misplace your anger now."

Pellaq looked at the Sayer, then into the marble black eyes of Cherry. "All right," he said. "All right. You're right, old friend." He rubbed his temples and shook his head. "All right," he said again. "We have to go. Now. Pellafinn will lead us to the chamber, where the Bright One, the Temple in the Deeps, sits. That's where this will be played out. Nuddfegh-Ho cannot move the Temple, and Baalor Dark-Eye will find his way there soon enough. We will have to fight. Cherry, you will have to face this – have strength. You must have strength. I believe in you – you are here, after all. You're with us. With me. And so, as I say, I have faith in that. How could I not?" He smiled weakly. "Woebeg, you asked me to put you to work. Very well then, now is your hour. I do not know what it is you have to do, what you can do. You will have to work that out for yourself. But whatever it is, do it man. See it through. Atonement was what you wanted. Earn it now, do the right thing. End this however you must, but end it. Show us that we were right in our choice and that you are who the Echoes-To-Be say you are. Do not question this, just act. Be the moment that your life has prepared you to be." At last Pellaq turned to Pellafinn. "Old father, this has been your fight, it was you who tried to awaken the world to what you saw coming. Thank you for giving me, however hard won, your trust. We have all learned more than we would care to about ourselves, our race, the crimes of our forefathers, and the horror we have visited upon this world that was not our own - and for these crimes you and I must also atone. Lead the way old friend."

Nuddfegh-Ho sat amongst a jumble of geometrical shapes, linked cubes and toruses, all the compound parts that had constituted the cube shaped temple, lit-up with arcane slithers of light. He stared transfixed at the torc that encircled his wrist, watching the green energies that crackled about it, sensing the Munger and Vile-Space, the chasm of eternity and the immediacy of nothingness in the all-pervading echoes of what might come to be. He smiled. There was peace in that moment. He had the power to draw that out now, to slow time such that it could seem forever. He could, if he chose, postpone the inevitable. But why bother? This was how it should be, and he felt no fear or remorse. He felt no blame.

As the small group of men and giants led by Pellafinn entered the chamber, Nuddfegh-Ho found himself only slightly surprised to see Iutse-Lai amongst them. He arched his eyebrows and found himself chuckling, and then laughing. It had been a long time since he had last laughed and it felt good.

"Iutse, my love, what are you doing amongst this rabble?" he asked at length.

"Nuddfegh-Ho, the Wayfarer has breached the walls. He's coming here." Said Pellafinn.

"I know that," replied the Ornish Warloq. "But look – what do I have here?" He held up his arm so they could see the torc around his wrist. "It's almost a disappointment isn't it? Almost.

But you should touch it, Pellafinn. It's really quite remarkable. I understand it, now."

"Nuddfegh-Ho," continued the old priest. "You know what will happen if the gemstone is reunited with the torc. We can't allow that."

"Oh, but you *must*." Nuddfegh-Ho turned his cold green eyes once more towards Pellafinn. "I've found the *solution*: If the Vile-Space is united, the torc and gem brought together, it opens a causeway into our own plane of existence. It operates on the laws of *this* realm - one space *within* one space. But should the the the Munger Itself emerge into *our* realm - and the Munger is a being made up entirely of Vile-Space matter – and should the two parts, gem and torc, *again* be separated... Well then, it's clear! The Munger will be ripped apart. Its matter won't be able to sustain itself."

"And you know this do you?" asked Pellafinn. "You know *how* to do this?"

"Not yet." Said Nuddfegh-Ho, chuckling. "I'm working on it Pellafinn. But I believe the *theory* to be sound. It's the practice that concerns me slightly."

Pellaq broke free of the group and ran towards the Warloc bellowing. "You bastard! I've had enough of this. You don't care about anything, any of it! I'll kill you now!"

"Beltan?" said Nuddfegh-Ho, raising a finger and stopping the bigger giant, his wronged brother, where he stood – frozen in painful bonds no others could see. "Beltan, is that you?" He stood, surprised for the second time, this time more deeply. "Of course. Of course! How fitting!"

"Nuddfegh, don't!" shouted Cherry. "You've hurt him enough!"

"Shut up!" The warloq sent his brother spinning across the room where he hit one of the great walls, slumped to its base and lay still.

"Cherry, don't do anything rash!" hissed Pellafinn urgently, a gnarled hand on her arm. "Go to Pellaq. See if he's alright."

"*His* people built this!" shouted Nuddfegh-Ho, gesturing at the pieces of the temple that lay scattered about him. "This monstrous device that *destroyed our world!* He tried to kill me, tried to kill us all on Althlathu! Look to him with your petty blame, it's not so clear, not half so clear as you think!"

Almost out of shadow, like a ripple on a black veil, there emerged into the room a horrific entity above Nuddfegh-Ho, barrelling into him and toppling him to the ground amongst the shards of the temple. It raised itself up, reconstituting itself several times before settling on a shape it felt comfortable with: The remnants of Thrall Brookbane, the semi manifest limbs of the Munger forcing their way into existence through him. The warloq, Nuddfegh-Ho, was up and facing it swiftly, laughing.

"Welcome home my Lordt," he said. "I expect things have changed a little since you left, no?"

"Dark deadly and flay. The wind-soft spears of wisdom say," hissed the Munger/Brookbane, the debris of the fallen wall still clinging to the smog that flitted about him like a spectral cloak. "I take this age iron cast and in fullness. I take this lovelost/ killer spawn. I take back me me mine." And saying that, the force that had birthed itself out of the wreckage of a blind Lordt heartbroken and an undead god that reached for the freedom to die fell upon the ancient Althlathun warloq, and both became buried under a chaos of detritus trapped in paranatural eddies, and a tumult of shifting realities.

Pellafinn looked on desperately, unable to ascertain how he should intervene. Cherry watched from Pellaq's side. The unconscious giant was bleeding badly from a head wound, but his breathing was steady. She looked back down at him and felt herself loving him anew. Not Beltan, not the echo of a mythic betrayed husband, but this soul-less Ornish man, Pellaq. He'd forfeited his soul defending the defenceless, she knew. He'd given it up knowingly, so that the travellers he had spent time with in Ypo-Polaria would live. He fought off the waylay men, killed two, and surrendered his soul – at least in the eyes of the modern Arddn Ornish. He'd then spent what many counted a worthless life studying the Echoes-To-Be, and attempting to avert a perceived cataclysm. This innate goodness reached her, and split the love she shared, returning it to one place: Pellaquial. Her Pellaq. It was Pellaq whom she *truly* loved, and the etherworks Nuddfegh-Ho had wrought were finally broken.

Cherry drew her sword and headed towards the thundercloud that was two near-gods in battle.

Woebeg watched everything in deep confusion. He recognised the man they were all referring to as Nuddfegh-Ho, and whom they seemed to perceive as one of the Ornish. The man was a Lordt of Tantrix-Alumnae called Hergal Ben Egan. He'd been a patron at The Sayer's Alms, had watched the contests that resulted in the ill-fated party destined to be descimated in the Ornisbach. He was not a big man, certainly no giant! He sported a large Torc around a slender wrist. Crafted for the Ornish it looked preposterous on the man, comical. He was clearly quite mad, as revealed by his words, the names he used, his manner. And yet his companions feared him. They were wholly in a different realm, seeing things he could not begin to perceive. He shook his head, looking from the crazy Lordt Hergal Ban Egan to Pellafinn and his desperate posse, and back again. Why couldn't they see it was just a man he wondered? Why were they so blind to the truth?

He watched, stunned, as Pellaq ran forward, seemed to halt, freeze momentarily, then turned to run at the walls of the cavern – a cavern like any other, certainly not the vault the others seemed to be witnessing – where he hit his head on the rock and slumped to the ground. Woebeg was horrified that a gesture could control the mind of a giant, the merest suggestion could send him reeling into a wall.

Woebeg almost gasped when his former Lordt Thrall Brookbane appeared, lurching, barely able to hold himself upright. He was covered in blood and dust. Nobody seemed aware of the man until he was almost upon Hergal Ban Egan - or Nuddfegh-Ho as he now called himself. The shock that rippled through the assorted company when they *did* perceive Brookbane was not shock born of empathy for such a tragic figure, but one born of fear in the presence of something terrifying. They staggered backwards to a man, looking on with slack-jawed awe.

Woebeg began to move towards the two figures, he heard the muttering Brookbane saying "Now, please. Home, my home. It's mine, you said, mine. Please, no more…"

Then the men before him were at each other's throats - no great spectacle, no martial prowess. Just two men, grunting and grabbing, strangely blind to each other, connected and yet not. Around Brookbane's neck he saw the stone hanging from its chain. Around the wrist of Hergal Ban Egan/Nuddfegh-Ho the torc still loosely dangled. Cherry ran at them suddenly to his right, so much bigger than they, so much more powerful, but Hergal turned his cool eyes on her and she collapsed.

"Stay there sweetheart! We'll talk about this later. I understand." he shouted, turning his attention back to the shambolic Brookbane.

I could just take them, thought Woebeg. *I can walk right up there and take the torc and the stone.*

Hergal/Nuddfegh and Brookbane both saw Woebeg at the same instant, and at once their attention was turned on him. Nuddfegh-Ho raised his arm with the preposterous dangling torc and yelled.

"And what the fuck do you think you're doing? Get back

there!" He pointed at the rest of the group but something happened, or rather nothing.

"How are you...? How can you...?" he trailed off. "No. Not now. Not after all of this."

Woebeg continued to walk towards the man. He was not going to be deterred. Why should he be? Why should he *get back there*? He was going to end this.

"Woebeg," said Brookbane. "My old friend. You've not deserted me then, eh? You see? We're here! We're at Da Derga's! We took it together!"

"No, my Lordt." He replied. "We didn't. I'm not your hound any longer. The man I served and loved died at the battle of Da Derga's the day he was wounded. The day he gave up, and fled, and left us to get by without him."

"You're wrong, Captain! Woebeg, look at me! See the powers that course through me! We can change things forever!" croaked the desperately wounded former Lordt of Da Derga's.

"I see no powers, Brookbane. I see a wretched coward and a traitor." Woebeg, with terrible sadness, hefted his sword and rushed toward the man, running him through. It was so easy, so very easy. Brookbane fell to his knees, clinging to Woebeg's shoulders, toppling sideways, pulling the warrior down with him. Blood gushed from his mouth, but he smiled, clutched Woebeg hard, hugged him as his life ebbed away.

"Thank you, my Captain," he whispered. "I knew. I knew you were my man. I knew... that I could trust you."

Woebeg rolled aside as a blade came down between him and the dead Brookbane, sending up sparks. Hergal Ban Egan was fast, as fast as he perhaps with the blade, Woebeg saw at once. This was a match of equals, a worthy fight, maybe a worthy death. He grinned.

Cherry watched, stunned, the invisible grip around her throat loosening. It was hard to make out what was going on. Nuddfegh-Ho had been visibly shocked when his paranatural energies had spilt around Woebeg leaving him unaffected and unaware of them. The madness had become starkly clear then, when like a child he had cried out, clutching the torc to his chest, wide-eyed and fearful. She watched, rapt, as the great energies that animated the remnants of Brookbane turned on Woebeg, and the soldier had boldly walked into the midst of them, becoming barely visible in the broiling dust and smoke that cloaked it. And within moments that energy had ceased, fallen away. It had gathered in on itself like an oily fire returning to its unlit state, played out backwards through time until it was nothing, just two figures caught up in an embrace. Woebeg had killed the Wayfarer, the vessel of the Munger. He had done so easily what they, with all their might and knowledge, could not.

Now Nuddfegh-Ho had manifested a sword, was running at Woebeg, the blade falling – but it hit only stone. Woebeg had somehow moved in his strange unnatural way to a new spot, ready to take on the Warloq.

For some time they clashed, incomprehensible to Pellafinn's party looking on helplessly. But what slowly became clear to Cherry was that Nuddfegh-Ho was winning. The old mercenary was a man of war, but he could not match Nuddfegh-Ho's vast experience, neither did he have his vitality. Cherry wiped her mouth. They were slowing. Sooner or later one of them would land the blow that tipped the balance. If they would only slow enough, then

"You're crazy if you think you can win this," said Hergal/ Nuddfegh-Ho as he and Woebeg circled each other in their time-shifting martial jig. "You don't even know what I am, what I can do! You have no idea what I'm capable of…"

"I thought you were a good man, once. I didn't know you

really, I admit, but you always seemed a man of honour. Maybe you were, I don't know," replied Woebeg, panting a little. "But you're here, you're part of this. You're a threat, I understand that. And maybe, just maybe, we'd be a lot fucking better off without you..."

The pair spiralled into another part of the chamber, scattering Pellafinn's terrified company. Hergal butchered two of them in passing for the sport.

"Don't talk good and bad!" he spat. "We're all worth nothing – Nothing! Don't you understand that?"

"Sure," replied Woebeg. "I understand. But I'm not *blind*, Ban Egan. Just because my life's been a wretched bag of shit it doesn't mean I can't see, can't appreciate love in *others*. Beauty in *others*. The stuff that *is* worth a damn, no matter how fucking fleetingly..."

"You're getting tired, old man. You need to rest. Let's stop this shall we? All I want is the gemstone from around that dead man's neck, and then I'll *gladly* leave this place! What's the harm in that?"

"It belongs to the Ornish!" yelled Woebeg, a deep anger suddenly twisting his gut, reddening his face. He thought of Tunny Mal-Tuboly in his shallow grave, Heron chastising him, telling him to do it *right*! Do it well. The Ornish gold he squandered - all for that stone. "If they want it back they should bloody well have it back!"

But Woebeg was stilled by a blade that pierced his side. "Well – I tried to make you see sense," said Hergal. "Now I'll just have to kill you."

Slowly, like the blooming of a flower, a red circle spread around the glistening tip of a blade emerging directly out of the centre of Hergal's chest. Woebeg watched tiny droplets of crimson arc through the air in an accompanying mist. Hergal/Nuddfegh-Ho looked down, shocked, and saw the sword-tip vanish back inside his body.

Woebeg looked up at the impassive face of Cherry Longorn as she yanked free her blade, heedless of the blood that spattered across her exquisite features. She turned slowly away from Nuddfegh-Ho - her lover, Beltan's brother - as though under water, and walked away without once looking back.

Hergal/Nuddfegh-Ho crumpled/rolled/fell silently to the ground, trying to stem the flow of blood and life, trying to comprehend this sudden and unexpected end. He looked up at Woebeg, mouthing words, pleeding. Woebeg could hear nothing but the thump of his heart. He looked at the blood on his hand, he had been holding his side without knowing it. He could feel nothing. Pellafinn was moving towards him, wide-eyed with wonder, and the few remaining soldiers wept and hugged one another. The two Sayers embraced. Woebeg saw Cherry crouch beside the still supine Pellaq before darkness stole away his vision.

"I wanted to kill him, Pellafinn," said Pellaq. "I wanted to do something…"

"You brought Woebeg to us, Pellaq. That was your roll. It was always his to finish, and that he did. We owe him his life at the very least."

The three giants gazed out over the ravaged Shea Pass from a tower balcony. So much of Da Derga's great structure lay in ruins below them, but that which was carved in the mountains themselves. It would be lifetimes before its like was ever seen again. But the world had survived, and in the light of this knowledge even the fallen walls were possessed of a great beauty, the trials and follies of men afforded glorious flawed nobility. The giants were filled with a joy born only of their being still alive.

"Woebeg will guard the gemstone, Pellaq," Pellafinn

continued. "Who better? The Munger cannot touch him. He's blind to it. And if any man can remain untouched by such power, and defend it, well that man it is Woebeg Ban Errieu. He's making his peace with himself and the world. It's out of our hands now, and thank Orn for that! We've done enough damage to the universe."

"What now?" asked Cherry.

"Home. For me at least. Back to Tantrix-Alumnae," said Pellafinn. "I need to write this all down before I drop dead, and that'll certainly be soon enough! I'm too old for all this."

"And what of the Ornish, Pellafinn?" she asked. "Are the beliefs to be rewritten? Are we to remain as Soul-less? I can't share those beliefs now, Pellafinn. We've seen too much. They're just a fabrication aren't they? Made to keep us from ourselves."

The old priest sighed. "I believe, my child, you're right. I no longer think of either of you as unburdened by souls. I can't think of myself as such either. But change will take time, and we are few. The terrible crimes committed at Orn will be discussed. The Ornish must gather, I think. We must corroborate our knowledge and learn from our misdeeds. Who knows? But all faiths are built from a substance that is no substance that remains tougher than the greatest wall, yet can be felled with reason. But, I fear, only rarely. We shall see."

Pellaq wrapped Cherry in the great circle of his arms as a cool wind suddenly whipped up around them. "The winter's coming." he said.

END

MACHIVARIUS POINT: ARDDN

THE DAGGERED ARM OF RESTRAINT

The noise grows thick and it's hard to concentrate as we pack everything, well, everything that we need. But how do you know what matters after so long? What will we miss? That is assuming we can never, will never return?

Come away from the window, I hiss, *for Orn's sake woman! You'll catch an arrow. Quickly now, out the back, there's time.*

But I don't know that. And it's my fault really. I kept us back here, wouldn't face the truth of it, the change that's come over this land. I thought...

It doesn't matter now. Whatever the reasons, they're irrelevant. They'll be forgotten, just as I will be – even as I craved immortality, justification, reason for my being. Just as I drove myself crazy with dreams of fame!

I will be, must be, forgotten.

And just-so my motives, everything that led us here. They matter not at all. Yes, how bitterly I see that, how markedly it's been made clear these last weeks.

We – myself, my partner Malettaine, and our son, our little boy, Ornis – spiral a ragged descent down the back of our wall-hugging refuge – Ha! Refuge! That I ever called it that! – at Golderga. (Bottom-feeder. Fucking saprophyte.) We came, I came, to make my name here, seeking patronage from the Lordt's and masters and moneyed at Da Derga's. My paintings would hang in those halls for a thousand years, I said. That's what I told Malettaine. That's what I promised. Aetuland proffered us no security, its money spent on wine and Tobbach, oils of whim and other intoxicants. That, or warfare. No, Golderga would save us – would make us!

Would make me.

I can smell burning, and I cry freely for my children left behind – children of oil and pigment on beds of canvas and wood. Birthed through the inelegance of my imperfect perceptions and untidy outpourings, children of passion and pain - and no doubt cliché and pretence - but beloved none the less for that.

All our children mirror our flaws, I used to say. *That's what makes them beautiful to us.*

We're caught in a rabble of flight, like rats, and I clutch Ornis to my chest as he sobs and we run and we run and we

Soon - that is only soon by the blessing of imperfect memory - we are spread through the bitter mountainous forest, fragile as embers thrown up by fire and cast out on a breeze.

I don't sleep much, huddled with my loved ones and frost-dusted beneath a black web of branches that do not protect us, do not protect us at all from the endless and pitiless sky. I don't sleep much, but when I do I dream of fire, and in that fire one painting stands out. Torments me.

Orn, three armed. The daggered arm of restraint fused with his torso. The great wings that give flight between worlds, across the vastness of space. Below, naked blind priests, the hooded and blind priestess leading unfalteringly. Our future – a symbol of the nations of the world, spilling forth to populate and people its corners...

A big painting, framed in metal.
A great painting.

I cry like a child bereft, as quietly as I'm able. Half a lifetime consumed in flame, and I only half a man without those props and seeded memories, those stillings of concept and time. And I try to perceive Orn in this, threaded between the stars that gaze coldly down at me.

But I see nothing.

I look for reason.

But there is none.

I beg for recognition, for the universe to see me – me! – and to acknowledge, love and embrace me.

But it does not.

I entreat it to be my mother, my father, and to take me home - to make all things better.

They're singing - it's caught on the wind that sets the thinning woodland a dance - the soldiers. They're not far behind us, and we know we'll most likely be captured or killed today – what use are we? I old, and a mother and child? Just a burden. And even if I had found my glory, would they know me? Would it matter?

Parem parum
The old men hum
Distract the child
And rape the mum
Love's yet adrift
When time begun
The old men hum
Parem parum

END

SED

They say it, say to my face they do, well they do - did. Mad Judd, mad Judd. So, well it's not it, it isn't. But they they

Well whatever they think, they think, it doesn't matter.

Thoughts they slip a bit is all, slip and it's a bit of a tumble, a rush, like lots of people lots of peopleallofthetime and I'm a bit eh? Eh? Eh?

But that doesn't mean doesn't mean I'm mad, no it doesn't.

The Sed the Sed library. That's where I live - lived. I stack - stacked and catalogue - logued.

The books, I love the books.

And when at night when it's dark - was dark - and there's none but I I me and the Watchers, with their sniff sniff Dogren about the place, that's when I read, I do - did. So much, the wealth of it, and that's when I get - got - the stilling, and a little, you know, a little peace.

Pollaqualaq Na Bo Tersium is my -was my - favourite. The spill and drift of image and metaphoric metaphoric metaphor, layers did you - do you - see? It's sweet calm dark thud thud, and you, you're out in motes, in light, dancing with motes, tiny tiny tiny. It all comes clear with Pollaqualaq:

Denizen of reflection
Call out the post.
React and do not oppose.
Occur but in harmony.
Reach wind forms to negate space and create form.
Trust not grounded feet.

Pollaqualaq, I sung to you and wept I did - I do. And the echoes they echo - echoed -around those sweet dusty cool halls bathed in the stuttered light fractured in panes of red and green and blue and blue and blue

When the wind gets – got - gets high and flutes amongst the wooded wooden housings, the nestling beds of these children of mind, I would - I did - must light a candle and seek – sought - out the higher stalls, the overhanging cherrywood circumference of the Pentatrixae, and there bury – buried - my head in the refuge of it, unfurling the scrolls of the Elder Lluddaddaq and his quixotic musing, the – mustn't mustn't did – banned and outlawed hubris of Manllann O Bo Naddarinn, whose howls from Vile-Space afflict yet the storms of night:

Damn you fools!
Cast not wan eyes red o'er flawed compromise,
Bite the tether red-teeth and spit into the grave!

No holding marriage of sin-blame for unbidden
acts of soul-peril mine!

Laugh I do – did! Loud, and bothered the sniff sniff Dogren, but let the Watchers curse me then, they need me - needed me - then here, so

And I think old Manllann, so damn his soul, was onto something, I really do – did - do.

They kicked me, and beat me when the Sed Library burned – but they didn't kill me. Perhaps they think thought think it crueller to leave me alive, to tell alone the tale myself, I the sole Ornish survivor of the sacking of Orn.

I blub blub blubbered, wet wet my cheeks streaked and dust streaked and

In, ripped, in rags, I watched, and the tower burned, the glass splintered and fell, I heard it fall inwards, part melting falling inwards, while the paper words paper soured and drifted up out grey black blue in the sky

Two days later the black bones of the Sed were warm still and I sleep slept amongst them blackened black myself. It cradled me even in death.

I dug I dug.

Dig.

Steps.

Low as high! Low as high, and it's there still!

Not the beautiful spiral, not the window – gone such and lost the echo of what we did to Althlathu. (I read the books, I know!) But the below is not gone. Few but the Masters and the mad knew the mirror-form of the Sed, and of how the lower floor, like Althlathu, was the sea, and in that surface a reflection: Below as above. Everything in duplicate.

As said Vertribulae:

Doom fled the silver tain
Echoes that be echoes and more
Kiazmic!
Cast into the wind wisdom and gather anew!

The city of Orn is gone, it's true, blasted by war and wind, snow and time and feet and the slow crawl of nature. Nobody came home nor back that fled. They do not wish to face it, so it's left to I I me.

Here, in the mirror-Sed, I dwell yet, and carry on.

The ghost of old Sed my memory creates above me, a towering delusion. The echoes a fiction. Much work is must be done yes, and black and blackened much is. But Orn and I know all is not lost. For I am the guardian of Sed, and guard it I will. Mad Judd! Mad Judd!

END

A STICKY MATTER, BEST FORGOTTEN

"Steady. Steady on. Old chap." gasped the portly swordsman. "No need for that."

The sagging, ancient walls of *The Fine Prospect* Inn were constructed of clay, Rafasi shit, straw and lime slapped by hand onto a crude latticework supported by a chunky timber frame. One of these walls had done little to halt the trajectory of Tunny Mal-Tuboly. He found himself in the courtyard looking back through a large, generally circular hole into the main bar - and at the Ornish Soul-less giant who hurled him there.

The giant was stooping, angrily knocking chalky chunks out of the wall with a balled fist to create a big enough gap for himself to climb through. At his back the landlord, Arun Ban Sheel, made half-hearted and blustery exclamations to do with the door having been a good enough exit for the past Orn knew how many years. The giant appeared not to register the observation.

Tunny was up and surveying his surroundings at a jog, engorged gut undulating uncomfortably above unsteady stocky legs. He belched loudly and whispered a cuss as he tried, and mostly failed, to brush the white dust and debris of his recent collision off his expensive vermilion velvet jerkin. He was sorry also to find a substantial tear in one elbow. Known and liked in Thurford, of which The Fine Prospect was the heart, there would be no inspired acts of bravery on his behalf from the locals. In facing the enraged giant Tunny was fully aware that he was on his own.

"Don't you dare, don't you dare run away from me!" the giant's voice was like a rabble in unison. "You! After all this time! I've a score to settle with you. Come back here!"

It was dusk and a fat moon cast filmy light through a blanket of low clouds. A drizzle of rain brought with it an earthy scent that suggested somehow spring, raising the dust and mingling with it. Firelight from The Fine Prospect danced over the damp cobbles and peppered the moonlit courtyard with gold. The shadows were deep, and Tunny plunged himself into the darkness behind a goods wagon. A Giant Sloth, whose lot was to pull it, stirred with vague unease in the stables nearby, snorting softly.

This is bloody hopeless, Tunny thought to himself. Weapons were removed before patrons were allowed to enter any public house in Aetuland, and were generally – as in this instance - stored in a locked outhouse. *All well and good, that. But not when you've pissed off a bloody Soul-less giant! Hardly an even pairing that. Not really.*

"If it hadn't been for you," the giant yelled, some distance away, "I'd still be, still have…" He was drunk, ageing, and not the largest of his race – no more than eight or nine spans – but more than a match for any native of Arddn.

The Ornish had a strict code, born out of a tumultuous near-mythic past, which denied them any act of violence. Such an act would result in a forfeiture of their soul, damning them to a living death beyond which lay no redemption. Most Soul-less Ornish became mercenaries, bitter and fearless with nothing to lose. They tattooed their woes in great spirals across their bodies, shaved their scalps like the priests, and strode out into the world to be killed.

Not an easy task.

"I know, I know it was you!" the giant howled, his voice near breaking. "I would not forget such a thing, not even in the circumstances. I would not forget!"

To be fair Tunny was hard to forget. He was colourful in dress and personality, rotund and hearty. Black coils of hair and a huge beard framed flashing white teeth, two sparkling eyes and a small bulbous nose that tended to redden as the evening wore on. His voice would ring loudest in any gathering and was punctuated by chuckles.

"Orn's bollocks!" hissed Tunny between gritted teeth. He had no recollection at all of the giant, could not conceive what offence he may have committed, what situation he had been involved in that would have lead to such a confrontation. He was in awe of the Ornish and he romanticised them. They were paranatural beings born of another world and who strode amongst men nobly bearing their tragic code.

As his eyes adjusted to their surroundings Tunny saw a possible escape route behind the stables, if he could just get across a brief open stretch of courtyard - and if the giant didn't find him first. The landlord was outside shaking his head and cursing quietly, studying the newly created entrance to his bar. Others watched the giant, squinting out into the darkness, waiting to see what would transpire.

The giant was now half way across the courtyard, swaying slightly, and looking directly at the spot in which Tunny squatted – increasingly uncomfortably and unnerved.

"Now then, Mallaq – you'll bloody well be paying for this, you know?" said the Landlord with the same uncertain and unconvincing bravado of earlier.

"It's a bloody wall!" replied the giant, hearing him at last. "It's nothing a little mud and crap can't fix!" He took a step forward. "Mal-Tuboly!"

Tunny's heart jumped. The giant had obviously remembered his name. What, what had he done? He obtusely acknowledged a weakness for beer and butterwine but wasn't prepared to fully sacrifice his whims to any blame. *Now then sonshine, this is bad*, he thought. *Orn, but this is not good, not good at all.*

"So, do I have to remind you Mal-Tuboly?" the Giant suddenly shouted, as though he had gleaned the swordsman's thoughts. "Would that help you, eh? Well, so I shall so I shall. Maybe ten, twelve years ago, in Aetullia we were. I a priest – can you believe it now? I mean, look at me! - wearing my robes then, fresh out of the Temple in the Flacks at Tantrix-Alumnae. I was late to the calling you know, but what else is there for the Ornish but prayers or battle? What? Can you tell me fat man?" The giant turned, walking slowly to the front of the inn, where the courtyard met the muddy single track through the village.

Tunny hurried across the courtyard in the opposite direction, heading for the shambolic stables leaning up against the outhouse – within which were stored the patron's weapons. He pressed himself against the wall, into the deepest shadows, and edged around towards the back as quietly as he could. A general stirring amongst those guests that had spotted Tunny's dishevelled dash caused the Giant to turn, and stride furiously - and mistakenly - over to the wagon, driving it easily aside with a bulky shoulder to peer furiously into the now empty darkness beyond.

"Where are you? Damn you Mal-Tuboly! Damn you to bloody Vile-Space and the Munger, man! Come out! Come out and take your dues!" he spat.

At the back of the outhouse Tunny found the shutters loose. It would be a stretch for a man of his girth to climb up through the gap, but his choices were few enough. However, reaching furtively inside he found he was able to find purchase on several of the stored weapons, pulling out a double-edged poniard and a long, curved briquet.

There was a drunken peal of bitter laughter. "All right then! All right then, Mal-Tuboly - you want to play Dogren and master? Well that's fine. Fine. I'll find you eventually!" the giant shouted. "Nine, Ten… I'm coming!" He made a pantomime out of looking under whatever object blocked his path or cluttered the courtyard for a while before eventually lapsing into a contemplative stillness. "So. So." he muttered at last. "Where were we? Aetullia, that's right. I a priest, and you, well you were as you are now, I suspect. I would have thought. You seem unchanged. A hired sword, a wanderer! You were already drunk Mal-Tuboly, when you challenged me – a giant! - to a drinking contest. I must admit I laughed, but you, you were determined. You said something, something like you'd never met a man that could out-drink you. So a giant seemed pretty fair game!" He laughed once more. "I confess, I thought you a fool and took you up on it."

Tunny barrelled out from behind the buildings armed and newly confident. "I was probably young and showing off. Probably still do from time to time. whatever, I'd rather this didn't end in a fight, giant." he said. "I've no issues with you old chap, none at all. But if it has to be that way, well, at least I stand a bit of a chance now don't I, eh?"

The giant grinned and the pair slowly circled as the patrons spread out to form a larger circle around them, muttering and making wagers.

"So," continued Tunny. "Did I win?"

"Actually, no." replied the giant. "No, you didn't. You passed out after another twelve or so long ales. But by then I was not in the greatest of shapes myself. I wasn't a big drinker you see, but you were already drunk, and I…" he lunged, slapping the poniard out of Tunny's suddenly dead left hand, but the swordsman spun nimbly and sliced a long cut in the giant's side, drawing a dark slick of blood and a gasp.

"Please man, let's stop this," grunted Tunny. "You said yourself, I was unconscious!"

"You were!" retorted the giant. "But you were the cause of my condition, and so too for what happened later…"

Mallaq, the giant, lunged again, the back of a massive fist thudding audibly into the side of Tunny's face as the fat swordsman simultaneously cut another deep wound across the giant's chest and through the triceps of his raised right arm. Tunny went spiralling to the ground as the Ornish Soul-less staggered back.

"This," panted Tunny, "this isn't worth dying over, surely?"

Mallaq furrowed a heavy brow, and a fleeting sorrow transfigured the flat, broad features. "If one's soul is not worth dying for, then what? What else is?"

The Ornish mercenary ran bellowing at Tunny, a landslide incarnate, earth and stone animated; anthropomorphesised. There was a collision, tumbling, and then stillness. The briquet had cut upward - under the Giant's chin, entering his brain and exiting through the top of his skull.

His expression was one of complete peace.

Tunny hauled his way out from beneath the fallen mercenary aided by a few of the locals. When finally he gathered his wits and breath he spoke quietly. "Why, Arun? Why did he do that? I never wished the fella the slightest harm."

"He told me a story once." Said the Landlord. "How he woke up in a cell in Aetullia. How he was informed that a group of drunken soldiers had decided to pick a fight - you know, fully aware that an Ornish giant could never fight back! But old Mallaq here was drunk, see, Tunny? He fended them off. A few insensible swipes, that's all it took. No harm intended. Broke one chap's neck and crushed the life out of another in falling over. It was just an accident."

END

DUST BOWL

There's wind, swirling up from the great dust basin below, carrying a taste of metal, a smell of death. And the dust itself dances, a whirling jig of broken chaotic grace...

The basin seemed preternaturally calm when first we arrived. Four thousand warriors born aloft on as many brilliantly coloured Wharghuls, fervent in our pious objective - to bring civilization and God to the infidels on behalf of Shevic-Rexae and the Emperor. The twin paired wings of our beasts beat furiously as we neared the ground, yet it seemed we barely lifted the dust, barely intruded on the silence.

The natives called the place *The Bowl of Barusch*. It became a joke among us, for the area was a barren wilderness hundreds of miles across, and Barusch was their god of plenty!

So, we had arrived. It had taken three months of perilous flight. Vents in the earth opened unexpectedly at Kallamae, spurting gouts of hot ash, gas - the excretia of the world - scorching the wings of the Wharghuls. Crossing the inland sea at Bardduhm we faced a storm. It seemed to rise up out of the water and blacken the sky in moments. Many were lost. Now we surveyed the "Bowl", considering how we might move forward.

Somewhere in this region, we knew, were they that sought to undermine the great work of Orn's Own Children. The barbaric masterminds of this heathen land, intent on imposing their own misanthropic ideology. They orchestrated the underground war that threatened us all, and so it was our duty to purge the area of their evil, and to deliver it into Orn's gracious hands.

The sun beat us with merciless zeal as we took to the skies once more.

The remaining Wharghuls panic, beating the ground alternately with ragged leathery wings, scraping the earth into furrows with their steel-clad claws. Their vivid blue eyes bulge with fear and accusation, blinking away the dust in free flowing tears. They strain at their tethers, grind filed teeth, but we cannot fly now, not with a new storm rising. Not with the conflict, which must surely follow, almost upon us...

At the centre of the basin there rises a pinnacle, *The Needle of Karnush-Rah.* A most impressive natural formation, it rises as high as the dusky Murtuhm Mountains that encircle it. From a distance it appears a fine, delicate thing suspended impossibly above the ground - it's base obscured in the shimmer of a heat haze. A half-day's steady flight later and its magnitude becomes apparent! We circled it at a wary distance, breathless in its shadow, dazzled in the light. To an observer we would have seemed no more impressive, for all our battle finery, than a murder of Croes, a flock of Seaghuls.

Eventually we landed upon the complex pinnacle, it being large enough to accommodate any of the great cities of our homeland, Umarica. It was a perplexing surprise that, though we looked diligently, we could find no discernible way up - other than flight. There were no rents or windows, nor carved out stairways or tunnels. The needle was of a smooth, polished rock, impossible to climb, and it resisted all our attempts to chip at it.

Yet clearly there had been visitors to the pinnacle - though Wharghuls are not native to these lands, and we are the first people to have mastered them - for an abundance of edible vegetation flourished in the cooler climate at that altitude. A large number of Ghotes were spotted, bounding over the curious terraced landscape, while in large grassy enclosures there grazed some native breed of cattal.

It was, at that time, a mystery as to how any of these beasts might have arrived there.

It's growing cooler now, as it always does, and all we survey is reduced to little more than flitting ochre-hued shadows as we are harried by the dust and wind.

Any time now they will come, and Orn help us when they do...

We spent a peaceful night on the Needle, praising the one true God Orn for his wisdom, and engorging ourselves on the bounty He had provided. The moon seemed close in the cerulean sky, and the scent of the flora was intoxicating after so long in such barren lands.

It was a wonderful thing, I felt, to be a soldier then. To be right there, doing our Lord's work, doing our Emperor's work.

This land, this corrupt, evil place, needed freeing of itself. We were here to do that - to bring to it all the benefits of our blessed civilization. To open up new trade routes, educate it, and welcome it under the wings of Orn. We, the Chosen Nation. We, the Children. It was our world to protect and to cleanse and to bring into order. I was moved by the greatness of our ambition, exhilarated by my being a small part of history in its creation. We were changing the world, and I was filled with a righteous fervour, the utter conviction of my belief.

I slept with the peace of Kings upon the Needle of Karnush-Rah and awoke early and refreshed as a fat red sun poured itself over distant mountains.

All around the needle the wind now swirls, The Bowl of Barusch *driving it, feeding it with dust. It broils like a wild oceanic squall, almost liquid.*

And riding this, on great carpets lined with ingenious wind-gathering pockets, directed by complex sail-like structures, they come for us...

END

MACHIVARIUS POINT: ALTHLATHU

THE IRASCIBLE BOR-BOR

The girl stood upon the bow of the Irascible Bor-bor, one of the Carpenter's Guild vessels, intent on what lay ahead. It was cool, late-summer, dusk, and the ocean swelled lazily below. Upon it the Napthacchi Ypopolype - one of Althlathu's greatest floating forests - dominated the horizon. She could hardly contain the thrill of anticipation at their imminent landing.

"Go on in now, Meg," grunted the girl's father. "You know it's dangerous for young 'uns up on deck at this time."

A tall, rangy man with sinuous tattooed arms and broken teeth, Gort Bulfitt was not endearing in appearance or manner. But his love for his daughter was writ in the crinkles about his steely eyes and sensed in the gentle touch of his hand upon her shoulder.

Begrudgingly, Meg made her way up the long spiral staircase to the lower viewing bridge. Slatted portals at least afforded her a partial view of the proceedings below.

The Carpenter's Guild were warriors to a man, and thieves. The floating forests of the Ypopolypi were not only naturally buoyant wood-stores; they were delicate ecosystems sheltering abundant life. Some of the inhabitants were deadly. Under a canopy of leaf, branch and vine the savage Sayers - whose glance, it was said, could steal a man's soul – lived in their Pack-houses. Clustered pods, dangling from and clinging to the trees like vast ugly fruit. To Sayers the Ypopolypi were not only home, they were sacred. They would scream in anguish when the carpenters plundered them, as though each felled tree were of their number, each hacked branch a limb of their own. The Sayers would drop out of the foliage in improbable numbers, all waxed horns and flashing canines. Black and white stripes against orange fur, they surged like a fire within the deep archaic jungle.

Meg had never seen a living Sayer. She had heard that some were lone travellers. That they went peacefully among the island cities of the north, such as Pella and famed Neptek. But mostly she had heard how Sayers stole souls and ate Ornish innards. They were the stuff of every child's nightmares. They were also the near-mythic beasts they each most longed to see. Meg was no different in this. She imagined them more as beasts; Primitive violent beings without thought, emotion. And yet their exotic beauty intoxicated her, as so many others.

"Let me see one." She whispered breathlessly to herself. "Oh Orn, please. Let me see a Sayer…"

The attack had been completely unexpected. Four biremes and a Quadreme had emerged from the cover of the Napthacchi Ypopolype and born down upon the Irascible Bor-bor with terrible suddenness.

"Eschatarchists!" the shout went up. "Hold steady! Prepare for a boarding!"

These were the last days of an aeons old war upon Althlathu. The council of Ornish Warloqs had long ago decided that they would not relinquish their powers and as such stood against the former might of the Eschatarchy. For a thousand cycles there had been an uneasy peace between the council of Ornish Warloqs and the leaders of Althlathu's Eschatarchists. Quarrels had been quickly quashed; the number of deaths kept to a minimum. There had, of course, been fiery debates, angry exchanges and threats aplenty, but an uneasy peace reigned.

That was until the rogue Thotlan - the most powerful Warloq on the planet in his day - took it upon himself to purge Althlathu of Eschatarchists once and for all. The Eschatarchy held the majority view at that time, but with a wrought ether-work of astonishing power - that used as it's source Vile-Space - Thotlan opened a gateway. Before the Eschatarchists knew what had befallen them one third of their number were dragged into that twisted realm and condemned to the hell they had themselves created.

The very act had driven Thotlan insane. He screamed for five cycles before being transfigured into an entirely alien state of existence. He had become *other*.

For a while after that Thotlan was worshipped by his acolytes as a god, sparking a new short-lived religion on Althlathu. But this new state was too much for his flesh to withstand. He ripened like a Blood-Por and burst before the next cycle was out.

The naturally aggrieved Eschatarchists at first bitterly complained, then launched their own terrible offensive. They gathered their flock and organised a final bloody counter-attack to seize power in Neptek and gain supremacy upon the waves.

They failed.

What remained were scattered forces, small bands of fighters, ragged remnants of the great Eschatarchic Palace-ships and their entourage.

It was a rare misfortune for the Irascible Bor-bor to have run across just such a band of desperate, hopeless fanatics.

Gort Bulfitt swung his double-headed axe with the mastery of a lifetime's martial discipline, yet the man he now faced was his equal in every way. The raiders had swarmed over the decks in greater numbers than the crew of the "Irascible Bor-bor" could have anticipated. The Eschatarchist pirates must have been crammed into the hulls like Kirkums, sustained by fanaticism.

Bulfitt countered a bullish swing to his head and saw an opening, quickly slamming the axes blunt handle into his opponent's face, breaking his nose and knocking him back. The axe swung round in his hands, gaining killing momentum, back, up, and over…

But too slow. The pirate almost blindly thudded one smaller axe unto Bulfitt's thigh whist raising his other to shield himself from the oncoming blow. Bulfitt toppled forward and the two found themselves entwined, almost like lovers, upon the ship's deck. There was urgency now in both their faces. Possessed of desperation, sadness and terror, they were, for that moment, brothers. United in their fearsome resolve to kill, their desperate need to live. They grunted, faces three thumb-widths apart, trying not to look at each other. Trying not to notice the warm living breath, the sweat, the underlying shudder, the hidden pleas and the prayers that hissed through gritted teeth.

Inevitably their small battle reached its pitiful conclusion. Whilst all about them warriors fought on or fell to the flight of an arrow, the heft of a sword, an axe, they reached their endgame: Gort Bulfitt slipped his short stabbing knife up under the man's chin as, at the same time, he felt a slick sharpness slide between his ribs.

He turned his head, groggily and blinked his eyes. Althlathu's bright moon danced above its twin, reflected in the calm waters of the ocean. The shouts and screams were growing faint. It was a beautiful night.

"Meg," he whispered.

Meg managed to leap clear of the flames that consumed the Irascible Bor-bor and scramble into the dubious shelter of the Napthacchi Ypopolype. The dawn found her at the waters edge, still gazing at the spot where the Carpenter's Guild ship had eventually gone down, praying for her father to emerge out of the morning's ink-black sea and take her home.

She had screamed, kicked and cried out in terror when the Sayer found her there and carried her off to the pack-house. But the house had been warm and comforting. The Sayers had fed her, washed her and left her in peace. Where could she go after all? They had not tried to eat her, neither (as far as she could tell) had they stolen her soul.

Several days later a huge one-armed Sayer had come to her. She had heard of these so called Readers of the Sed and was terrified, for ghostly limbs were said to sprout from the stumps of their self-maimed arms to reach inside you, driving away your sanity. But again, no such thing happened. Rather, he bowed to her and sat, studying her intently with large golden eyes, a gentle smile curling his thin black lips.

And eventually, much to her surprise, he spoke.

"My child, may it be that we are well met." He said in a voice like an echo of thunder.

"I had read it in the tells, the signs of things that might be, that I would find you here. Of how one day you will lead your people to the wells at Amalthus. You will safeguard all that your people hold sacred, all that is left of your world. A fire upon the deep comes, and all that we were shall be lost – but what you save, what you glean, and what you remember. When the seas have dried up they shall sing of you in ages to come – Aletha Ruatha Meg. They shall sing of you and weep, for you will be the death of the old and the mother of the new. Within the carcas of an ancient and petrified tree risen from prehistoric land newly revealed to the sky they will carve for you a temple, and Orn will be kept in the hearts and minds of the few remaining, until such time as they find anew the Kiazmus, and return at the last to His embrace.

"*Child of Orn*, I have much to teach."

END

KIAZMUS FOREWORD

by Professor Frank Scopegate.
Tangiers. 1978.

Whilst it can hardly be doubted that the text translated in this book is of an Earthly origin, much of it can only be explained by visual placement within the context of the Universe at large. Obviously this represents some major problems for orthodox archaeology. The apparent age of the Kiazmus tablets recently unearthed near a Berber settlement in the Moroccan desert, some two and a half to three thousand years, suggests that the composer could not have had any true understanding of the greater nature of the physical universe. He would have had no concept of planets, stars, wormholes or genetics that the text implies. Yet attempts to translate the prose as metaphor have, for the most part, yielded unfathomable results. For the purposes of this translation I have chosen to interpret as literally as is possible, and so while it may be rooted in mere analogy, I choose to read it as fact. Where the text implies 'planet', I have written planet. Where it appears to be describing voyages that span the universe, then that is what I have interpreted it as meaning. When it apparently speaks of extra-terrestrial races, that's how I have referred to them.

In essence I have intentionally placed myself outside of orthodox study, and attempted to present the most literal translation of the Kiazmus text to date. In this abridged version I have striven to provide a more consistent narrative and have chosen to omit the *Book of the First Cycle of Relevance through Rational Rememberance and Reason*, starting instead with the first chapter of the second book from which the text takes it's name; *Kiazmus*. Much of the first book describes what appear to be the belief systems, legends, demographics, flora and fauna of the desiccated 'planet' Althlathu, the setting of this epic. The second book, Kiazmus, stands as a bolder, more narrative work, the controversial nature of which has led it to be much overlooked by academics as a work of fancy, with little or no relevance to either history or archaeology. There is little indeed to tie it to what we know of our world today, but it stands at the very least as a great work of the imagination in the truest tradition of the Epic poem. From Gilgamesh, through the Odyssey, to Beowulf. And perhaps most startling of all is that it's primary protagonist is female, while her familiar is not of any race we know of today, or have encountered in other primitive mythologies currently studied.

The Kiazmus tablets stand unique as a vast work that draws no parallel with any period of civilisation known to man. It is as elusive as it is alluring. It defies categorisation and leaves us reeling at its implications.

Where possible I have included information from other tablet segments that apparently relate to the saga, depicted upon the main *Kia* tablet, and deepen our perception of the mythology - or as I'm fancifully suggesting, the flora, fauna and legend of this incredible alien landscape so richly and vividly depicted by a hitherto undiscovered civilization so very long ago.

KIAZMUS

The Coming of the Lost

Catspur has only just danced for us. Soon the scatter-
shower will come, glittering where her trail fades.

A holy time.

I have learnt well, so they tell me.

But I am a child of the Weeping God. If I do well it is
because He so wishes it.

They tell me that once this was a land of lakes, and that
more than half the world was submerged beneath water!

Not so now.

But by the will of the Weeping God, whose tears bring life,
I may wring from the hard rock that is our home enough of this
sacred element to create beauty.

An offering.
And though I'm told I have no eyes, I can sense every part
of it as I can our world.
For it is I as I am it.
Not long will it last, this precious bloom, but its brief glory
will be sung of.
And I will mourn.

And so the second cycle of Relevance through Rational
Rememberance and Reason begins.
This brightening-fade the scatter-shower comes.
And the Weeping God will test us.
We will go down to the Bitter Lake with all the sacred
trappings of our blessed God, and there we shall await the pure
bright moment of the scatter-shower.
And should its brilliance awaken such beasts as legends tell
of, then perhaps it is good that I have no eyes...
The Weeping God will mourn us should this be our
Transition-manifest.

And so with great joy we enter into the celebrations that
honour the Macra and eternal Son, our Lord.
As one of descent, in whom the blood of the Weeping God
flows, I am Raised in my Sixth Cycle to Macran; Holy Mother
of the Tribe of Amalthus.
My aged Maga-Macrain bears witness and gleans to source
with joy! The Silent garb me in the mantle of Macron. And the
Sacred Rhoag, born in the image of the Weeping God, is bound
and brought forth.
And we rejoice that a new cycle begins.
And I rejoice that it should be my good fortune to be
Macran at this time.

Excerpt: The Book of the First Cycle of Relevance through Rational Rememberance and Reason.

"And Catspur did dance, signalling that the Weeping God required His children to do Him great honour. And Alepha Rhuatha Meg, the fifth Macran in the cycle of Past Relevance and Contemplation, did lead into our midst a mighty Rhoag bearing the mantle of the Blessed Weeping God. And the Rhoag was raised high upon the altar and washed and fed and clothed in the finery of our God. And for three flights of Ashar he was our God. On the forth flight the Daggered arm was struck from him and the Rhoag was split open with the God's own Dagger of Restraint. And a great fire was built within the Ashen Hall of the Petrified Tree, and the gifts that the children of Lineage had raised in honour were harvested and Stuffed into the Rhoag. And the Rhoag was impaled on a mighty spike and roasted, that we may eat of our God, and in so eating be him, and he us. And the great head of the Rhoag would be stripped of it's tough hide and fashioned into a new helm for the Macran that the God be within the Macran, and the Macran be within the God. And the leathery wings would be made into gauntlets."

And together we raise up a feast from the earth, and when we are spent the Rhoag is slaughtered, and eaten, so that we are all one with the Weeping God and he with us.

And after five flights of Ashar we trek north to the Bitter Lake.

KIAZMUS

Awaken!

Oh! Awaken! Awaken!
The mountainous Sleeper arose!
Stirred by who knows what powers when the scatter-
shower gleamed!
And, in it's bitter anguish that there still swelled but dust in
it's ancient basin, it carved a deadly trench with thrashing, and
honoured us with the promise of a Transition-manifest Opus.

I have heard it said that in the second cycle of Relevance
through Rational Rememberance and Reason one will come:
One who would be lost.
A Messiah-eh.

I have run my fingers over the carvings and gleaned their
contemplation's.
I have immersed myself in complex thoughtscapes, passed
through the Analogous, to the Conceptual-pre-emptive, to
source.
I found nothing anomalous.
And therefore have I found anger such as I've never known
when those that raised and taught me, those that have called
themselves seers and servants of the Weeping God were blind
to the wonder of what transpired.

From the sky he fell, as the scatter-shower glistened,
encased in the very sign and symbol that it is my right to bear
upon my chest!
And with that unfaltering providence that is the Weeping
God's way, he brought down upon the ancient Sleeper a
Transition-manifest that ended mightily it's desiccated
loneliness, sending it finally to the seas of it's dreams.
And how they fled, my teachers!
And how lost my saviour.
He came to me then. A mighty burden across his wide back.
Quiet. Gentle. Knowing.
And he saw my mark, my pride, and was attentive. And
drew it in the sand.
And I saw within, and trusted.

Excerpt. The Book of the First Cycle of Relevance through Rational Rememberance and Reason. "...And did the tears of Catspur not call on the mighty Sleeper? And did not that monstrous son of Orn awake? Did he not bring down upon your people a Transition-manifest Opus in his anger that the seas of his father no longer surged and eddied in his halls? Were not all but the very swiftest crushed by those vast shanks never meant for land, as he dug once more a new chamber in which to sleep away millennia? Oh, Khallus! Was this not enough?"

KIAZMUS

The Passage

Long it was, and hard our passage through bitter lands I had
heard no tell of.

In sign and touch he put his trust in me and I in him.

And I learned there that though my lost benevolent saviour
was of a race and form I had never imagined it was the very
same Weeping God he put his faith in.

And he saw in me a vessel of that power, for I am a
daughter of that God, and he bade me do my God's bidding,
trusting my senses to show us the way.

And it was in this way that we crossed first the whole of the
dead sea of Truth to places I'd been told no longer existed.

We dined on the gifts of the God that I raised in his honour, and my Lost One was all hung about with vessels full of more water than I'd drunk in a lifetime.

And the relics I saw! Glimpses of what was to come! Vast petrified husks of vessels that once glided over seas, and yet others that I was to learn sailed the voids between worlds! All these I reached out and gleaned by the will of the Weeping God, beloved of sailors.

And I wept for the lost and the Lost One wept with me, for he had sailed in the void and dreaded such a lonely fate. My teachers I came to pity for their ignorance, and I came to see them too as stranded sailors unable to return home.

Their seas long-since dried up and gone.

Oh sailor, know you well what heart you take on returning to land after years adrift! So was I moved to find in the low lands and valleys, where once plunged the depths of our mightiest oceans, fertility and life! Tough plantation bristled at our passing. Hardy bitter blooms spread over exposed rock and stabbed at the tender probing of my fingers.

And, wonder of wonder! There were, in the gaping potholes that lay commonplace about these parts, free-flowing underground streams of the sweetest water it has ever been my privilege to taste!

Excerpt. The Book of the First Cycle of Relevance through Rational Rememberance and Reason. "It was with heavy hearts that the last of us finally came across the Dead Sea, named by Alepha Rhuatha Meg as "of truth" for that which was revealed to those who yet lived. No more than 300 of the 10,000 who left Neptek made it to the wells at Amalthus, that once frozen and terrible land, and of that 300 only 100 survived."

KIAZMUS

Rememberance and Reason

It was within the depths of a cavern, one marked with the sacred symbol of the Weeping God, that the cycles of Rational Rememberance and Reason were made valid and clear to me. Their purpose no longer hidden.

Sad it is that we do forget what we strive so hard to remember, no matter the rituals we build for Rememberance.

Leaving behind my lost saviour who seemed to sense it was a journey to be made by one of the lineage alone, I journeyed into the sacred heart of that deep place. And in the light that danced through cracks and holes in that vast cavern roof there flourished life in such abundance that my whole being wanted to be out, over, in, and of it.

And by it's wanting; so it was.

He found me then.
A Sayer.
Speaker of the Sed. Reader of Reason.
His sight of me set him atremble, and he shook as he knelt,
gasping words I almost recognised as my own.
He was of a stature far bulkier than the men of my kind.
A hunter of prowess.
Yet he became as a child at the gentlest of my touches!
And there happened a union.
In contemplation we gleaned harmony.
And in harmony we gleamed Rational Rememberance at
source.
He touched my eye sockets with a gossamer arm of ether
and I joyously Remembered with Reason.
And I swam.
I swam till I had not the strength to swim further; then I
swam on some more.
And I drank till I feared I would anger my God.
And here I fell, for I drank still more.
I remembered our beautiful blue and green land as it had
been.
And in every gathered hub of union there was, watching
over us, a vast effigy of the Weeping God.
And we would remember we were not alone.
Then as I swam up towards the light I became confused.
The water was hot, and rich in salts.
Devoid of life as our own precious wells.
Atop an ancient water tower I gleaned the putrid sulphurous
sea that had swept all life before it.
And still, looking down on me, the image of my God.
And I saw then why he wept.

I would have stayed there, lost in despair for all eternity,
had not the Speaker called me back. And here he told me that
the Weeping God called to me, and required of me a service.
That he had not forgotten us, though we forget the Reason of
Him.
And he bade me return to my Lost One and lead him to the
God.

Then, as we walked, I felt him slip away into his ancient
forest, and it was to a distant echo of rapturous, feral song that I
emerged new into the light.
And I thought of the Weeping God gazing out over
creation, and felt my resolve strengthen.

Excerpt. The Book of the First Cycle of Relevance through Rational Rememberance and Reason. "Have you so soon forgotten? Did not Ashar, thwarted as he was in his lust for fair Catspur, curse forever her father, mighty Orn, god of the Oceans and Wind, for fanning the flames that entrapped him? It is he who has boiled away our seas in his madness. And we, may the Weeper forgive us, have helped him."

KIAZMUS

Travails

Many the perils we faced in the long period following my awakening. Often I believed I saw my God, like the Benevolent Mother Macra, the Universe Herself, wide armed, inviting embrace, almost near enough to touch.

Many the times I was week, and cried bitterly to return to my home, wishing that I could blissfully retreat into the comforting embrace of that ignorance that had hitherto been my life.

And sometimes the Lost One wept. His strange, haunting moans echoing across the bedrock. Often times he railed at the skies, bellowing like a great beast.

There were days I was too week to walk, and he silently

bore my weight along with his own great burden. And yet other
days where we both rested in the shade of the bleached bones
of ancient Levithians.

On days like this my companion would draw maps of
the heavens in the dust, moving my hand over intricate web-
like patterns and marking these strange lands with the sign of
the Weeping God. When I had the strength I would raise the
gauntlet of the God, the symbol of the Third Arm of Creation,
and bring forth a bloom for us to dine on.

But I was week, and the blooms were wretched and
insulting.

There were times when I was reminded of the Second
Daggered Arm of Restraint, such was my frustration and
anger, but it was the First Arm of Fate and Guidance that saw
me through. This was my connection with the God. Where by
providence I was eternally bound to both blindly lead my God
and be herald for Him and those who sought Him.

And through blindly leading would I be led.

I also learnt that not all races of this aged planet were
benevolent. There were those who sought to stop us in our
travels. Those that jealously guarded their territories with a
violent hand.

Many indeed were the times our lives faced an immanent
Transition-manifest!

And the day came when no route of passage availed itself.
A vast fissure, as though Althlathu herself smiled, opened like
a wound in the scorched earth. And at this time our hunger and
weakness was great, and there seemed no hope in that desolate
place.

And the Lost One laid down his mighty burden and set
about it. And with tugging and pulling and gentle coaxing it
swelled to an even greater size.

And the greater the size, the lighter the load until it swayed in the hot desert breeze an undulating bubble, barely brushing the earth.

And the Lost One affixed this once more to his broad back and took firm hold of me.

He leapt then, as though in leaping he could cover that vastness of space in a single bound! And at first we fell, but with more tugs and pulls the great bundle began to rise, so that we were the burden of it!

To fly is a wondrous fearful thing. We soared like a great mountain Roarche above that lethal canyon and were a fair way across when, like a scatter-shower, deadly projectiles whistled by, thudding into the heavy sacking of our support. With a terrible hiss it shuddered and swayed, and we began a fearful descent into a dance of arrows.

We hit hard that jagged edge. The lost one digging his mighty red fingers into the very rock itself so it seemed. I climbed up over his broad blue back and hacked at the ropes that attached him to his salvage. It's weight, once more great, threatened to dislodge him and drag him with it into the depths of the fissure's dark maw. But at the last it came free and fell away into the gloom.

Whatever treasures he had saved for himself were now gone, and with it what little stored water we had.

Excerpt. The Book of the First Cycle of Relevance through Rational Rememberance and Reason.   ""I shall have thee, accursed hulk! Thou that hast torn mine very heart from its port and moorings! I shall avenge my beloved son and noble captains, beast, by Orn's will I shall! So swears King Amalthus!" And in so saying, the great Ornish King leapt from the rigging of his palace and into the dark broiling embrace of the sea below. And days it was the Levithian thrashed in that awful embrace, and oft times threw it's vast bulk at the very rocks that jutted as it's own foul teeth from beneath the waves. But it could not shift the vengeful king."

Kiazmus

How many the Flights of Ashar after that we walked
I cannot recall. I have lived my whole life knowing the
harshness of my world and it's many ways to surprise you
with a sudden Transition-manifestation. But I had gone farther
than any of the Tribe of Amalthus since the times of Ragnorax,
and the Fall. And before then never more than two Flights of
Ashar's distance from the wells.

And then we saw him, as I had seen him, a colossus
straddling the horizon! The long curve of his wings, faded
behind thin clouds, bearing the heavens!
The Weeping God!

And I found in me then the strength to raise a little offering
to the God, and we fell upon that little bloom as hungry
children.
And in another Flights walk we reached his base and began
to climb.

Round and round that spiral path, the symbol of the God's
Heart, we traipsed. Each footfall an agony. At Brightening-
fade we rested, and indeed we slept. And I don't believe I slept
better before or since than I did in the lap of the Weeping God.
And when Ashar raised his head over the rim of Althlathu
we climbed the length of another flight till at the next
Brightening-fade we reached the Temple carved within the
shadowy cowl that was the head of the God.

And I Gleaned the Kiazmus for the very fist time!

How had we lost our way? How could we, the Weeping
God's children, have forgotten this, His very soul and nature?
How had we come to wander so far from His myriad pathways,
His all-encompassing embrace?
And how had we come to miss the point of the teachings?
To glean so wrongly what the ancient carvings imply?
Oh foolish we! That the very mark and sign adorns me is
an offence I can scarce bare, and I weep with knowing that I
know not.

But the Lost one found strength then and came to me,
lifting me up to face the God. He embraced me, and weeping
himself, stood back, gesturing that I should mount the steps to
the podium and glean my God.

So I traced my fingers over those ancient stones, and they

felt familiar to me. I gleaned the gossamer trails that spread out over the symbols and carvings of this sacred place, and the light spread into me.

And I unfolded into Him with joy.

And so my Father opened himself to me and we became One.
I, the Weeping God.
I the Magogaplex.
I am on every world, the Gate Keeper.
I am older than I can remember.
I am infinitely powerful.
Infinitely helpless.
Blind leading blind leading blind.
Tethered strength.
Wondrous creator.
Child of Macra, the Universe.
I surge through the Kiazmus, a swarm.
Vortices of probability entrance with tantalising variables, googaplexian beauty.
Hokum wedges shatter carefully cast vortex maps.
Flux craters shudder on the mapscape's apex as fanned fool denominations hastily spin neutron hexes in the etherwhere.
Some are lost.
There are also many sentients I would not wish to be here, but other matters press me.
And at my heart are the lost sailors of this infinite sea, guided by my children.
By me.
And I would see them safely home.

And at once the unbearable loneliness of being just one hits me, and we are out.

I unfold my mind to better glean this new place as a sensation I have never felt before tears into me and fills me with rapture.

I am cold!

I don't know how far we must travel to find the next opening. What perils we might face. But I shall find the door to the Kiazmus and reunite with myself once more.

I know now what I am and what I must do.

We will dance across eternity.

Tread mightily upon the stepping-stones that weave their way between the stars.

I have gleaned the sum of all things.

My Lost One must be taken home.

I shall lead him there.

END

Excerpt. The Book of the First Cycle of Relevance through Rational Rememberance and Reason. ""Has it come to this, brother Khallus, that I, Ragnorax, who have loved you always, must be the bringer of transition manifest in you? Let me tell you that my heart bears such an Opus as has never burdened a man as wholly as it does me. Nay, nor as completely. That you bade me lead our people into that accursed land be crime enough! That I did it denies me forever the transition-manifest that is my birthright. I shall see an end to this, beloved brother, though it shatters forever the sacred ring of our ancestors, and tears down the house of our noble lineage. And, when you no longer walk in this world, I shall return to the Dead Sea of Truth and see that my soul burns forever in the pit of it's vast belly.""

Excerpt. The Book of the First Cycle of Relevance through Rational Rememberance and Reason. "All manner of maker, of mason and wood-smith, erector of temple and tower was employed in its craft. And slowly, over 300 cycles, the people of Neptek raised from the island-city a statue of their God. And within the cowl that hid his face they built him a temple and housed there his heart."

ALTHLATHUN GLOSSARY

ALTHLATHUN GLOSSARY

Compiled by Prof. Frank Scopegate

Alepha Rhuatha Meg: Macran *(see Macran)* referred to in
The Book of the First Cycle of Relevance through Rational
Rememberance and Reason. Alepha Rhuatha Meg is famous for
'gleaning' the location of the springs (later turned into wells) at
Amalthus, thereby saving her people from certain death.

Althlathu: The 'planet' on which most of the first chapter of
Kiazmus takes place.

Amalthus: The site of the wells 'gleaned' by Alepha Rhuatha
Meg referred to in The Book of the First Cycle of Relevance
through Rational Rememberance and Reason. Amalthus was a
legendary King of the sea-faring Ornish race. He purportedly
killed a Levithian with his bare hands, but at great cost. He was
able to restore his strength and save his own life by bathing in the
creature's blood. Amalthus is also the name of the tribe, after the
wells, to which the narrator belongs.

Ashar; flights of: Ashar is the sun of Althlathu. 'Flights of' refers to the sun's passage across the sky. Ashar is the ancient Althlathun God of mischief referred to in The Book of the First Cycle of Relevance through Rational Rememberance and Reason. Ashar boasted he could fly up to Catspur and steal her silken trail, and he built a winged ship that sailed on a wave of fire and set off into the heavens to claim his prize. Orn, the God of wind and sea, and Catspur's father, was angered, and fanned the wave of fire with a mighty gust of his breath, causing the flames to engulf the flying ship. Thus Ashar was forever doomed to circle Althlathu in a ball of fire and in so doing became the sun. Ashar's revenge is that he evaporated all the sacred seas of Orn in his passage over millennium. The Scatter-shower is sometimes referred to as the 'Tears of Catspur.' Has strong similarities to both the story of Icarus and the god Apollo.

Ashen Hall of the Petrified Tree: A temple dedicated to the Weeping God carved out of an ancient petrified tree by the wells at Amalthus.

Benevolent Mother Macra: A spiritual representation of all things. The "mother" of all things including the Weeping God.

Bitter Lake: The dried up basin of an ancient lake on Althlathu.

Brightening-fade: Widely interpreted as dusk or nightfall.

Catspur: Earthbound interpretations have suggested this might be Haley's Comet. For the purposes of this translation we fancifully suggest that it is indeed a comet, but not one bound by our own sun's gravitational pull.

Conceptual-pre-emptive: A meditative state in which the worshipper/priest(ess) is able to 'pre-empt', or predict the cycle of possible events by 'gleaning' the larger concepts related to, or preceding that event. The mental state in which the future, or futures are predicted.

Dead Sea of Truth: The name attributed to one of the numerous ancient seabeds.

First Arm of Fate: (See also Second Daggered Arm of Restraint/ Third Arm of Creation.) The arm of the Weeping God *(see also Magogaplex)* most commonly depicted as guided/symbolically joined to the figure of the blind priestess, or fate. It represents the unpredictable future and faith. It is also the symbol of the God's bond with his/it's children, and his/it's faith in them.

Flux crater: As with all terminology referring to the experience of passing through the infinite pathways of the Kiazmus, our interpretations are sketchy at best. What this appears to be describing is a natural fissure(s) within the fabric of the Kiazmus.

Fool(s): From later texts it appears that Fools are like drone soldiers of the Weeping God. Their principal role to clean, maintain and protect the Kiazmus.

Glean: The method by which a blind child/ Priest(ess) of the Weeping God "sees" his/her surroundings. A form of meditation in which the immediate environment is understood without the aid of physical eyes.

Gossamer arm of ether: Referring back to the book of the First Cycle of Relevance through Rational Rememberance and Reason, the 'gossamer arm' is an arm of pure energy/ light that an ancient Althlathun race (see Speaker of the Sed/ Reader of reason) used to communicate with each other at a higher level. According to these earlier texts the right arm of the priest(ess)'s would be struck off at puberty. The 'gossamer arm', usually interpreted as a "ghost" limb, would grow in its place.

Hocum Wedge: Later texts reveal these as often intentional means by which one can damage either the material of the Kiazmus, or "kill" Fools. The exact nature of a Hocum Wedge remains unknown.

Kiazmus: Usually interpreted in the same way as the various mythological versions of the underworld. This translation reads the Kiazmus as literally being a vast network between the stars created by the Weeping God for the purposes of getting stranded sailors home. Each planet is seen as having both an entrance and exit to this apparently stable wormhole. Stranded travellers must find one of The Weeping God's genetic children to access it. Sometimes, as in this book, the travellers may have to cross many worlds before they are able to return to home.

Levithians: bleached bones of: Enormous sea creatures. Once a great threat to sea-going vessels. Hunted for the restorative nature of their blood.

Lost One: Legendary traveller who would restore the seas of Althlathu.

Macra the Universe: (see Benevolent Mother Macra.)

Child of (above): (see Weeping God.)

Macran: Chief priestess of the Weeping God.

Maga-Macrain: Former chief priestess, Mother of the tribe.

Magogaplex: (see Weeping God)

Mapscape: Appears to be both the structure of, and means by which one travels within the Kiazmus.

Messiah: (see Lost One.)

Neutron hex: Energy fields that can both heal or destroy within the Kiazmus.

Orn: (See Weeping God.) Orn is mostly understood to be the God of the former oceans of Althlathu in the time of the author of the Kia tablet. Older sources suggest that Orn is also inextricably tied to the Kiazmus, and only later became a separate divinity after the dreadful purging of Althlathu – an event seen as relating to flood mythology wherein the world was consumed by a sea of fire, turning it into the desiccated realm of this saga.

Probability Vortex(ices): Vortexes of infinite possibility harnessed to form the main structure of the Kiazmus.

Reader of Reason: Ancient Althlathun race of Kiazmus worshippers. Believed long dead at the time of this narrative, they are frequently referred to in the more ancient text of the book of the First Cycle of Relevance through Rational Rememberance and Reason. They were once the major power on the planet when it was still heavily forested.

Rhoag: A large winged reptile with three arms that closely resembles the Althlathun interpretation of the Weeping God. The wings are more likely to be a blood warming mechanism than for flight, though it may have glided short distances. The Rhoag was often sacrificed to the Weeping God on holy occasions.

Scatter-shower: Most likely a meteor shower. Once again this features heavily in the book of the First Cycle of Relevance through Rational Rememberance and Reason as a measure of time, and precursor to momentous sacred events. Sometimes called the 'Tears of Catspur'.

Second cycle of Relevance through Rational Rememberance and Reason: Refers to the dawning of a new age and the arrival of the Lost One. By the time of this story the few natives of Althlathu still practising worship of the Weeping God had such reduced understanding of the ancient ways that they were practically just ritualised habits. It has been forever unclear whether the Lost One refers to the teller of our tale or her companion. The suggestion is that she, as her people, had lost the way, and in the journey recounted in Kiazmus regains what was lost.

Second Daggered Arm of Restraint: Represents the virtue of restraint from the use of violent power. This is typically shown as the Weeping God's powerful single right arm merged with his torso, and cumulating in a dagger.

Silent: Attendant priests of the Macran. Teachers and Seers. Sometimes one eyed in deference to the Macran. It appears the males of the tribes of Amalthus could not 'glean' outwardly as the women who were part of the lineage could, so actual sight was imperative under such harsh living conditions.

Sleeper: This is described more fully in the book of the First Cycle of Relevance through Rational Rememberance and Reason as a great sea-faring creature somewhere between a turtle and a Lungfish. It could survive hundreds, if not thousands of years in a state of desiccation, buried in the dried seabed. The appearance of the scatter-shower seams to have triggered the awakening of such creatures as referred to in the legends of earlier text.

Source: Point of origin of all rational thought.

Speaker of the Sed: (see Reader of Reason.)

Sulphurous sea: The book of the First Cycle of Relevance through

Rational Rememberance and Reason talks of a Sea of Death that swept the planet. It is hard to know what could physically cause such a catastrophe though there are many parallels with the Noah myth.

Third Arm of Creation: The arm most often depicted as raised, sometimes breaking free of its chains. The gauntlets worn by the Macran, the Maga Macrain, or the Silent represent this arm. It, in turn, represents the Weeping God creating the Kiazmus. The broken chain represents freedom.

Thoughtscapes: Much like the Australian aboriginal Dreamtime, or indeed any shamanistic realm, where matters of the tribe, or the future, are contemplated.

Transition-manifest: The final transition to the world beyond. Death.

Transition-manifest Opus: Death on a huge/ dramatic/ memorable scale. A heroic death. As with many ancient civilisations this was considered the best kind of death.

Unfold: Appears to describe the means by which one 'gleans' and enters or exits the Kiazmus. One can also 'unfold' into different states both physically and mentally once one has 'gleaned' the Kiazmus.

Weeping God: Also called the Magogaplex and in other texts is also the God Orn. In literal translation this is the god-like being that created the Kiazmus. Indeed the Kiazmus may in fact be read as being part of Orn, or the Magogaplex. It is one consciousness that shares countless physical manifestations. The Magogaplex has spawned children on every planet capable of maintaining life. These are the guardians of the Kiazmus and the beings capable of accessing the Kiazmus and guiding lost or stranded 'sailors' home. Fools appear to be the lower end of his sentience, acting almost as antibodies within the Kiazmus.

Weeping God; Child of the: Any being who is genetically related to the Magogaplex and can access the Kiazmus.

Children/Daughter/Son/Offspring /Vessel of the: (See above.)

Gauntlet of the. (See Third arm of Creation.)

Sign /Symbol of the: An elongated square above a circle. Often in red, sometimes carved in relief. According to the texts this is universal. Basically identical on every planet.

GOD KILLERS

METAWHAL ALPHA

The corpse was roughly one hundred and twenty feet long. The greater bulk of it gathered at one end in a festering turd-like swirl some thirty feet across and fifteen deep. The specifics of its anatomy were elusive, as was the smell, which escaped any attempt at comparison and was not entirely unpleasant. It occupied two thirds of the length of the Clock Warehouse's fourth floor, and there was not the slightest clue as to how it had come to be there.

Kevin and Tamsin Milner were the bar managers of the family pub-come-restaurant that now constituted most of the old Clock Warehouse in Shardlow. The two centuries old structure had an industrious heritage. It once housed the village clock, whose bell paced the day for the wharfmen. A central arch straddled a short branch off the Trent and Mersey Canal, beneath which working narrow boats had been stocked and un-stocked. The village boasted several coal and timber wharfs, a large warehouse for iron, others for cheese, corn and salt. For years it had been an industrial hub, until speedier competition from the Midland, and other railways, set the canals and their sluggish trades into decline. The clock stopped long ago, the bell gone, and with it the sounds of creaking cranes, rattling chains, falling timbers, the shouts of working men - all the din associated with an inland port.

Now the Clock Warehouse traded on nostalgia, a crude facsimile of a working boat, fixed in three inches of stagnant water below the arch, proclaiming it's faux-romantic heritage.

An arrogant man, of average intellect and pedestrian ambition, Kevin took his managerial role extremely seriously and enjoyed shouting last orders at closing time. All the clocks in the working part of the building were five minutes fast. Kevin's wristwatch, however, was precisely set. He would tap it and wink at Tamsin, as if to remind her how clever he was. The couple lived in a purpose-built flat above the pub. It was connected via a fire door to the only section of the mill remaining undeveloped. The curious smell had prompted Kevin to venture through that door at 7.00am one Tuesday morning, and he had almost walked into the great bulky thing decomposing in mote-filled gloom. Gagging, he backed out and yanked the door shut.

Kevin stood, wide-eyed and ashen, a hand still clutching the doorknob. Eventually he gave it a jerky twist, opening the door again - just a fraction, just enough to make out a sliver of the slick black corpse.

He spent the next two hours locked in the toilet.

Kevin pinched and picked his nose - which itched infuriatingly - stroked his moustache to calm himself, as though it were a pet curled up on his lip. His glasses felt too tight on his head. At around 8.30am Tamsin knocked on the door, her small voice relaying staff work queries, asking if he was all right. He gave her terse answers, brushed her off.

"I'll be down soon. I'm fine."

Initially he thought he'd have to call the police. Clearly some rival had orchestrated the whole thing, creating this huge whatever-it-was for - what? Revenge? To maybe put him out of business? How would that work? Did somebody want to scare him? But he realised that no one he knew would or could go to such lengths. He wasn't important enough to merit such hatred - though he tried not to think about that too much. He didn't know anybody capable of dreaming up such a thing, let alone putting it into action.

So just what the fuck was it?

His next thought was that the pub's owners might have something to do with it. Perhaps the brewery had competitors with a macabre imagination? Or maybe it was an elaborate publicity stunt? Shardlow had its share of ghost stories: "The Lady in Grey" that haunted the bridge by the wharf. The "Witches Oak" that stood untouched in the middle of a grit quarry, safely entombing the (fictional) witch buried below it (the farmer had loved that old tree and contrived the tale to save it when he sold the land.) But this wasn't a ghost, it was a corpse. A bloody big corpse. In the end he remained stumped, and, frustratingly, the only person he could talk to (he was surprised to realise) was Tamsin.

Reluctantly he slunk down to the kitchens to look for his wife.

"It was right here!"

"What?" Tamsin asked, with a hysterical warble in her small voice - so unaccustomed was she to questioning her husband. "What was here love? I don't understand..."

"I don't know. Something BIG, something... dead..."

"Like a cow?"

"No! BIGGER! Much MUCH bigger. More like... more like a whale..."

"A whale?"

It wasn't anything he could rationalize. He had seen it, twice. He had smelt it. Yet there really was no explanation for how it got to be there. No entrance was wide or high enough for it to get through. The double-doored loading bays that once graced the front of the building either side of the arch had been replaced with tinted plate-glass windows in the 1970s. And anyway, they had only reached as high as the third floor. The thing had been on the forth.

And yet it had somehow vanished, in broad daylight, and in under three hours, without a trace.

Later that Tuesday evening Kevin passed by the now dreaded fire door and gasped. The telltale odour had returned. He forced himself to open the door again - just a fraction. Just enough for confirmation: The monstrous corpse was there, just as though it had never been absent.

He neglected his work the rest of that night, even missed the last orders call. Instead he scoured the Internet looking for an explanation, something to pin his fears upon, to rationalise everything. Google obligingly unearthed pictures and accounts of wretched giant squid and whale corpses washed up on lonely beaches; great rotting Basking Shark corpses, strangely reconfigured into "pseudo-plesiosaur" forms. The "Cthulhu" mythology of Lovecraft tantalized and terrified him with fictions of a monstrous "dead but dreaming" entity, deep below the Pacific Ocean - waiting to displace humanity and return the world to madness and chaos. Alistair Crowley loomed large and fearful in his searching, yet ultimately proved hollow and fraudulent.

Tamsin found herself frustrated that she was unable to get on to the computer. She usually spent an hour or two conversing with invisible global friends before bed, but this time she was denied even this brief respite from her unhappy life. The tap tap of his fingers still registered distantly in her mind long after she had fallen asleep.

By Thursday Kevin was barely recognizable. Unshaven, he had not brushed his thick wavy hair. His usually immaculate crisp shirt was crumpled, unevenly buttoned, unchanged for three days. He was distracted and foul tempered, waving off questions and letting the staff fend for themselves. Tamsin ran about organising everybody in a newly energetic shrew-like manner. She was rising to the occasion, proving her worth - not that Kevin noticed. He had been into Derby and joined the library for the first time, taking out a wide-ranging and substantial pile of books covering mental health and the occult.

On Thursday afternoon he galvanized himself to conduct a survey of the unwelcome rotting thing in his mill. Revolting though it was he had soon realised that he had no reason to fear it. He pulled on an old overall, a dust mask, some thick rubber gloves, a pair of Wellington boots, and went through the door to confront his personal nightmare.

He found he could only squeeze past one side of the corpse as its other side was rammed up against the wall. What he could see of it was a dappled red-black, slug-like in texture. Great rents and gashes punctured its flesh, revealing a sickly white interior that grew pinker with depth. There were bones too, jutting at odd angles from tears, up to nine feet in length and as broad as a man. He could not make out any limbs as such, though numerous protrusions jutted in blood red explosions of pigment. Strange fin-like shapes, or rudimentary wings, to propel it through whatever it's native element was. Kevin could not distinguish any eyes, nose, mouth or ears - making it unclear which was the front and which the back. Maybe such things had no relevance where it came from, but Kevin Milner was not a man to ponder such possibilities. With shaking hands he took as many photos as he could, noting down dimensions and attempting to describe - entirely unsuccessfully - the smell.

He was becoming obsessed.

On Saturday morning Kevin's visiting corpse had manifested once more - sign-posted, as usual, by it's frustratingly evasive odour. This time things were further complicated when he discovered a huge chunk of it was missing. A livid hole now exposed a vast area of its extrinsic innards, slick with viscous matter. He had taken to posting his finds on an Internet site that dealt with the unexplained, but as yet he had not given away the corpse's location or his real identity. Nobody had posted anything that remotely came close to an explanation for what he was dealing with. Various crackpots had led him down blind alleys with their theories. Others thought him a hoaxer. So he hid behind the on-screen name of "CaptainX" and waited, hoping for answers while his monster was eaten away, chunk after hefty chunk.

The following Tuesday provided him with an almost overlooked breakthrough. On one messageboard at an Internet site called "The Fauna of D17" there was a new post by somebody calling themselves "Lilyth88". The post was entitled "Missing God" and Kevin very nearly didn't bother to read it. After browsing several other messages detailing UFO abductions and astral plane wanderings he found himself staring at the cryptic words again. He became drawn to them, intrigued. Missing God? What the hell was that all about?

He opened it and read.

<Hi all.

271

Unfortunately I have some distressing news. Those of you who have studied the various meta-beings that exist in D17, the seventeenth dimension, may have heard allusion to - or perhaps even had contact with - the God known as "King Frederick VI", or King Fred as we like to call him. (Obviously not his real name, merely an affectionate epithet given to him by his discoverer and beneficiary, Dr. Knight.) King Fred has befriended many of us astral wanderers and enhanced our understanding of the metascape tenfold. His patience has been, dare I say it, godlike! His charisma has enhanced the lives of we few lucky enough to have shared, however briefly, his path. So it is with very great dismay that I report his absence.

Dr.Knight - whom you should know is amongst the most respected and widely travelled astral wanderers, not to mention 17th planers, and an expert on inter-dimensional life - realised King Fred was missing a week ago. We have subsequently spent a goodly portion of that time deep planing wherever possible, including some organised group-planing, but to no avail.

Most worrying are signs of a killer Metawhal hunting within the dimension. It's unlikely that a Metawhal could pose much of a threat to King Fred, and Dr.Knight urges us not to jump to any conclusions about this, but never the less we should not entirely write off the possibility, however unlikely it may seem. It's possible such a threat may have some sort of knock-on effect we can't begin to foresee.

How little we know!

PLEASE keep your ears to the ground, and for the time being it's probably best to stay clear of D17 until we're sure the Metawhal has moved on to pastures new...

King Fred is very dear to a great many of us, so any news would be gratefully received.

Thanks,

Lilyth88 >

Someone called Gator4T had responded:

<Terribly sorry to hear that Lilyth88.

:(

I'll listen out. >

Another, Headspaceeddie, had simply written

<Metawhals suck! >

Kevin punched the reply button and typed:

<Hi Lilyth88.

Sorry, but what's a Metawhal? It might sound crazy, but I have a 150ft corpse that keeps materializing in my mill. Could there be a connection?

CaptainX. >

It was less than an hour before Kevin noticed Lilyth88 was back on the messageboard and his heart skipped a beat. He left it a few more minutes then checked the thread. Lilyth88 had posted again.

<Is this a joke? Why are you even reading this if you don't know what a Metawhal is? >

Kevin typed furiously, afraid she would go again and he would be left to wait who-knows-how-long until she returned to the board.

<No joke. Seriously. Either this IS happening, or I'm completely insane. I have no experience of anything as weird as this. I just run a pub.

Please help... >

He waited a few more long minutes before Lilyth88 replied to him.
"Oh thank Christ," he gasped to himself, reopening the topic.

<OK CaptainX.

I'll give you the benefit of the doubt.

A Metawhal, for those of us who DO know about "weird" things, is like a shark in astral seas. He's the biggest danger to us astral planers (that's "people who travel outside of their bodies in different dimensions" to you) and big ones have been reported to have even killed lesser gods.
So don't try it unless you know what you're doing!
It's unlikely your so-called corpse is connected, as the gods of the seventeenth dimension can't cross over to our own. And no god as big as King Fred has ever been reported killed by a Metawhal. Not even a big one.

Good luck with your problem.

Lilyth88>

<But what about Metawhals? > Kevin punched into the keyboard, <Can they cross over? >

<Metawhals are pan-dimensional, so theoretically, yes. They sometimes manifest in dreams. But there's never been a Metawhal sighted that was large enough to drag a god's corpse from one dimension to another, and nobody has ever actually seen one manifest physically...

I think you're safe! >

<This corpse. It's being eaten - I think. There's only half of it left now.

If it IS a Metawhal, and - please bear with me Lilyth88, if just for arguments sake - if that IS the corpse of King Fred, what should I do? >

<If I had actual evidence of a Metawhal big enough to kill a god manifesting in my back yard then there's only one thing I would do:

Get away.

Get as far away and as quickly as possible. One thing you don't want is for a Metawhal to pick up your scent.

You might never sleep soundly again... >

"Are you mad?" Tamsin's voice had garnered some steel in the last week. She had worked hard to cover up her husband's descent into apparent lunacy. She had finally forced him to shave and put on a fresh shirt each day - for the few moments when he had ventured out into the sunlight to stand squinting up at the top floor from the car park. She had pretended to be passing messages directly from him to the staff, keeping everything running smoothly. She had made up excuses for him, created a fictitious family tragedy that was causing him great anguish. It was a terrible lie, she knew, but what else could she do?

"I'm serious. Tamsin, I can't stay here..."

"We can't just go Kevin! You know that! Do you want us to lose our jobs, our home, everything we've... you've worked for..."

"You have to believe me, if we stay it'll be much worse..."

"For me or for you? I don't bloody believe this..." Tamsin turned abruptly and started to march in the direction of the stairs leading up to their flat.

"Wait, Tam! Tamsin, please! Where are you going?"

"You know where I'm going..."

"But what if it's not there? There's no smell... there wasn't a smell…"

"Of course it's not there!"

Tamsin raced up the stairs, Kevin close behind, trying to stop her, to reason with her, until presently they were at the door. She stopped then, her hand on the doorknob, looking back at him.

"Well?"

"All right..." He muttered. "What if... What if I could show you? What then?"

"What then?" Tamsin looked with uncertainty first at the door, then back at Kevin. "You don't see anything do you Kevin? You don't see me at all. What am I to you?"

"What?"

"What am I Kevin? Who am I? Do you even know who I am?"

"You're my wife... You're Tamsin..."

"I'm not just Tamsin! I'm not just your wife! Look at me! I'm not just a board to pin your medals on! A... a mantle piece, all stacked up with your trophy cups, pointless bloody awards...

I'm not just here to make you feel great about yourself!"

Kevin looked confused. "I... What are you talking about? I know who you are..."

"No! No! No, you don't Kevin! Who am I? What do I do? What TV programs do I watch? Books? How about books! Do I like books Kevin? What are my interests? Who am I?"

"What's all this about? I thought y..."

"You didn't think at all... Kevin, you're just a bloody landlord for Christ's sake..."

There was a stalemate as the two strangers regarded each other with uneasy new eyes. She was right, he knew that. He had completely lost interest in her years ago. He never thought to praise her for anything she did behind the scenes. She was the manageress after all, but you'd never guess it. He had taken the credit for everything they did together, such that it was. He ran - they ran - what was little more than a glorified theme pub. The food was hot and rarely took more than twenty minutes to arrive. The beer was good. And it was a clean and relatively comfortable environment. He - they - had a spotless health and safety record. But that was the sum of their success. No more, no less.

"You're right. Tamsin." Kevin said at last. "I've not been much of a husband..."

"You've not been much of a friend, let alone anything else. And what about love, Kevin? Where does that feature in your life? What about children..."

"Tamsin, stop! Tamsin, please – please just listen to me: It's back. Oh shit, it's here again."

The smell had returned, increased as the corpse continued to rot. Her eyes widened. "That smell... Is that... is that... it?"

Kevin nodded, pointed at the doorknob. She looked at it, unsure, and afraid now.

"Go on. You have to see it. You have to believe me."

"Oh god, I don't know."

"But there's nothing there, is there? It's just a figment of my imagination!"

"I'm scared Kevin."

"Don't be." he said, suddenly grinning. Elated. "It's dead."

Tamsin opened the door, and gasped. Filling the far end of the mill's floor space was a mass of rotting matter, exactly as Kevin had described it, though now greatly diminished. The black mottled skin was greying and sloughing off the pale brown flesh beneath. It was almost unbearable to behold, defying the imagination, challenging perception.

"Let's go." She whispered, backing up against him. "Kevin. Please. I've seen enough..."

"No!" Kevin was angry. He grabbed her arm, dragging her towards it. "You have to see it, really see it. You didn't believe me... well. Too bad. I want you to see it close up Tamsin! No time to be shy about it! I want you to have no doubt at all about what you are seeing here."

He pulled her slight frame easily across the dimly lit mill, the floorboards resounding with scrapes and footfalls, her protests magnified in the vaulted space. He threw her to her knees before it and tears began to track down her piqued cheeks. She was shaking.

"It's a God, apparently," he hissed. "How about that? I've got a dead god in my mill."

"Kevin. Please. Let's go. I've seen it now OK baby? Let's go, OK?"

"Fuck it - what is it? I'm not mad am I? It really is fucking here!"

He turned to face Tamsin, the last great chunk of the thing still clearing his head by several feet.

"I'm not going to feel guilty, Tam. Yes, you're always there, organizing, doing your thing - but it's me that made this place what it is and I am a fucking success. And you can moan all you like, but you reap the rewards. You benefit from all of this too, I know. So don't give me that fucking crap. You know how I feel about children. And don't you ever, ever doubt me a-fucking-gain you little bitch, all right?"

But Tamsin wasn't listening to her husband any more. She watched, awed, as the space directly behind Kevin distorted, like a flaw in an old mirror magnified a billion times, and then, through the inevitable tear, there emerged something. Something terrible and quite... quite wonderful...

Kevin turned in time to see his own death arrive - to register it, and to fear it. The dead God, he now saw, was no horror at all. Not really. The corpse that had reduced him to an obsessed internalised wreck had been just that. A corpse. The real horror had been hidden from him. It existed between the hours he spent with the dead God. It was a God killer. And now it would kill him.

Its head resembled nothing so much as a fresh mass grave turned inside out. Tentacles, like flayed limbs, thrashed wildly above a cavernous maw ringed with backward facing ten inch long serrated teeth. Multiple tongues twisted and spun, tipped with black stings, like scorpion tails. A pale, segmented body, lit from within by a putrid phosphorescent liquid, wound its way into reality behind the charnel head.

New topic:

<King Fred is dead.

We're asking all planers to stay away from D17 - at least for the time being - for your own safety. It's been confirmed that a newly recognized species, an "Alpha Metawhal", was responsible for the demise of King Frederick VI. The reported

Metawhal was at least five times bigger than any previously identified. It is also the first of its kind to have fully manifested within our own dimension. Amazingly the Alpha Metawhal was able to store the body of King Fred in an undisclosed location upon our own plane of existence, only returning to feast upon the carcass periodically. What the long-term ramifications of this are, well, only time will tell.

As ever, we still have so much to learn.

Long live King Fred. We will all miss you terribly. >

Tamsin Milner punched in her signature.

<With much love,

Dr.Knight. >

END

DEATH AND THE MYRMIDON

The sun curled fingers of gauzy light through the gaps, and around the edges of the lumpy thunderhead congress above Derby. Death liked this particularly gloomy guise frequently assumed by the midland skies. The pall it cast masked the melancholy associated with his presence and he could walk more or less unnoticed through the patchwork streets of the small city. He made himself a mug of sweet milky coffee and absently gazed at the impending storm through his kitchen window.

Later, standing in a queue that congested the isles of the Kedlesden road branch of "Jackson's", Death noticed the uneven heartbeat of the elderly Irish lady, two people in front of him.

"I've only got two pounds twenty five, dear." She was saying to the shop assistant. "Could you tell me what I can get for that? Anything'll do, I'm not bothered." The assistant held up two cans of Special Brew.

"How's this Ashleen?"

"Sure, that would be grand dear."

Not long now, Death thought to himself, though - as is so often the case with the terminally near-death - she had for decades evaded what should have been a much earlier acquaintance with him. He chuckled. Perhaps I'll leave her be for another decade, he thought. He did, after all, rather enjoy the farcical chaos her prolonged and drunken existence wrought within her narrow world and upon its denizens.

The assistant felt a faint contraction of his skin and pinpoint beads of sweat formed upon his forehead as Death's voice swirled mellifluously into his ears, like syrup down a plughole.

"Just a small pack of Golden Virginia and some green Rizlas please." He said. "Oh, and I'll take a disposable lighter too."

Precariously poised on the curb at Five Lamps, sucking on a damp hand-rolled cigarette in the bluster of near horizontal rain, Death waited for a gap in the flow of traffic as it surged around the island. It was a spot he knew well. Eventually he seized his moment, dashing out into the road and attaining the further side as a renewed onslaught of vehicles growled at his heals. He felt himself invigorated, imagining what it must be like to know the touch of his own hands, the chill of his breath and hush of eternity that inevitably followed.

Death came at last to the "Seven Stars." The old pub sported a "bikers welcome" sign outside, a faithful clientele within. He ordered a pint of Marston's Pedigree and sought a corner in the back room - near the glass covered well that plunged thirty feet into dark, evil-looking water.

It was not long before Pantagruel the Myrmidon emerged, slick with pond scum. He slipped through a crack at the edge of the glass circle like a foul gas seepage and reconstituted himself before the ancient angel. If any locals noticed they did not let on.

"Evening. I'll get us a pint in," He drawled, sibilant and malign. "If you fancy another?"

"Cheers mate." Said Death absently, yawning.

Death and the Myrmidon often met in the "Seven Stars" on a Monday night. They shared a taste for real ale, and both enjoyed the jukebox - which contained a generous selection of the Devil's own good Rock n' Roll. Death was just about to order another round when the door opened and in strode Erlking Yulegrave.

"Bloody hell!" He bellowed. "Is everyone moving to Derby now?"

Behind the red-bearded giant came eight of his Wild Huntsmen, clearly already pissed. They grinned sheepishly at Death, whom they had all met several centuries earlier, but whose final snares they had somehow avoided.

"Night off, Erlking?" Asked Death, amused by this latest development.

"Agh!" Grunted the old master of the hunt. "You know how it is. Nothing is quite so dramatic as it used to be. I blame drugs. And television."

Death fell out of the "Top Chef" kebab house in the midst of the long-dead huntsmen.

"You're alright." Said one to his left. "No hard feelings, eh?"

He watched as they staggered round the back of the "Seven Stars" to the car park where their spectral horses were tethered. Shortly, with a great cry, the Wild Hunt thundered into the sky behind the Yulegrave on his monstrous white mare, heading in the direction of Nottingham.

Pantagruel waved after them heartily, his laughter bringing unwelcome blasts of acrid, sulphurous breath laden with chilli and garlic to the nostrils of Death. It was time to call it a night. After lovingly mauling the old Angel, the Myrmidon slid under the pub door and back into his well. Death took a last bite out of his large Chicken Tikka Kebab and dropkicked the rest with unerring accuracy into a nearby bin.

The sky was depressingly clear now, bright stars punctured the darkness and a fat moon bulged contentedly low above the houses. As he weaved his way back along Kedlesden road towards his house in Bromley Street Death clearly heard the plaintive warble of a Nightingale.

END

FLUXIUM

It was a distractingly swift, darting motion Prof. Aaron McLaren noticed bothering his peripheral vision as he worked late one September.

His garden shed was fully kitted out with all his choice paraphernalia, the reference books and his Mac. He liked the solitude. It was a good environment for working – if he could fight the ever-prevailing urge to procrastinate (or masturbate).

McLaren was a public intellectual. A passionate and vocal atheist, he had in recent years taken his initially tentative forays into the dismantlement of monotheist "delusions" to ever grander, more public arenas. The more he did it, the longer he survived it, the braver he became. It was now a calling, and all his hard-won academic status, his much-vaunted scientific methodology, was brought to bear upon this vigorous belief. The world needed to hear the truth, and to wake up from its protracted slumber of ignorant institutionalized mollycoddling and ethics-by-numbers. The bronze-age warrior sky-god did not exist.

The book he was currently writing – his third on the subject – was taking shape under the working title "The God's Father". He had charted the anthropological "birth" of religion world wide, the understanding of nature via anthropomorphic elementals; Gods; The eventual political motivations that resulted in the cult of monotheism, a mere 500 years before the birth of Christ. And he had woven through his narrative the science that had made his name; The popular (memes; the notion of ideas as replicators, belief systems as viral); The fashionable (String and Membrane theory; the – in his view – absurd notions of the agnostic hedge-better, and likelihood of there being a giant teapot orbiting the sun, because, of course, everything is possible); The true (Evolution and Darwinian theory, natural selection, the question of purpose in replicators such as DNA); And the classical (Astronomy, mathematics, physics, chemistry and biology – the working mechanics of all that is and all that is alive.) He had jumped through time, comparing the natural misunderstanding of the universe as witnessed through the primitive eyes of our hunter-gatherer forebears, with the wilful refusal to abandon archaic and redundant belief systems by the modern indoctrinated ill-educated masses and their institutions. He had savaged the word "institution" along side "conformist", which he saw as the blinkered unimaginative heart of the conservative. They both suggested stagnation, and the desire to remain forever the same, as though everything was right and good as it stood and everything that opposed or threatened that was somehow dangerous.

McLaren had been deeply entrenched in a theoretical passage

about the what-ifs of deity, enjoying the fantastical nature of it while somewhat smugly marvelling at the incredulity of it all; the notion that there could be a single entity – whose origin is not ours to question, all power be to he – who built a vast and mostly empty universe, found a tiny corner (some ball of magma with a thin earth crust mostly covered in water, and wrapped in a veil of gas, pelting around a nuclear fusion factory hundreds of times its size) to sprinkle the seeds of life upon, and form man in his own image. A being that created dinosaurs then wiped them out – presumably because they never developed enough brainpower or self awareness to question the nature of their existence, and therefore had never discovered their maker. Or maybe he just planted the bones of giant beasts to further test us? That'll be it. And this God made pigs, whose flesh even the cat will not eat of (except, of course, for sliced ham which his own cat, Erasmus, was very partial to) merely, it would seem, to make our paths yet more hard to find, our lives still more complex to live. He created endless holy things we must not damage or slaughter, and menstrual emissions that might taint a god-fearing man indelibly. He made a perpetual place somewhere at the end of days for us all to be delivered unto, either to burn for our earthly sins, or to live in eternal peace – possibly with a great many virgins. And all these differing monotheist beliefs were the clear and true and righteous and only correct one, though they all stemmed from the same geographical historical origins.

Why? Why would any being bother to do that? What might motivate it? What might be its reason for such an act of cruel creation? What father would give his children the right to slaughter each other for not believing in him in the correct manner? And how might we find the correct manner when it is determined by the random nature of the culture we are born into? For his amusement McLaren attacked this section from the point of view of somebody who truly believed in a genuine – he thought – attempt to understand what it was that convinced the faithful of such a deity's existence. He tried to conjure the beliefs of his childhood, the unquestioning naivety of the child listening to a trusted adult. He tried, as a personal experiment, to find his faith again through rational means. But as always, the more he looked at it the more he found misdirection, memeic transference, indoctrination, delusion, fear and cultural perception.

The flickers and blurs that intruded left and right of his monitor, seeming to come from behind his head, burnt themselves out like shooting stars before they actually entered his field of view long enough for him to grapple with their structures. He initially put the experience down to tiredness, chemical abhorations in the working of his eyes, though he did not feel it. He'd give it another hour – he was enjoying himself – then call it a day. But within five minutes the blurs were becoming more insistent, to the point that they engendered the sense of moving backwards through something at speed, as though his head – he mused fancifully – were entering the atmosphere of a planet. He could almost hear the whoosh; feel the heat, as he blazed earthward, still tapping away at his Mac as he descended in a bright arc through an alien sky.

Suddenly he was desperately afraid to turn round. The powerful logic he relied on at all times began to exert itself. This was internal, he knew that immediately. It was certainly some mental condition he was experiencing. The motion blur that now dominated his peripheral awareness had become almost a tunnel. But for the screen and keyboard, his stilled fingers upon their designer squares, all was motion. It would surely pass, this episode, but he would have to ride it out – if, that is, it was not to be the end of him. He was aware that his fear of turning around was entirely irrational, but fear it was, and very insistent.

After a minute that might have been an hour – a cliché he associated with being at the computer – McLaren began to notice that there were shapes in the streams. He had started to think of the phenomena as a kind of slipstream. In reality he thought it likely to be the result of undetected blood pressure, something like that. He liked his cheese and port a little too much for it to be healthy. There was possibly pressure being exerted upon his visual cortex, or it was something physical to do with his eyes. Maybe he was having a mild stroke; there was damage happening to his brain. Whatever the disconcerting and worrying physical cause, it soothed and amused him to imagine it as a nonsensical metaphysical phenomena. And it looked and moved like a stream of some sort or other. It had eventually passed beyond the edges of the monitor, and was also now "happening" upon the screen itself. He watched it as though it were a particularly beguiling screen-saver. The monitor edge remained, as did the keyboard, his fingers. But there were shapes in the stream. Living shapes. And they were looking back at him.

As a scientist his instinct was to observe first and theorize later. Hallucinations were not entirely a new experience to him, though it had been almost forty years since he had experimented with psychotropic drugs in his student years. That experience, however, had remained a fresh and vivid memory, and quite unlike what he was currently enduring. For a start his mental faculties were at present sharp and focused in as much as he could judge it. He did not feel woozy or out of control. His mind was not wandering. He was not, for want of a better term, high. The other distinguishing factor was that the strange manifestations in this instant were occurring in an alien but somewhat logical progression. There was an awakening sense to it, like the pealing away of perceptual fascia. It had not the flowering randomness of waking dreams that he had experienced taking acid, nor the clench-jawed, vaguely hysterical anxiety it had provoked. Though it was a stark sense of fear that prevented him from moving his head, (the irrational nature of which angered him greatly,) he had found that simply not doing so left him free to witness the experience in a calm and entirely lucid manner.

What prompted the conclusion of "life" in McLaren's mind - and he admitted to himself it was fanciful - was the evident interaction, and subsequent reaction between the shapes. Their 'heads', or frontal regions, were highly evolved. They were made symmetrical by clear features. They had mouths, his first and easiest starting point. These openings were vertical, splitting the head with a thin dark line. They occasionally gaped and snapped at other less-distinct passing shapes. Were they eating? He took the two sets of watery spherical bulges to be eyes. There were other complex, quite beautiful he thought, blooms of sensory equipment in what seemed to be golds and reds. They waved, retracted and dilated, prehensile and delicate, occasionally brushing each other's faces.

McLaren found he had dubbed them *Metafauna* without even really thinking about it. A passionate Darwinian, he began to explore the experience like a Victorian naturalist. Within a short time he had identified three distinct species. The largest - being the shapes he had first noticed, and which seemed to him the most sentient - he called *Plateids*. (It seemed the great philosophical speculations of Socrates and others detailed by Plato regarding the possible layers of the world, and how the earth may be the sky to beings that dwelt in rock, were entirely relevant to his own immediate experience.) The sluggish, amoeba-like worms - that the Plateids apparently ate - *Vermiculus-Alucinor*. Darting around the Plateids like indistinct silvery fish were the *Piscil-Ignis*, whose only notable feature was the globe of light where there might ordinarily be a head.

By now McLaren was fully emerged. All sense of the physical had gone.

Anthony Thorpe-Beaston was wrapping up questions at Seattle

town hall in relation to his new publication "Un-Holy Diver", a brutal autopsy on faith. The question of Prof. Aaron McLaren's recent book "Meta Fauna" had arisen - the two had been great allies in the debunking of myth. Thorpe-Beaston took a deep breath. Though his response was much practiced the subject still rattled him. "My once great esteemed colleague and friend, Aaron McLaren, has me very worried indeed. Not, I might add, with regard to the fanciful, speculative flight of science fantasy that is his latest book - rather I am concerned for his mental well-being, as I'm sure you are aware his entire output and major hypothesis has centred around the notion of faith being necessarily a creation of the mind, and as such a delusion.

"To suffer quite such a delusion as to believe one has potentially - and accidentally, I hasten to add - broken down the fabric that separates us from this world and his realm of the Meta Fauna - the Astral plane, or the land of the Flying Spaghetti Monster (may she reign eternal) - McLaren's 'Fluxium', well let's just say I find it's all rather heartbreaking. That he has witnessed such things I have no doubt - though I do doubt the veracity of it. That he now claims to be able to enter this Fluxium at will and progress our understanding of it is a concept that fills me with enormous misgivings, if not utter contempt."

A shout from the audience caused Thorpe-Beaston to pause and squint into the gloom of the auditorium. "I'm sorry what? Have I tried it? What - opening my mind to the possibility of tooth-faeries? No I've not tried one of professor McLaren's workshops, nor do I intend to. I would say I'm as likely to do that as charter a flight to the North Pole to complain to Santa about the goodwill and peace to all men he didn't bring me last Christmas - to cram two meaningless faith-based myths built round a pagan fertility festival into a single metaphor.

"As I understand it, there's no physical manifestation on view when such venturing occurs - by which, of course, I mean that witnesses of those travelling in the so-called Fluxium will observe no outward sign of the said traveller actually going anywhere at all."

Thorpe-Beaston waited for the laughter to subside before going on.

"My learned friends, need I say more? The truth, with regard to McLaren, is that no matter the very right and proper paths of inquiry which he brought to bear in documenting and studying the phenomena - the diligence and intelligence he used in assessing the behavioural patterns of the species and subspecies he witnessed, the professorial intellect displayed in the understanding of the Fluxium and it's admittedly fascinating inhabitants is peerless, as always - it is still improvable, entirely delusional non-science. I cannot be emphatic about this enough. It is shocking that such a great voice of reason in such difficult and uncertain times should, in the midst of breaking new ground in the public understanding of science - on a pretty global scale! - not only present us with something so starkly against all he taught, but may also have the potential to start a whole new delusional cult to muddy up these deep and turbulent waters yet further. It has all the hallmarks.

"With that I think we can call it a day. Except to say if you have any further questions please buy my reasonably priced lucid and informative book. You'll find ALL the answers in there."

END

FROGSPAWN

It was Tain's habit to rub his palms together in small, energetic circles when nervous or enthused. In this instant the former engendered it. He was having one of those grey days, in which nothing seems quite substantial. There lingered within him a sense of impending doom, as if he had forgotten something important - something he should be afraid to remember. The sensation reminded him of a particularly stubborn dream - one that, more often than he cared for, infused his nights with terror.

In the dream he had killed a man. Who, or why, eluded him. He vaguely perceived that the murder had been committed using a hammer blow to the man's head. In the back of a white Ford transit van - which he drove only in this dream - Tain would be worryingly aware of an old Hessian-backed Persian carpet. Rolled up within it was the corpse.

People knew; they had figured it out. An old clerk with characterless glasses and a tobacco-stained moustache leafed through the minutia of a decade-old paper trail leading back to a time and a place. Policemen asked innocuous questions of old friends. They were getting closer. He knew it was only a matter of time before…

Perhaps there was truth in it. Perhaps he had murdered somebody and the intense shock, the horror of it, had caused the memory to bury itself - surfacing only to haunt him in dreams. Perhaps. But more likely it was attributable to some guilty secret, half-forgotten and un-confessed. Whatever the cause though, on grey days it leached at his spirits and left him bleak.

Tain stood on the corner of Bromley Street rubbing his palms together, mouth ajar in a gormless aspect. Without the exertion of any particular will he found himself heading home. The Street boasted red brick terraced houses, built during the reign of Queen Victoria, which would have been grand had they not been so narrow, and not quite so near to the road. A stumpy Hawthorn provided an ideal perch for Sparrows and Magpies to crap on his pointless out-of-service car. He scratched the knuckles of his right hand on the thorny overgrown bush outside his front door, and sucked at the sudden red line as he let himself in.

His pregnant wife, Kristina, was in Ireland, county Cork, with her parents and both their kids. The house felt as though nobody had ever lived there. It offered no comfort. Tain wandered into the kitchen, placed his coat on the back of a chair. The plastic bag, containing a movie magazine, a half drunk bottle of coke, a toothbrush and yesterdays underwear, he placed upon the table. He felt a distinct kinship with an earlier self; unwashed and dry-mouthed, stale smoke and alcohol on his breath and clothes, the aches of not enough sleep on an unfamiliar sofa in his legs. He reverted often to this prototype-self when left alone any length of time, uneasy in his own company and seeking the shallow solace of others. The radio had been left on, but for some reason it was no longer tuned in to any station and was quietly broadcasting the white noise of stars. He didn't think to turn it off. There was nothing engaging on the television so sleep became inevitable and descended uncharacteristically swiftly.

Given the timbre of the day it was not restful. His hands swelled to three times their normal size, like purple balloons, within the uneasy confines of his imagination. They undulated, listless spumes filled with corrupt liquid matter that separated the flesh from the bone. He stared at the blackened fingernails morosely with dream eyes. This was another regular and unwelcome night-visitor, he realised, lucid though asleep, and probably just deep-rooted paranoia born of his trade as an illustrator. But the rationale of his reasoning did not bring him any peace.

A storm awoke him. He guessed, by the shift of light, that he had slept maybe an hour, an hour and a half. Just long enough to make his head swim, his limbs feel heavy. He must have been lying on his arm, because it hurt, and he couldn't move his hand. Having drunk far too much the previous evening he decided to spend this one at home with a couple of DVDs, rather than rally another mate or two for a few pints down the Seven Stars, or the Dolphin. A quick cup of tea and he was outside again, hood raised against the rain, heading for Blockbusters, the video/DVD rental shop on Ashbourne road.

By the time he was half way across Markeaton recreational ground it was getting dark. The horse chestnut trees loomed either side of the road, unchanged, it seemed, since his childhood. Britannia Mill - black, monolithic, and punctuated with ineffectual pits of yellowish light - loomed before him. It was students and their tools, not factory workers and their machines, that now laboured within it. Turning left at the top of Merchant Street, he noticed that Ashbourne Road was empty. It should have been swarming with vehicles, and yet...

Under the old Victorian railway bridge up ahead there were flashing lights, a huddle of cars and figures. Tain could hear an indistinct voice shouting through a loudhailer. From where he squinted in the gloom it appeared to be a police roadblock. Now all the buildings lining Ashbourne Road had been boarded up, when only hours earlier they had not been. Wooden planks and thin, corrugated metal sheets had been nailed over windows. Those still visible were more often than not smashed. The few remaining cars were all raised up on bricks, their tyres stolen. None of the streetlamps remained unbroken. It was as though he had stepped through time somehow, slipped into another reality almost his own but not quite. His heart thumped faster. Trying to remain calm under what he judged to be reasonably frightening circumstances, Tain kept his head down and his hands thrust deep in his pockets. His pace quickened to match his heart rate. He made up a tune in his head, matching the rhythm of his steps, repeating a mantra:

"Sordid, you know the one? He stopped your heart one night, but the silence never came. Sordid, you know the…"

He should have been surprised if Blockbusters had been open. He stood looking at the shattered windows, the torn shreds of posters, with an almost detached air. He found himself grinning, but he didn't know why.

"Come on, son-shine," a loud voice in that quiet road.

"The've gone inside again - for now. Let's get you out of here. It 'i'n't safe."

The Policeman steered him firmly by the elbow toward the railway bridge.

"'S goin' on?"

"Not a bleedin' clue."

A sudden peal of automatic gunfire exploded behind them. They ran as bullets sent sparks up from the pavement at their feet.

Under the shelter of the bridge the policeman bustled Tain through the barricade and sat him against the wall, next to a thin looking youth in a shell suit and baseball cap.

"A'right?"

The youth did not reply.

"'S 'appenin'?" Tain pushed.

"Fucked if I know. They's fuckin' loads of 'em!" The youth finally spluttered, eyes bulging. "They're in all t' buildins! Wearing Batman cowls, th' bastards! Batman cowls! What th' fuck's tha'r all aba't?'

The youth raised his right hand, which he'd kept jammed under his armpit.

"Chopped mi fingers off, di'n't they? The've got bags full o' fingers! See-through plastic bags, full of fuckin' fingers..."

It was the storm that woke him.

He felt like he should have been sweating, but his skin was dry, crisp like mapping paper. He remembered the dream, and shivered. The image of a plastic bag full of severed fingers sloshed in his head.

"Fingers..." He thought. "Always fucking hands and fingers."

Work had not been good recently. Until a year ago he had lived in Brighton. He'd foolishly imagined, when he moved there, that the white Georgian houses were full of like-minded creative types. The "hippest city in Britain" had been fun at first, but in the end it was much like everywhere else. And so when they had been forced to sell up and move back to his small industrial home city of Derby it had not been the wrench he expected. And yet work had not come to him there either.

He had begun to suspect he lacked the talent, that his artwork was somehow marred or ugly. He could no longer see the good points, nor could he find pleasure producing what had once come so naturally. He tormented himself.

His right hand hurt.

On closer inspection he found the scratch had become infected. The skin was cracked and sore all around a weeping cut. A grey pallor was spreading up his arm.

"Shit," he whispered. "What the fuck?"

The phone was dead, and as he stood at the kitchen sink gazing out into the garden with it still at his ear, having pointlessly dialled Ireland for the seventh time, Tain noticed the Frogspawn. It covered their tatty little law end to end, and inches deep. It hung from the trees in saggy loops. Shrouded a stocky rose. The image sent a shock through his body. He recoiled in horror. How had he not seen it sooner?

"Christ!" he gasped. "What the fuck?"

Then the first of millions fell. He didn't know what it was right away, just a grey lump falling past the window, bursting upon the wall. Gingerly he opened the kitchen door and peered out.

It was raining toads. And frogs. Huge frogs. Large fat African Bullfrogs. And bigger. They fell and burst, or landed in the bushes, the trees. They slid off the roofs and crashed through conservatories and green houses. The carnage of their bodies mixed with the slime of the Frogspawn turning Tain's world, his safe suburban middle-class haven, into a writhing crimson nightmare.

The phone fell to the ground, his hand still holding it. He held the brittle grey stump of his arm up to his face.

I'm dying, he thought, Dead. *I'm already fucking dead..."*

Without warning the horror fled him. He was consumed with

a white calmness. A peace. The house too, he now saw, was a decayed husk. Layers of crumbling paper curled away from the walls exposing the pockmarked brickwork. Above him, through holes in the ceiling, he could see there was no longer a roof. The moon was visible, shining, full. Ancient. Older, much older, than he remembered it. Had the dead muscles of his cheeks allowed Tain would have smiled.

Above the city centre a vortex whorled. The toads were stacking below it, forming a column. Out in the streets the dead walked, shuffling blindly to fates they had no interest in. Tain joined them, crushing the wretched amphibians beneath unfeeling feet as he and they marched towards the ever-growing tower of frogs.

Soon they were climbing it, spiralling upwards...

END

Visit the online Machivarius Point gallery
www.machivariuspoint.weebly.com

Liam Roger Sharp (born May 2, 1968) is an artist, writer and publisher. He lives in Derby, UK, with his wife Christina, three children - Matylda, Lorcan and Jeff - and their cat Molly.

PREVIEW
CAGED AURORA

BOOK ONE of the upcoming series set on Arddn, the
homeworld of MACHIVARIUS POINT.

CHAPTER ONE: A BETTER LIFE

Kia fell hard. An ill-placed foot, a small slick of traitorous crushed moss on smooth stone, and she was down in a spin of limbs. Tears forced unbidden passage as immediate as the pain that exploded in a knee, an elbow. But it was not the pain that drew tears as much as the sure knowledge she was caught.

The Nefars had erupted from of the foliage, a savage swarm of mixed races, mercenaries all. It was a hunting party, but their prey was not food, rather it was people - future warriors and those who would serve the Empire as slaves.

"Orn, no…" she whispered, and as she rolled onto her side breathing hard the Dogren were on and around her like a burst dam; teeth barred at her face, serrated feathers tearing jagged little cuts in her arms as she tried to fend them off. Then she was off the ground and over a massive shoulder, a rolling guttural voice mimicking - as near as it was possible - the squall of the flightless pack hunters below. He was the Ghull-Master of the raiding Nefars, and they answered only to him.

Kia felt nauseous - but it was brief. Dogren saliva - which they used to coat their blade-like feathers, licking each other in a bonding frenzy - was poisonous to men. (Only the Ghull-Masters were immune, and many died in the effort of becoming so - their arms a mess of feather-cuts, groaning as greedy Dogren licked the wounds.) Soon she was swept to oblivion as the poison gripped her, wracking her body with miniature convulsions and casting her in a sweat. It would be days before she regained her consciousness, and by then she would be a very long way away from her mountain home in Ypo-Polaria.

The High Temple was a simple circular space ringed by eight squat, broad columns, of varying heights, which once bore a domed roof. Mahratt Spenk watched his pupil with eyes that could penetrate the fascia of substance and glean the dance of time; courting it. Moments would unravel before him into a loose weave of possibilities, and, again, he saw where Lai-Mai faltered, and failed, where she might otherwise have succeeded. The ghost of that success faded into another future as Mahratt stepped smoothly into her Now. It did not matter. It would not be long before she learned to master the skill. She was strong and adept.

"I'm sorry, Myfather." She said. "I was afraid, I…"

Mahratt silenced her with a gentle tilt of his head. "You gleaned well, Mydaughter, Lai-Mai, but you were overwhelmed by possibilities. What is your fear?"

Lai-Mai began to feel the bitter winds that whipped at their robes, the bite of the snow within which her small bare feet were buried. Below her lay the Southern steppes of Ypo-Polaria, a wilderness of silt plain dressed in a patchwork of hardy grass and low, twisted trees punctured by startling eruptions of granite, as though the earth were about to be devoured from below by a vast magma-dwelling Levithian. Stretching either side of her in an arc that sliced into the distant horizon like a scythe, separating land from sky, were the great Yg-Djinn Mountains. Lai-Mai watched her sigh spiral away in little eddies before being swept to nothingness by the mountains own more powerful breath. She felt entirely inconsequential.

"Myfather, I grew afraid." She said. "I grew afraid because it seemed as though a million voices called me. And then somewhere else I was already dead. I feared the confluence that sprang up, the air had become like water. I lost my purpose, Myfather. I couldn't see which way I should go."

"But, child, you saw the possibilities." Said Mahratt. "And that is what you must take from this: Tonight, when you next Glean, I want you to go back to what you saw, and there look again, and learn. It will reveal itself."

"Thank you Myfather. All honour be upon you."

"And upon you also, Mydaughter. Orn preserve us, but it is cold!" The Ypo-Polarian Priest threw a cloak around Lai-Mai, proffering a momentary squeeze of her narrow shoulders in the act. "Put your boots on Lai-Mai. We've still a long walk back to the Temple." He said. "If only we put so much effort into the speeding up of time as we do in the slowing then we should have no care at all how far it is we have still to walk!"

Mahratt watched the young orphan Priestess weave her way down the steep path ahead of him. The sisters, Kia and Lai-Mai, had been at the Chio-Wei Temples in Ypo-Polaria since childhood. Kia had been a stern-faced rogue even then, aged no more than three. Lai-Mai, barely six months old, had been unnaturally quiet, but her eyes burned with a kind of fury that

3

made even some of the priests uncomfortable. Never the less, she was possessed of a disarming smile, and could, on occasion, let forth a peel of vulgar laughter that would make the most seasoned mercenary blush. Mahratt was entirely devoted to them. Their parents had been mountain Slothherds. The huge shaggy beasts of burden were also a source of meat, clothing, and milk. They were all but gone from the plains now, brought into captivity in the Empire by raiding Nefar mercenaries. Such a raid had orphaned the two sisters, and it had been providence that kept them alive and delivered them safely up to the Temples. Kia was now on the cusp of womanhood. Dark and slender, the lose robes of the priesthood were struggling to confine her voluptuous but powerful physique. Her shaven head did nothing to dispel a sullen beauty. Lai-Mai, on the other hand, was still a child, though her amazing advances through the priestly disciplines lent her an air of wisdom far superior to her years. The aging priest knew well that at any moment the girl would master the slowing of time, the priesthoods most highly prized and hardest attained of skills. It was an ability achieved by a precious few, and usually deep into adulthood. The girl gleaned well. She had found harmony with the Echoes-to-be, touched lightly and easily upon the Source. She was as called by the paranatural as any one Mahratt had ever met, and the depth of her talent moved his old heart near to rapture.

As they walked the sky grew steadily darker under a mantle of clouds, gathering itself into a thunderhead. They quickened their pace as a light fall of snow inevitably turned to blizzard. The most dangerous paths were behind them now, but even the eldest, most travelled Priests could get lost in such conditions without supreme vigilance. But almost as soon as it started it was passed, leaving four or five thumb-widths of fresh snow behind, softening the harsh contours of the mountains, until the wind chiselled it back into swathes and blades. But all was not

4

well. The sky remained full of black and broiling forms, though not cloud; smoke. Ahead, through the failing last fall of fine snow, deep in the snug protective valleys of the Steppes, there was the unmistakable glow of fire.

Mahratt and Lai-Mai ran the last distance, heedless of their footfalls now and trusting their instinctive knowledge of the place. The Priest cursed himself. What was that, in one possibility he had gleaned? What had he neglected while watching the girl? But it was ever the case - to glean was always to see the possibility of death and to embrace that, along with all the possibilities of life. They had been too far away. No blame rested with them, but still...

Lai-Mai stood at the top of the flight of steps down into the Temple vale, rich with the spoils of it's own microclimate. In the heart of the smouldering Borachial Ferns, as tall as trees and warmed all year round by volcanic streams of steaming water, there rose a series of spires, twisted and lumpen like inverted stalactites of incredible size. Into and upon these were carved and built the Ypo-Polarian Temples, now aflame.

"Kia!" screamed the girl, and she was gone over the edge, her robes hitched up above her scrawny knees, desperation in her posture. She vanished into the canopy of Fern, legs a blur and as quickly as though she had fallen, the old priest in her wake, panting and fearful.

At the base of the main Temple mound Lai-Mai stood screaming for her sister, looking up to find a way in through the flames. All about her the Ferns crackled and shed large flaming clumps. The ground hissed, smoking and damp. There were bodies too, cooked and shapeless like blackened maggoty Dolomites, bereft of identity. A few of the survivors were gathering them, tending them, those that could. Others awaited eternity and the Munger, beyond help.

"Nefars." Said Mahratt.

Lai-Mai crumbled, coughing between sobs, while tears began the task of cleaning sooty smears off her olive-pink cheeks.